EVERLASTING PASSION

Savannah stared at Jake for a long moment before she silently admitted that she had indeed picked a fight. She wasn't proud of herself. She had wanted him to talk about his feelings for the plantation and instead she had turned the discussion into something else entirely.

"I don't know why I did that," she replied awkwardly. But she did know. In her heart, she knew what had happened. "Maybe I wanted to be reassured."

"About what?"

"You, me. Us."

In less than five seconds, Jake maneuvered the car from the far left lane to the shoulder on the right side of the road.

"Jake?" Her expression was incredulous. "What are you doing?"

In answer, he reached out, hooked his hand behind her neck, hauled her across the seat, and kissed her hard. "You're something else," he told her when he finally lifted his head.

"Why did you do that?" she stammered, all eyes and genuine wonder.

"To remind you of where you are in the 'grand scheme of things.' Remember that the next time you fall back into your old insecurities." He stroked his thumb over her cheek. "You aren't alone any longer, Savannah. You've got me in your life and whether you like it or not, you're dead center in mine."

* * *

Advance praise for NOW AND FOREVER:

"Another engaging and engrossing story from the pen of Elizabeth Sherwood."

—*Affaire de Coeur*

Books by Elizabeth Sherwood

VIRGINIA EMBRACE
LOUISIANA ROSE
NOW AND FOREVER

Published by Pinnacle Books

NOW AND FOREVER

ELIZABETH SHERWOOD

P

PINNACLE BOOKS
KENSINGTON PUBLISHING CORP.

PINNACLE BOOKS are published by

Kensington Publishing Corp.
850 Third Avenue
New York, NY 10022

Pinnacle and the P logo Reg. U.S. Pat. & TM Off.

First Printing: December, 1995

Printed in the United States of America

For Fran and Donna

Acknowledgments

Special thanks go to

the Reverend Sandi Staylor
for sharing her
insights into the world of paranormal psychology

and to

Capt. Louis J. DeFidelto, USAF
and Col. Chip Griffin, USAF (Retired)
for insight into JQ

Prologue

"Savannah Davis can go suck raw eggs!"

"Jake, I know how you feel about the old plantation house—"

"Then you should have known better than to have called me."

"I'm only asking that you listen to the woman. She's a critically acclaimed photographer."

"BFD." There was a silence in the phone conversation, and Jacob Quaide could almost hear his attorney cringe on the other end of the line.

"Jake," George Howard began again. "It doesn't have to be a big fucking deal. She's only asking for a few minutes of your time."

Jacob stood behind his office desk and shoved a hand deep into the pockets of his dress slacks. "The same way that half-assed owner of that car dealership wanted a few minutes of my time?"

"You couldn't blame the man for trying. Oakwood Plantation is centuries old, it has an air of permanence and stability. From an advertising point of view, it suited the venerable image he's created for himself."

"Hell, George, it suited his ego and his bank account. Both would have profited while my ancestral home would have been reduced to an exploited backdrop."

"You won't have to worry about that with Savannah

Davis. That's why I'm asking you to reconsider and talk to her."

"For what? She's already got my brother's permission to photograph the old house. Why does she need to speak to me?"

George Howard released a sigh that transmitted his waning patience across the telephone lines. "Because you and I, and even Miss Davis, know that your cooperation would make her job a whole hell of a lot easier."

"And whatever Miss Davis wants, Miss Davis gets, is that it?"

"No, that isn't it. Look, she's going to take her pictures with or without your agreement. The old house is on your brother's portion of the land. You can't legally stop her if Doug has given her the okay."

Jake swore succinctly. "I'm aware of who owns what, George. I was there at the reading of Dad's will, remember?"

George Howard ignored the question and the acidic sting of its delivery. "She'd like a chance to explain what she's trying to do."

"You've already told me what she wants to do and you've already given her my answer."

"Apparently she'd like to discuss the matter further."

"I bet she does. The minute she found out that the only road giving her easy access to the old house is on my portion of the property, she was on the phone to you."

"Can you blame her, Jake? If she can't use your drive, she's going to have to pack all of her equipment in."

"Then let her hike in."

"That would be close to five miles."

A nasty smile creased Jake's face. "What's the matter? Is our 'acclaimed photographer' afraid of a little hard work?"

"I didn't get that impression. In fact, I found her to be very pleasant. And reasonable."

"Meaning I'm not?"

"Meaning that when it comes to Oakwood, you're never impartial," George shot back with an alacrity that spoke of the no-nonsense kind of relationship that had developed between them over the years.

Jake absorbed the verbal jab and swore beneath his breath. He couldn't fault George Howard for his observation. The man was right. When it came to the plantation, Jake knew he wasn't impartial. He was defensive and protective and with good reason. The land was more than his inheritance. It was his heritage.

That might mean nothing to someone else. To Jake, it was part of who he was. Inherent to Oakwood was the legacy of the Quaide family. He couldn't separate himself from his association to the plantation any more than he could sever himself from his own face.

"Jake, are you there?"

At Howard's voice, Jacob heaved a sigh. "I haven't gone anywhere."

"What do you want me to tell Miss Davis?"

Jake chewed back his immediate response, then loosened his tie and unbuttoned the top button of his white shirt. "Tell her . . ." *What? That I'm unreasonable and I know it?*

Howard urged, "Talk to her. Hear her out. That's all she's asking."

That was enough. "All right. Tell her I'll meet with her the day after tomorrow. But that doesn't mean I'm going to change my mind about this whole thing. If it were my decision, she wouldn't have a camera anywhere near Oakwood. The old house is special."

"She already knows that."

"See that she doesn't forget it."

One

Something was wrong. Savannah didn't know why she felt that way, but she did. Absently, she ran a hand across the back of her neck, and then realized that this was the third time in the last hour she had tried to rub away whatever stress was nagging at her.

So much for her horoscope, she mused as she eased her car off northbound 17 and into the left turn lane. That morning's column of astral advice had promised that this was going to be her kind of day. Well, she had a news flash for the local paper; her kind of day did not come with the type of anxiety that raised the fine hair on the nape of her neck. Nor did it come with the unshakable feeling that something was . . . well, wrong.

It was the only way she could describe the sensation that seemed to have a hold of her. It was the same kind of feeling she had when she was a half-hour from home and couldn't remember if she had left the iron on or if her hot rollers were roasting toward meltdown on the bathroom counter.

The light ahead turned green, thankfully distracting her from her thoughts. Mentally, she reviewed the directions she had received from George Howard. Left onto Longhill, past the pond to Aunt Mable's General Store, left at the store and bear left at the fork in the road.

Her kind of directions. In the three months she had been traveling the back roads of Virginia and North Carolina, she had learned not to rely on route numbers. Those little numerical markers were useful, if they were present at all and if the local teenage boys hadn't turned them around in order to get a few laughs.

It was the solid, unmovable landmarks she looked for to get her where she needed to go. And some of those places, she reflected with a crooked smile, had been out in the boonies. She didn't mind though, in fact, she hadn't expected anything else when she'd begun her search. After all, architecture that had somehow managed to survive from the eighteenth century had to have done so partly because it *was* in out-of-the-way places, safe and protected from the mainstream of the careless and sometimes destructive twentieth century.

Just thinking of her latest project eased some of the strange tension gripping her. Of all the work she had ever undertaken, photographing the once grand buildings of a bygone era had to be her favorite. How could it not be? History and antiques had always fascinated her.

That explained why she was an absolute sucker for anything colonial. There was a richness to that period of American history, a sweetness of mind and heart and soul that was gone forever. America in its infancy, before the age of industrialization, before the Civil War—the essence of that time had been most superbly captured in the houses that had been crafted then.

A great many of those buildings still stood up and down the East Coast, but especially here in Gloucester County. Defying the odds without restoration or renovation, they had resisted the combined tests of the elements, fire, desertion of families, vandalism, and even pollution. Structures once filled with the spirit of pioneers, of fortitude and romance and graciousness, stood as silent, crumbling sentinels to the past and reminders to the present.

She had thought that capturing the vitality of all that would make for a powerful, deeply poignant photographic study. Her editor in New York had agreed. Of course, he might not have if her last collection of prints, a book titled *Centuries,* hadn't gone into a second and then a third printing.

So there she was, in the southeast corner of Virginia, turning left at Aunt Mable's empty store, looking for the fork in the road that would bring her to Oakwood Plantation, complete with its house dating back to 1690.

Over three hundred years. She hadn't thought to find a house that old. In other parts of the world that kind of age was barely a scratch in history. But in terms of European influence in America, things didn't get too much older than that, and the idea that she had the chance to photograph such a treasure nearly had her missing the sudden end to the road.

Her little red Ford came to an abrupt halt, and Savannah let out a sigh as she took note of her surroundings. To the right was a dirt track cutting through the remains of a harvested cornfield, to her left lay a pebbled path dissecting another plowed-under field.

"Oh, lovely," she muttered to herself. Mr. Howard had assured her that Oakwood's mansion was at the end of the road. Well, here was the end, but where was the mansion?

She scanned each of the dirt roads, as well as the colorful November forest that bordered the edge of the field, but didn't see a sign of any building, three hundred years old or otherwise.

With a flick of her wrist, she turned off the ignition and got out of her car to stand at the poor excuse of a crossroads. She should have become accustomed to intersections such as this, but the truth was, they never failed to amaze her. Time and time again, she had had to leave the pavement behind only to find herself in the middle of nowhere wondering which way to go.

Sighing again, she turned back to the car with every intention of finding the nearest phone when she caught the glimmer of metal shining out from behind a clump of bayberry bushes near the left path. On closer inspection, the metal proved to be a mailbox, its discreet nameplate stamped QUAIDE.

"Ah, the elusive Mr. Quaide. Thought you could hide from me."

Eyes narrowed slightly, she returned to the driver's seat, mentally gearing up for the meeting to come. Mr. Jacob Quaide did not want her anywhere near his ancestor's deteriorating home and he had been brutally blunt in having that sentiment relayed to her via his attorney.

Unfortunately for the Q Man, as she had come to think of him, Oakwood's plantation house and the surrounding two hundred and fifty acres belonged to his older brother, Douglas. *He* had been more than happy to give her his permission to photograph the place.

Unfortunately for her, Douglas Quaide did not own the entire plantation. His bother, Jacob, the Q Man, lived on the portion of the property that had been willed to him, property consisting of a couple hundred acres of farmland, the overseer's house, a few dependencies dating from the early nineteenth century, and the plantation's only road.

To get to the old house, she had to get past Jacob Quaide. Hence, the appointment today.

It still surprised her that he had agreed to meet with her. She didn't know much about him, but she got the impression that he was not an accommodating man. Not an optimistic thought since she hoped to convince him to cooperate with her by letting her have access to his drive.

Was all of this why she felt so uneasy today? She didn't think so. She had dealt often enough with standoffish, even rude people before. It wasn't her favorite thing to do, but it had never given her a case of the willies.

The crushed stone drive stretched out toward a thick tangle of woods. As Savannah carefully negotiated the numerous ruts, she had to consider what kind of man chose to live in such isolation. He had no close neighbors that she could see. It also seemed the Q Man didn't mind a fifteen minute drive to pick up a carton of milk. The only convenience store she had passed was back on Route 17 and that was at least ten miles away.

Steering around a water-filled hole, she figured that Mr. Quaide was probably an eccentric old coot who liked to run people off with a twelve-gauge shotgun, most likely the very same gun his grandpappy used to shoot squirrels. Well, whatever he was, she surmised that he either drove a Jeep or else he spent a fortune in keeping the front end of his car aligned.

The path curved behind a towering stand of oaks and elms, and then broke abruptly to reveal a two-story brick house. The dark green Jaguar parked in front was definitely not a Jeep.

"You've got expensive tastes," she told the absent Jacob Quaide as she got out of her car. "And an eye for detail." She noted that the exterior of the house held no modern fixtures or appointments. From the shingles on the roof to the color of the wood molding, the house gave every impression of appearing exactly as it would have over two hundred years ago.

Making her way to the brick walkway, she smiled for the sheer aesthetic pleasure she derived from the structure and its dependencies off to the left. Whoever had converted the one-time stable into a garage had sacrificed none of the historic feel for modern conveniences.

In the back of her mind, she made a mental note to ask if she could snap a few pictures of these buildings, too. However, before she could pursue the thought, the sound of a low growl caught her attention. Her instant and wary attention. The growl turned the corner of the house a split second ahead of the dog it belonged to. Savannah's reaction was immediate.

"Oh, shit," she muttered, eyes rounded.

The largest, angriest Airedale she had ever seen bounded straight for her, blocking her only escape route back to her car. Given no other option, Savannah scrambled backward up the brick steps, pressed her back to the front door and pounded with all her might.

"Go away!" she commanded, her voice shaking as much as her hands.

The dog answered by bursting into a spat of fierce barking, lunging forward and back in a threatening display meant to frighten.

It worked. Savannah gasped and blindly sought the door-knob. Instinct propelled her to get inside as fast as she could. Her fingers fumbled with the cold metal, but without warning the door was swung wide from within and she tumbled backward.

Steely arms caught her about her waist and chest, literally choking off her alarmed cry as she struggled to get her feet beneath her. Her legs went in one direction, her torso another. She didn't care. She was so grateful to be out of reach of the Cujo impersonator, she grabbed hold of her savior's arms and even managed to ignore the fact that one of his hands had a firm grasp of her right breast.

"Hold still," a deep voice ordered sharply from above and behind. Then, "Ares, stay."

The dog quieted at once. Savannah wished her heart would do the same. It thumped wildly, making breathing more than a bit strained.

"Are you all right?"

It wasn't the most dignified entrance Savannah had ever made. She could tolerate that. Not so easy to overlook was the fright she had been given.

"Yes, I'm fine." She wasn't, though, and she felt the surge of an adrenaline-induced temper. Her voice carried a bit of sting when she added, "Does he greet everyone this way?"

Her question went unanswered and she was released to

stand on her own. Still shaking, she watched the man step out onto the brick landing. He gave a snap of his fingers and Ares took the three brick stairs in a single leap. Panting excitedly, the dog buried his head between his master's knees.

" 'Atta boy." Firm male hands scratched behind the dog's ears. Ares's hind end wiggled from side to side, making him appear no more ferocious than a puppy.

Savannah turned away, slightly miffed. Apparently, the dog's owner had other priorities in mind, an apology for scaring her not among them. Adjusting her jacket, she had to consciously remind herself that the dog had only been doing what he had obviously been trained and instructed to do.

Determined to go on as pleasantly as possible, she threaded her fingers back through her hair, turned, and drew in what was supposed to be a fortifying breath. Unexpectedly, it got caught somewhere in her throat when she found the man leaning against the closed door staring at her with narrowed eyes.

Instantaneous recognition. The feeling slammed into her with an intensity that had her heart racing again. His black hair, roughly chiseled features, and crystal-blue eyes all seemed familiar somehow. Even his casual, long-legged stance struck a cord within her. Searching her mind, she tried to recall a time or a place in which they might have met.

"Mr. Quaide?" Out of sheer habit, her mind clicked off more observations. Six feet three, one hundred and ninety pounds, thirty-eight-ish.

"Yes." He returned her gaze with one of his own. Steady, purposeful, probing, it was intrinsically masculine in its appraisal.

"I . . . I'm . . ." Savannah mentally cringed at the awkward stuttering sound of her voice. It really couldn't be helped, though. She had the most compelling urge to stare at the dynamic features: the hard curve of lip, the clean line of jaw, the bold slash of brow.

One of those black eyebrows quirked up in a mocking gesture. "You are?"

She snapped out of her confusion, deciding at the same time that she had to have been mistaken in her first impression. For one thing, she was too visually oriented to have forgotten Jacob Quaide's face if she had ever seen it before. And secondly, the sensation of recognition had changed, becoming something less definable. What she felt edged closer to an intense awareness of the man; intimacy on an untouched level.

"I'm Savannah Davis."

He silently seemed to absorb that for a bit. "Right," was all he finally said.

Savannah gave him a questioning look, and waited for him to continue. He didn't and she restrained the disgruntled sigh she wanted to heave.

"I assume you were expecting me." She offered him a polite smile, her most professional voice, and silently congratulated herself on her poise. Part of her dearly wanted to get in the man's face and tell him what she thought of taciturn, unreasonable men with unfriendly dogs. "I spoke with George Howard the day before yesterday."

"He called." Tipping his head to the side in silent invitation, Jacob Quaide crossed the foyer with its wide, random-planked floorboards and entered the living room. "Have a seat." He indicated one of the wing-back chairs set before the windows. He chose to settle back against the front of a mahogany cabinet and stretch his long legs out before him.

Savannah made her way to the chairs, finding that with each step more and more of her irritation slid away. She was entranced by the room, more specifically its ambiance of age. It was there in the slight buckle of one corner of the ceiling, the wavy distortion to the glass panes in the windows, and the scent of old wood that saturated the air. The essence of duration touched her deeply.

Rooms like this one, similar buildings and homes, had always had this effect on her. Inside, she could feel a lovely warmth begin to blossom and capture her heart.

"This is wonderful," she murmured, taking in every detail and committing it, almost lovingly, to memory. "I can't imagine living in a house that has so much history. You're very fortunate." Eyes soft and mellow, a gentle smile curling her lips, she dragged her attention from the carved scrollwork around the mantel, then stilled instantly under the impact of the hard gleam in Jacob Quaide's sapphire gaze.

"This house has been part of the estate for generations," he stated, his tone nothing short of a warning.

Savannah felt as if she had been jerked to a jarring halt. And then her temper flared again. He was the most defensive man she had ever met, nearly to the point of rudeness. Did she pose some kind of a threat to him? Did he think she was going to steal his house and his property with a few honest comments?

She left the queries unanswered, rising to the challenge he presented. "I'd like to thank you for meeting with me," she began, noting for the first time that by standing, he had assumed a position of authority. On top of being defensive, the man was positively overbearing. "Mr. Howard explained your feelings in regards to my photographing the mansion house."

"They're more than feelings, Miss Davis."

"I can appreciate that. From what I gather, the plantation has been in your family since its inception." She paused to choose her words with infinite care. "I also have been made aware of the fact that you are opposed to my photographing the plantation's original mansion."

"If you understand all this, then why did you ask to see me?"

"I was hoping we could reach an agreement. Your cooperation would make my job much simpler."

Jacob scoffed. "My brother owns the mansion house, Miss Davis. You don't need my permission to take your pictures."

She tried to ignore his scorn and laced her fingers together, letting her hands rest lightly in her lap. "That's true, but the only road giving me easy access to the house is your drive."

His chin came up, a humorless smile quirked one corner of his mouth. "Figured that out, did you?"

Savannah bristled, and forgot about the finer points of keeping her temper in check. "Tell me, Mr. Quaide, is it me you don't like or do you have a thing about photojournalists as a whole?"

The blue of his eyes edged toward black, the line of his mouth lost any hint of humor. Through gritted teeth, he grated, "I have a thing, *Miss Davis,* about anyone who would exploit Oakwood for their own gain."

His anger had erupted out of nowhere, taking Savannah completely by surprise, but only for a tense, silent moment. During those few seconds, her indignation grew until she glared at him with a lethal load of her own anger.

Leaning forward, she insisted, "I have no intentions of exploiting Oakwood." She was insulted that he would think such a thing.

"That's exactly what you'd be doing."

"How, by taking a few pictures?"

"No, by using those pictures for your own financial gain."

She was skewered on his logic, impaled to the seat by the facts. The pictures would be part of a book whose royalties she would earn. That much was the truth, she wasn't going to apologize for it.

But for her, there was so much more involved in the

project than money. The art she loved so dearly, the craft she had spent years perfecting, was the ultimate concern.

Exhaling sharply, she sat back and regarded him with sad, albeit, indignant eyes. "I'm sorry you feel that way." Absently, she rubbed at the back of her neck. "But you couldn't be more wrong. My true interest lies in the process of capturing images, of manipulating light and form and line, in drawing out the special qualities unique to the subject matter. It is not, it has never been, in something as crass as exploitation."

The edge of his jaw gave new meaning to the word hard. "Over the course of the years, too many people for too many reasons have tried to use Oakwood for their own selfish purposes. Don't try to convince me that you do what you do purely for the sake of art."

The arrogance of that brought her out of her chair, an irate flush staining her cheeks. "I wouldn't dream of trying to convince you of anything." Pausing only to catch her breath, she continued in hard-won smooth tones. "I can see now that my coming here today was a waste of time. You've got your mind made up, but just for the record, let me fill you in on a few facts."

She didn't do this sort of thing very well. Some people could argue or rant and remain as cool and collected as the old cucumber. She wasn't one of those people and as she fought her own outrage at his taunting rudeness, she also sought to keep her knees from buckling and her voice from breaking.

"Photography *is* an art to me. I love what I do and it clearly shows in my work. Because of that, I'm able to make a modest income, *modest,* not extravagant, not even great. If I was all that concerned about money, I'd have gone into commercial photography where exploitation is a true art form.

"I didn't, and I've been fortunate, maybe even lucky enough, to work at something I enjoy. If people like the results, it's a bonus, but I work to meet my own standards, my own needs."

"A woman of principle."

"And practicality. But you're too callous and insensitive to handle the fact that I have to eat and pay my rent."

Jacob shoved away from the cabinet, his stance as unyielding as granite. "Sit down, Miss Davis."

"Go to hell, Mr. Quaide."

She stormed off with her words, more infuriated than she could ever remember being at anyone for any reason. Hands shaking, legs quaking, she flung open the front door and marched off toward her car, not giving a damn that Ares came running at the sight of her.

"Stay out of my way, dog," she snarled, jerking open her car door. She never gave the animal a second thought as she grabbed her key out of her pocket and shoved it into the ignition.

"I should have never come, I should have cut my losses . . . I'll get to the mansion, all right, even if I have to crawl in and just let him stand in my way."

Jamming the car into reverse, she fumed, "Just let him say anything." The gear shift was shoved into drive. "Arrogant, nasty, sonofa . . ."

She sped down the drive too quickly, hitting most of the potholes she had avoided on her trip in. After the fourth shocking bump, she eased off on the gas petal.

"Damn him, damn him," she raged. She had never been so insulted in her life. God, how could he have thought her so low?

That hurt. Deep inside her, a small pain erupted and tears came to her eyes.

"Damn him. Now he's made me cry."

Resenting him even more for causing this small outrage, she blinked furiously. It didn't do any good. In seconds, she couldn't see clearly enough to continue. Feeling as if she had been wounded in her heart, she slammed on the brake, braced her forehead on her steering wheel, and broke into sobs.

From the end of the drive, Jake watched the car race off, taking a small bit of satisfaction when the front left wheel connected with a deep rut.

"Good. She deserves to ruin her car." If for no other reason than for coming into his home and insulting him.

He narrowed his eyes when he thought of how she had called him callous and insensitive. The little shrew. Who the hell did she think she was? Even his ex-wife had never been so galling.

Shoving his hands on to his hips, he continued to glare down the lane. The car slowed for about a hundred yards and then came to a stop.

"What the devil is she doing?"

From this distance, he couldn't tell. He told himself he didn't give a damn. Still, he stood there, waiting to see if she got out to check a tire, or lift the hood. She did neither. Nor did the car move.

"She's cracked on top of everything else." The everything else being obnoxious, rude and opinionated as all get out. No one, and there had been more than a few, had ever told him to go to hell with such honest depth of feeling.

He gave a grunt at the unwelcome thought. He didn't want to associate Savannah Davis with anything as noble as honesty. He'd be lying, though, if he said that she hadn't been sincere in her emotions. And there had been quite a few: anger, resentment, irritation.

He could understand her more hostile responses. The very nature of their meeting had its basis in a true conflict of interests. But when she had walked into the living room, her expression had yielded to a yearning she hadn't cared to hide. At the time, her blatant admiration of his home had sent all his defenses into overdrive. Now, every instinct he possessed was challenged to see that Miss Savannah Davis understood that she had messed with the wrong man when she had decided to mess with him.

He scoured his lower lip with his teeth and mentally raked her about. She wasn't what he would have called beautiful. Her dark eyes and high cheekbones leaned more toward the exotic, while her lips were full to the point of being sensual. Her coffee-colored hair, swept back from her face, was shoulder length and as rich in appearance as the feel of her body had been. When she had fallen into his arms, he had discovered first hand that the oversized tweed jacket and tan slacks she wore disguised some very choice curves.

He focused on the little red car again as it began to move off at a cautious speed. When it was out of sight, he entered the house and settled into his den and called his brother.

Douglas Quaide picked up on the second ring. "Yes?"

"There are times when I think you should have your head examined," Jacob started right in. "Either that, or pull it out of your ass."

"Hello, to you, too," Doug returned, unperturbed at his brother's tone. "What's this about?"

Jacob shifted in the leather desk chair and propped his right ankle against his left knee. "As if you don't know."

"Let me guess, Savannah Davis."

"Bingo."

"Meeting not go well?"

At the too-innocent inflections, Jacob sneered, "You know goddamned well how it went."

"No, I don't, but I can imagine." Clear from Norfolk, the sound of Doug's sigh was weighty and when he spoke again, his voice was saturated with a taut impatience. "Leave her alone, Jake."

"Why the hell should I?"

"Because I think her project is worthwhile. The old house deserves . . ."

Silence traveled between them. Jacob pictured his brother squinting in his quest to find the right words.

"Don't pull that defense attorney crap on me, Doug. I'm not some jury you have to sway to your way of thinking."

"I know how you feel," Doug threw back sharply. "The plantation is a legacy. Hell, Mother and Dad drilled that shit into us from the first moment either one of us could understand what was up and what was down. That's why what Miss Davis wants to do has real merit." Doug paused, silence returned. And lingered. "Hell," he muttered sarcastically at length, "the old house isn't going to be around forever. This is the perfect opportunity to capture it for posterity."

"The old house has been there in one form or another for three hundred years. Unless the coast takes a direct hit from a class four hurricane, or the Naval Weapons Station across the river blows up, the house isn't going anywhere."

Doug didn't reply at once and Jacob had to wonder why. Doug was his best in a debate. He thrived on deliberation, commanding words the way generals commanded troops.

"Jake, look, I've gotta go."

Jake's brows slanted up at the coarse tension he heard. "You all right?"

"Yeah. Just . . . just leave Miss Davis alone to do her job. Catch you later."

The line went dead before Jacob could say anything more. It was just as well. He and Doug weren't going to agree on the issue. There was no use beating it into the ground.

He could, however, find some answers to the question of Savannah Davis herself. He dialed his office.

"Hi, Mary Beth, yeah. How are things there?"

As expected, his secretary assured him that everything was fine.

"Good. I'll be in tomorrow. In the meantime, I'm going to need some information on a woman named Savannah Davis." He spelled the last name. "Yeah. Everything we can find on her. Have Louis look into that." Bold, hard determination glinted in his eyes. "I want a file on my desk first thing tomorrow morning."

Two

The brass nameplate beside the solid wood door read QUAIDE AND ASSOCIATES. No one looking at the discreet panel would ever be able to tell what services the company offered. Nor would anyone flipping through the yellow pages ever find the name anywhere under any listing.

Jake preferred it that way. The general public didn't need to know that *Q and A* was in the business of collecting information. Or that the information at times was of a "sensitive nature," as his partner, Phil, liked to phrase it.

As far as Jake was concerned, caution and discretion were essential in his line of work. And there were several United States senators and a long list of major American corporations that appreciated that philosophy. Jake liked to think it was one of the reasons Quaide and Associates was as successful as it was.

Parking in front of the brick, colonial style building that housed his offices, he ran through a mental list of the day's agenda, noting at the same time which cars were present and which were not. Phil hadn't arrived yet. Their secretary, Mary Beth, had. She greeted him with her usual morning salute as he came through the door.

"Major."

He took the comment in stride. The title was left over from his days in the Air Force. No one other than Mary Beth used it any longer.

"Any calls?"

Mary Beth swiveled her hefty weight around in her chair, her half-glasses perched on the end of an impressive nose. "Four." She handed over the messages.

"Thanks."

The secretary pulled a pencil from the knot of graying hair at the back of her head and shook the slim instrument his way. "Don't thank me too soon. One of those calls was from Congressman Ipsell's aide. Some subcommittee of a subcommittee in Washington wants you to give a report next week on those projected statistics we dug up on Japanese telecommunications."

Jake flipped past the message from the aide. "Hopefully, Phil will want to take that one."

Mary Beth gave a wickedly smug smile, her fifty-four year old face showing a network of fine lines. "I don't think so. Ipsell's been asking for you."

"Ipsell's a dweeb." Jake scanned the other messages. "Anything else?"

"Yes, as a matter of fact."

He looked up in time to see Mary Beth lift a large, bubble-wrapped envelope from behind her desk. "This came from Louis."

The information he had requested on Savannah Davis. He had been expecting the standard file, several sheets of data. What he held appeared to be anything but standard.

Black brows slanted over suspicious eyes, he took the package and made his way down the hall to his office. Sitting behind his desk, he tore open the envelope and removed a bundle of magazines rubber-banded together. Attached were the several pages of Louis's report. Under the entire stack was a book with a note from Louis.

JQ—as the saying goes—a picture is worth a thousand words? LT

Jake stared at the assortment and gave the matter of Savannah Davis his full attention.

A half-hour later, his booted feet propped up on his desk,

his lap and the floor around his chair covered with magazines, he read through the two pages of Louis's report for the second time.

"Must be interesting stuff," Phil commented from the doorway.

Jake looked up and gave his partner a distracted half-smile. "Something like that."

"Anyone I know?" Phil gestured to the array of weekly news publications.

"You tell me." He flipped one of the five year old magazines onto the desk. "Ever heard of this photographer, S. Davis?"

Phillip Stewart came forward to peer down at the gut-churning picture of a starving child in Somalia. The photo had as much impact now as it had had years earlier when it had first appeared.

"Jesus," Phillip muttered. "I'll never get used to it."

"It's sobering."

Shoving his hands into his pockets, Phil shook off the disturbing effects of the black and white images. "I remember seeing this picture and a great many just like it a few years back. I've never heard of this"—he craned his neck to get a better view of the name in tiny print beneath the picture—"this S. Davis. Any reason I should know him?"

"Her. The S is for Savannah."

Phil grimaced slightly. "Why do I know that name?"

Jake reached to the floor for the hardback book and handed it over.

"Centuries." Phil's face lit with recognition. "Yeah, great stuff. Francie got me a copy for Christmas last year." His gaze dropped to the name on the cover then shifted to the array of magazines on the desk. "The same Savannah Davis?"

"It would appear so."

"So why are we gathering info on her?" Before Jake could answer, he held up a hand and sighed in disgust. "Oh, don't tell me she's pointed her camera somewhere she shouldn't have."

"Nothing like that."

"Thank God. I hate to see great talent wasted." He set the book down and gave his partner a shrewd look. "So what's up?"

"She wants to photograph the old house."

Phil smiled broadly. "Oh?" The smile dropped away like a ton of lead. "Oh." Jake had never made any secret of how he felt about the plantation. Phil, better than anyone, understood. "What does Doug have to say about this?"

"He gave her the go ahead."

"Then what—"

The phone buzzed, cutting off Phil's question. Jake took the interoffice call from Mary Beth.

"You've got a call on line one," he told Phil. "National Enterprises."

Phil was already heading for the door. "Thanks. We've been playing telephone tag for days. I've got at least five messages from their CEO."

Jake considered the messages he had ignored since he had come in. Thankfully, none had been urgent because reading about Savannah Davis had been consuming. He fingered the dossier Louis had compiled and contemplated all he had learned, starting with the most obvious.

She looked younger than twenty-eight. Except for her eyes, he decided abruptly. Propping an elbow on the chair's arm, he scrubbed his fingers over his chin and mentally scrutinized those eyes. Deep brown and heavily lashed, they had somehow seemed older than the rest of her, as though they had witnessed more than twenty-eight years of life.

One of the magazines on the floor stared back at him with a full page image of a wretchedly pitiful child in Sarajevo. There was no doubt that Savannah Davis had seen her share of living . . . and dying.

He scanned the rest of the first page of the report. Her

personal life read like a maiden aunt's compared to most modern women. He read further and found no great surprises, except perhaps, for the mention of her having seen a therapist for a short while. If it was to curb her temper, whatever money Savannah Davis had laid out had been wasted.

She had graduated from Rochester Institute of Technology at the age of twenty and been scooped up by *World News Magazine.* No mean feat there, since the publication was noted for the raw power of its photojournalism. Within a year, Savannah Davis had been given her choice of assignments.

The woman was accomplished. There was no doubt about that, but why had she chucked it all? According to Louis, she hadn't worked for any newspaper or magazine in over two years. Her energies and her lenses had been focused on a more private subject.

Centuries. Jake leafed through the book of portraits again. Not for the first time, he found himself firmly caught and held by the intensity of each face. Babies, teens, the elderly, Asian, Caucasian, Native Americans, Africans. Without any prejudice to race or color or age or ethnic group, Savannah Davis had captured far, far more than a collection of features.

He shoved a sigh out in a hissing sound, studying the photos. This wasn't what he had expected—or wanted—to find. Pretty pictures, fluff photography without depth or feeling or even artistic merit would have been preferable. Those would have given him confirmation of what he wanted to believe about Savannah Davis, that she was a miserable little opportunist.

Instead, using nothing but a camera, she had managed to draw out the vitality and spirit of each person, and cold-cock the viewer right in his emotions.

He stroked a long finger over the smiling face of a new mother holding her tiny, naked son. From that still picture came pride and trepidation, hope, fulfillment, supreme satisfaction, fierce protectiveness, and love; unending, limitless, from-the-soul, unconditional love.

Only the blind or the insensitive could have ignored the strength of such a photo. Only a fool would have believed that the strength of that photo wasn't due solely to the photographer.

It had been a whole day since she had driven away from Oakwood and Savannah still felt the remnants of yesterday's temper and tears.

Putting water on to boil for a late afternoon cup of tea, she tried not to dwell on the fiasco with Jacob Quaide, but she couldn't shake the episode. Too many turbulent emotions had arisen from her few minutes with the man. Taken individually, the emotions would have been manageable. Dumped on her in a heap as they had been, she was feeling nearly as edgy now as she had when she had stormed out of his house.

She took a seat at the kitchen table and tucked her bare feet up under her so she could wrap her arms about her knees and simply reflect. She wasn't proud of having told him where he could go. Then again, he had gotten her so angry, the words had just burst out.

Angry words for a hard, austere man. She didn't even have to close her eyes in order to see the severe planes of his face and the intensity in his chilling cobalt gaze. His expression had been as grave and intimidating as his manner, and his ordering her to sit down in that deep caustic voice of his had only added to her temper.

Her stomach knotted at the memory of how she had cried. It wasn't like her to be reduced to a puddle of tears. At the time, though, her mind, and body, and feelings had been driven to that outlet. It was a little demoralizing to realize that the thick shell she thought she had developed over the last few years was tissue thin.

The whistling kettle brought her to her feet. Hiking her

slouchy blue sweat pants up about her waist, she made herself a cup of tea and hoped the caffeine would help get rid of the drained feeling that still nagged at her.

She didn't like the hollow sensation. It reminded her of other times in her life when she had felt void of energy; after her father's death. And after everything with Eric.

Eric.

Out of habit, she shied from that train of thought, gripping the cup's handle in a reflexive move. Only when the door bell rang did she gently uncurl her fingers.

Cup in hand, she made her way to the front door, peeking through the living room window as she went. Instantly, she stopped at the sight of a dark green Jaguar parked out in front.

Unease clenched the muscles around her lungs and heart, followed closely by the stroke of irritation. What was *he* doing here? Exhaling sharply, she opened the door and faced Jacob Quaide squarely despite the fact that she had to tip her head back to do so.

He stood tall and imposing in well-worn jeans, his hands tucked into the pockets of a bomber jacket, his eyes hidden behind aviator glasses. The same air of power and command that had surrounded him yesterday all but pulsed from him in formidable waves that had her swallowing.

"Mr. Quaide." Every one of her defenses was up. She hadn't forgiven him for treating her the way he had. She was on the verge of resenting him for just standing there, making her feel insecure.

He returned her look, and behind his glasses, squinted slightly, noting, she was sure, the subtle nuances of her misgivings. "We need to talk."

She didn't know what she expected him to say, but that wasn't it, and her brows rose in twin arches. He spared her none of the polite hellos. Directness seemed to be his style, and he apparently expected her to accede to his directive in as straightforward a manner.

The gall of that had her biting the inside of her cheek.

"May I come in?" he asked, when she remained silent for a second too long.

Her first reaction was to tell him to get back in his car, and this time, he could drive to hell. Common sense nudged aside her abused feelings and pointed out the simple fact that *he* had come to see her, *he* wished to speak to her, presumably about yesterday. She couldn't find any other reason for his being there. If that were the case, it would be to her benefit to hear him out.

She swung the door open and he stepped in, filling the small living room at once with his presence. "How did you find me?" She lived in Richmond. This cozy river-front cottage in Gloucester belonged to a friend of the family. She was using it for the duration of her stay in the area. As far as she knew, only her sister and her mother knew where to find her.

Jake gave the room a cursory once over, tucking his glasses into his pocket. Only when he had seen his fill did he turn to Savannah with his answer.

"I have my ways."

She didn't think that was any answer at all. Her fingers tightened about the cup she still held. "You obviously do. Well, you've found me; what do you want to talk about?"

Her brittle tone confirmed what Jake had already noted. She wasn't pleased to see him. Nor had she been prepared to do so. Under the faded red T-shirt she wore, she was clearly braless, and the comfy sweats that hugged her legs revealed the sweet curves of her thighs. All in all, she looked better suited to a relaxing, intimate evening at home than to a verbal skirmish with him.

That didn't deter her, though. Her chin was up, her mouth set just enough for him to rise to the challenge she presented.

He removed his copy of *Centuries* from under his arm and handed it to her. "It's very good."

Savannah held the book in one hand, her cup of tea in

the other and once again, felt at a loss. After their heated exchange, the absolute last thing she expected from him was a compliment, one that oddly enough, jarred her.

Gazing from the book to him and back again, she stood there not quite certain how to react or what to say. Praise and accolades were not unusual to her. Everyone from her agent to the booksellers had at one time applauded her work. The kudos were nice, but she didn't always agree with the assessments. She was her own toughest critic and as a result, she appreciated the acclaim, but didn't always take it to heart.

And yet three simple words from the Q Man struck her deeply. For no logical reason, she was inordinately pleased that he liked her work, and she didn't know why. Maybe because he hadn't been so nice to her yesterday, and by comparison, the compliment took on some value. Or maybe it was because he was such a blatantly bottom-line man that his approval reeked of an honest opinion.

Then again, perhaps it was because he was so potently male and she was reacting to him on a purely feminine level. He was more dynamic than handsome, more virile than attractive. The combination was impossible to ignore.

Disturbed by where her thoughts were headed, she turned away and set her cup on a nearby table. When she faced him, it was with an expression of confusion.

"Would you like to sit down, Mr. Quaide?"

They settled into chairs facing each other, his legs stretched out and crossed at the ankles, hers tucked up beneath her. She gripped the book on her lap.

"Did you track me down just to bring me this?"

"I didn't track you down. And the book is part of the reason I came."

"That surprises me."

"Why?"

She wrinkled her nose in an attempt to proceed tactfully. "Would you be insulted if I said that I wouldn't have thought you the type to be interested in a collection of portraits?"

"That would depend on why you would think such a thing."

"Given our association so far, I've come to certain conclusions."

His unwavering blue gaze taunted her. "In this case, your assumptions would be wrong."

She returned his gaze for as long as she could endure its masterful force then flicked a glance to the familiar paper cover on the book. "I guess so." Since he did have a copy, that said something about his appreciation of her art. And, of course, there had been the compliment. She might not know him from Adam, but she did know that he wouldn't be one to offer meaningless praise.

"Was there something you wished to discuss about *Centuries*?"

"No."

"But I thought you said it was part of the reason you came here."

He shifted so that he braced his left ankle on his right knee. "It is. The quality of the work in *Centuries* convinced me that we didn't finish our discussion yesterday."

"I see." And she did. She had passed a test of sorts. Impressed with her work, he now was willing to consider whether or not he would give her easy access to Oakwood's mansion.

Clenching her stomach muscles at the jab of irritation she felt, she silently and truly hoped he had a valid reason for such arrogance. It would help her tremendously in keeping from hitting him over the head with his book.

"You're very attached to the plantation, aren't you?"

He cocked his head to one side and laced his fingers together over his stomach, knowing that she was struggling with her temper. He could see it in the flash that came to her eyes and the way she angled her head so that her chin jutted out a fraction of an inch.

The last was a dead give away that she was pissed off. She had done the same thing yesterday and he wondered if she was aware that her body language spoke volumes.

For some reason, he was glad that he could get a rise out of her. "Yes, you could say that Oakwood is important to me," he drawled, unwilling to keep the smile from curling the edges of his mouth. "Why do you ask?"

"Because I'd like for *this* discussion to remain civil."

"And you think it won't?"

"Not if you continue to see me as some money-grasping bitch out to swindle you, or abuse your property."

"I don't think that."

"You did before you happened to flip through this," she charged, lifting *Centuries*.

"I thought a great many things about you before I studied those prints."

"None of them good."

"I didn't know you then."

"You don't know me now."

"I know more than you think. Your pictures are extremely telling."

"And now your opinion of me has changed?"

He lifted one shoulder in a negligent shrug. "To some degree."

"Enough so that you'd . . . what? You'd cooperate in letting me shoot the house?"

"Something like that."

Savannah swallowed a string of curses. Why did she have to prove anything to this man? She was the exact same person she had been yesterday, before he had viewed her work.

In a more reasonable vein, she reminded herself that she had just gotten what she had come for: his help. There was no turning her back on that.

She gave a sigh that eased her tension and expressed her relief. Even though she did have a temper, at heart, she was an agreeable person. She didn't like confrontations and rose to the unpleasant occasions only out of necessity. She'd stand her ground if she had to, not out of instinct, but because she had learned that at times in life, it was the only way to survive. Having survived this skirmish with Jacob Quaide had been taxing.

"Thank you," she offered graciously, passing him his book. "I don't think you'll be disappointed with your decision."

He came to his feet and lifted one black brow. "See that I'm not."

The warning wasn't even subtle, and her uncertain temper flared for a second. He wouldn't hamper her efforts, but he expected superb results from her in return. And she knew he would hold her to that.

Following him to the door, she watched him dig into his pocket for his glasses. "I'd like to come out tomorrow and walk through the house before I actually start shooting."

Sunglasses back in place, he asked, "What time?"

"Late afternoon, I'd think." Lifting a hand, she rubbed at the slight tension at the nape of her neck. "I'm shooting a house in Urbana from dawn until noon. It'll take me at least an hour to pack up and drive back."

"Fine." The cotton fabric of her shirt stretched over the softness of her breasts. Behind his glasses, Jake studied the contours of her nipples. "I'll meet you at my place."

"Wouldn't it be easier for you to just give me directions to the old house? I don't want to put you to any trouble."

Studying the twin impressions against the front of her shirt, he gave her a crooked grin. He turned for his car, and over his shoulder drawled, "You already have."

Three

It was back—the haunting sensation that something was wrong nibbled away at the nerves at the back of her neck. As Savannah maneuvered her car around one of the holes in Oakwood's drive, she pressed her left hand into the spot between her shoulder blades, and then ignored the feeling away.

Her morning had gone well. She expected her afternoon to be even better. If all she had heard about this particular house was even one-tenth accurate, she'd be one very happy camper. There wasn't time or reason for her to be concerned with imagined impressions of apprehension.

She pulled up behind Jacob Quaide's car parked in front of his house and spied the source of a more real apprehension. Ares. The Airedale stood at the foot of the brick steps, looking as if he couldn't wait for her to make a mistake. Any mistake.

"Damn dog," she muttered to herself. "Why couldn't you be a cat or something? A parakeet would be better."

As if he had heard and chose to tell her what she could do with her suggestion, Ares broke into a round of barking that bared his teeth and had his front paws leaving the ground.

Savannah glared back at him from the safety of her car and waited for the Q Man to rescue her from his own private warning system. As much noise as the dog was making, she figured Jacob Quaide would know she was there. He'd have to come looking for her though, because she wasn't getting out of the car until Ares, the raging hound from hell, was out of the way.

She didn't have long to wait. The front door opened and Jacob came down the steps. He bent slightly to one side until he could see her through the windshield. She lifted her hands in mock surrender and smiled a smile that was undiluted sugar.

Ares quieted immediately, at a command, no doubt, from his owner. Savannah appreciated that. She would have liked it better, though, if the dog were the roly-poly kind that lapped at your knees.

"I used to like animals," she said, getting out of the car.

"He won't hurt you."

The laugh she gave was just as much a scoff. "As long as you tell him not to."

"That's the way it's supposed to work," he told her with a short, tight grin.

It was the first sign of humor she had seen from him. Too bad it was at her expense. The sides of his face creased, softening the hard planes, although not in a boyish sense. He was so overtly mature and masculine that he could never be confused with anything as young and inexperienced as a boy.

No, his smile and the humor behind it, made him seem approachable. In command, fully aware, determined, but approachable.

Savannah didn't misconstrue that for anything else. She knew that he would prefer her not to be there at all. And she couldn't forget that he was going to hold her accountable for treating his ancestral property with respect and dignity.

As if I would do anything else, she thought. "Thanks for meeting me. Again. I appreciate your taking time out from work to help me this way. I hope your boss doesn't mind."

"I'm my own boss, Miss Davis."

It didn't surprise her. She couldn't picture him taking

orders from anyone. As she came to stand near him and tuck her hands into the back pockets of her jeans, she told him as much. "So you get to come and go as you please." Her gaze skimmed the navy sweater and faded jeans he wore. "What do you do, Mr. Quaide?"

"I run an investigative agency." It was his pat answer, much simpler than getting into the finer points of what he did. And besides, they weren't there to discuss him or what he did to earn a living.

He had agreed to help her, make her job as simple as possible. Having come to that decision, he wanted her to get to work. *Centuries* had convinced him of her talent, but in his mind, she was still on trial for one very basic reason. He didn't trust anyone other than Doug when it came to Oakwood. Savannah Davis had yet to prove to him that she was as good as his gut instinct said she was.

"Come on, I'll take you up to the house." He gestured off to the stand of trees spreading toward the York River.

Anticipation was like a tingling blanket wrapping itself about Savannah's nerves. She hugged the sensation close, trying not to let too much of her delight show. As touchy as Jacob Quaide was about the entire situation, she thought it best not to appear as if she were gloating. Still, there was no suppressing her smile when she joined him in the quiet hush of the forest.

Tangled underbrush and vines grew in thick clumps, while low bushes and thickets nestled between the larger pines and oaks. Autumn's ripe colors were everywhere. Savannah studied the grove in silence for as long as she could, but finally gave into her excitement.

"How far is it from here?"

"About a quarter mile."

"I've heard a lot about the house. It's supposed to be one of the best examples of early American architecture anywhere."

"It is."

At the pride in his voice, Savannah's smile grew and a spark of pure joy lit her eyes. Jake noted both, deciding the effect had her looking like a little kid at Christmas.

She wasn't. If the remembered feel of his hand on her breast didn't confirm that then the fit of her jeans did. The denim hugged the long length of her legs and cupped her bottom with no pretense of childishness.

He liked that. The sway of her hips was subtle, the gentle bobbing motion of her breasts an understatement of sensuality. Cocking his head to one side, he scanned the front of her blue work shirt with an appreciative eye.

"Were these trees here when the plantation was in use?" she asked.

"No." *She's wearing a bra today, damn it.* "The mansion was last used in 1910. Fire destroyed most of the west wing and my great, great-grandparents moved to a second house they owned further upriver."

"So they allowed the land to grow wild?"

"Only the acres that weren't directly used for farming. They continued to use the rest of the acreage for growing soy beans and corn."

"Is that what you still grow?"

"I don't grow anything. I lease my fields to a local farmer." He stepped between a shielding border of undergrowth and held the tangled thicket aside. "Through here."

Savannah ducked through the opening, straightened and came face to face with Oakwood's mansion.

"Oh . . . my," she breathed. The visual impact of the house shoved all the air from her lungs in a single stunned exhalation.

She was awed, transfixed. Eyes wide, her mouth formed into an "O," she felt a thrilling rush that inspired and humbled at the same time. All the strange tension she had experienced in previous days collected at the base of her neck as she tipped her head back to see the house in its entirety.

It was massive. Three stories tall, constructed entirely of

a mellow red brick, the main portion of the house consisted of six bays. From the east and west sides, extended the two-storied wings that added to the overwhelming sense of unity and perfect, peaceful symmetry.

The craftsmanship was superb. Savannah visually absorbed each detail, taking great satisfaction in the keystones that highlighted each window, the remains of the dentiled cornice that edged the roof, the remnants of the marble that had at one time flanked the front door.

Each corner of the house boasted a whimsical display of decorative masonry work that was repeated in a border between each story. Three of the six separate chimneys could still be seen, as could some of the wood lintel around the doorway.

Savannah took it all in. It was beautiful. Even with its scarred, burned out west wing, even with a portion of the roof gone, the mortar discolored and crumbling, and windows gaping holes without glass, it was simply magnificent in construction and ambiance.

Her lungs squeezed themselves about her heart. Everything she had hoped to find in the house was there. Artistic workmanship, timeless beauty, and the steadfast essence of generations who had lived and loved and died there. From the pit of her insides, Savannah felt a surge of welcome that brought her to tears.

"Oh, Jacob," she whispered, pressing her fingertips to her lips, wanting to give into the urge to go to her knees.

Jacob held perfectly still, studying Savannah as intensely as she studied the house. She practically vibrated with a pleasure so profound, he could almost feel the chaotic cadence reach out to him.

She was captivated, truly captivated with an admiration that bordered on reverence, and it wasn't an act. Rosy color rode her cheeks, and those gorgeous brown eyes of hers were half-filled with the tears of her emotions.

More gratified by her reaction than he cared to admit, he said, "I assume you like it."

She swallowed, grinning at him with a smile gone wobbly. "I never expected anything like this. Just looking at it . . . I don't even know what to say. How could she describe feelings that ran clear to her soul? She asked questions instead.

"How have you managed to keep it in such good condition all these years?" She didn't wait for his answer as her gaze went back to the structure, seeing all the obvious signs of the extraordinary protection the house had been given. "I can't believe it. No graffiti . . . and there's so much still intact. The keystones are the first things to be stolen from houses like this."

"We weren't so lucky with the doors."

Sadly, the panels were missing, as were the shutters. "Were they mahogany?"

He nodded. "Taken from timber here on the plantation."

What she wouldn't have given to have seen them. "Is it safe to go in?"

"The first and second floors are," he said, watching one unguarded expression after another march across her face. "The third floor has caught too much rain damage. Parts of the ceiling are crumbling and I don't trust the walls. Of course the west wing is completely off limits. The rest is fine." He gestured toward the front doorway for her to precede him.

She laid her fingers lightly, momentarily, on his arm. "Would you mind if I went in by myself?"

Her touch, brief as it was, stopped him. He jabbed a look from her hand to her face, wary out of habit alone. Few people were allowed entrance into the old house. He had preferred it that way for too long for him to become instantly nonchalant about the matter.

"Why?" The query was a concession, giving her the benefit of the doubt as he tempered life-long instincts.

"I'd like to spend some time visualizing, without a guided tour."

"Don't you want to know what each room was used for?"

"Function will come later. Right now I want to go with my first impressions of light, form, structure, textures."

His brows arched up. "And I'll just get in the way, is that it?" he concluded in a droll voice.

"No, it isn't that," she quickly countered, even as she grimaced. "Well, actually . . ." She spread her hands wide in a gesture that was a little helpless around the edges. "You will interfere with my concentration by just being with me."

Her confession pricked him on a primal male level. He gave her a long, lazy stare, gratified as only a man could possibly be, by the fact that he had the power to disrupt the attention of an attractive woman.

"All right. I'll wait for you back at my house. Watch out for mice."

"You don't have to remind me." She shuddered in distaste. "The last building I was in, I carried a long stick."

"Did it help?"

"Not really."

Turning to leave, he kept his smile well-hidden. "I could send Ares in with you."

She gave his back her nicest stick-it-in-your-ear smile. "No thanks. I'll get an old tree branch."

"Have it your way. How long will you be?"

Her gaze went from her watch to the house. "About a half-hour, forty-five minutes."

"If you're not back by then, I'll send Ares out to bring you back."

She shook her head as she watched him step through the tall hedge of underbrush, having no doubt that he would send the damn dog if she was even one minute late.

"Arrogant man," she muttered around her lingering smile.

The mice were in the walls. She could hear the scratching

noise of their feet when she walked into the mansion's wide entrance way. That was the only thought she gave the little critters as her mind focused completely on her surroundings.

The odor of disuse hit her first. Old buildings carried with them the scent of mold and rot, earth and wood, sometimes even a trace of smoke. This house smelled of all of that. She could understand why. Amazingly, there was an abundance of wood that still remained.

Decaying wainscotting paneled the lower half of an entry way that bisected the house. At the other end of the hall, in typical Colonial Virginian style, was a back doorway identical to one on the front side of the house. Off to the left was the oak stairway, complete with broken wooden spindles and banister, leading up to the second story.

Savannah stood at the base of the stairs, struggling to keep from racing upward. She was giddy with excitement and wanted to take it all in at once. It took a conscious effort for her not to touch anything, to leave it all exactly as it was until she could take her first shots.

Methodically, she slowly entered the first room to her left, advancing only by a few feet. Sunlight poured fiercely into what she assumed was a parlor, illuminating the stains on the plastered walls and the thick layer of dust on the floor. She squinted to filter out extreme colors and found that beneath the blatant wash of gray that predominated everything, was a warm yellow hue.

Her gaze lifted to what remained of the crown molding at the ceiling. To her absolute delight, she discovered that the trim had been etched with a pattern of twined flowers and Cupid's bows. The elegant decoration was repeated on the mantel and its chimney pieces.

"This is unbelievable," she laughed out loud. Already, she was anticipating how the details of the room would look in the muted mistiness of dawn or with moonlight throwing stark shadows over the old surfaces. Autumn cast its influence with sweetness, but winter was coming, and she intended to use its subtle powers to the fullest.

Smiling broadly, she continued the rest of her inspection. Each room was a treasure with a special point of interest, with a unique feel of its own. Six rooms on the first floor, six on the second; Savannah died a little inside at not being able to go up to the third. The east wing, however, was its own reward. A ballroom and two smaller chambers.

The sense of peaceful symmetry she had noted from outside was repeated again and again within the house. Everywhere she looked, she saw poetry of form enhanced by the type of craftsmanship that simply did not exist anymore. From the smallest detail, she derived a feeling of timelessness, of enduring grace and ageless comfort.

It was no wonder Jacob felt as he did.

Thinking of him, she glanced to her watch, realizing with a start that she had been in the house an hour. It was nearly five o'clock. The Q Man was not going to be happy about that. She was already fifteen minutes late.

Her steps quick, she left the house, her mind crammed full of angles and lighting, lenses and filters. The subject matter was rare and beautiful, its potential priceless. The possibilities were endless, and she couldn't wait to get started.

Once through the tall concealing hedge, she stopped to give the structure one last loving look, turned for the forest again and was hit suddenly with a wave of dizziness. Automatically, her hands reached out in an instinctive move to gain her equilibrium.

"Oh, God," she groaned, pressing one arm to her stomach and a hand to her head. Neither helped. Nausea rolled in her throat, sweat broke out on her forehead, and she ended up bracing her hands on her knees and letting her head drop forward.

That effort was useless. The ground seemed to tip up at her. In defense, she straightened, sending the blood from her head so quickly she sucked in a deep breath and shut her eyes against the drumming sound in her ears.

She was going to be sick. The miserable thought snapped her eyes open . . . to the sight of Jacob Quaide stalking toward her, looking as if he intended to chew her up and spit her out in little pieces.

"Just what I need," she muttered to herself. She was going to throw up and he was going to be there to see her loss of dignity. "Please . . ." She tried to hold him off with a raised hand.

"Do you know what time it is?" he demanded in a voice that could have put frost on the nearby trees.

"Not now," she managed, looking around to find some place, any place that would give her a little privacy.

His hands caught her by her shoulders and held her in place. "You better get something straight right now. I don't work well with people who are irresponsible. And I don't give a rat's ass for liars."

Even her misery couldn't prevent his accusation from hitting home. "What are you talking about? I'm one of the most responsible people I know. And I am *not* a liar."

"No? You told me you'd be forty-five minutes. Well, I gave you that and an extra seventy-five minutes."

She frowned in disbelief. "It's only been an hour."

"Wrong."

Swallowing against the pain that began to throb in her head, she checked the time on her watch . . . and the world tilted. Her watch read a little past six.

It couldn't be. She had noted the time just a few minutes ago and it had been a little before five. She was sure of it.

That was her last thought before the dizziness became unconsciousness and she felt herself fall.

Four

"Lie still."

Savannah blinked her eyes open at the deep-throated command. "What? . . ."

From his squatting position beside the sofa in his den, Jacob held her right wrist in his hand and checked her pulse against his watch. "Just be still for a minute."

"What happened?"

"You passed out. Quiet." Under his fingers, he could feel her pulse, steady and regular. A good sign since less than a minute ago, she had been dead to the world. Laying her hand over her stomach, he scrutinized her pupils and found them evenly dilated. "How are you feeling?"

Lying on a sofa with her feet propped up on the arm rest, Savannah took inventory of her body. The nausea and headache that had attacked her were gone. Her mind was clear and alert. "Better."

"Meaning what?"

"Meaning I don't feel as if I'm going to throw up." She eyed him with a pained expression, hoping she truly hadn't fainted at the feet of the one man who viewed her as a tolerable nuisance. "Did I really pass out?"

"Yup."

"Sorry."

Jake shrugged her apology away, but his gaze was sharp, penetrating, reading the signs of her embarrassment. "What happened?"

With his query, she shifted to her elbow in an attempt to sit up. His hands shot out and held her firmly in place.

"Don't move for a while," he told her, sitting beside her so he could search for any signs of a relapse. Her color had returned, her skin was not overly hot or cold. If she pushed it too quickly, though, she'd be right back where she was. "Give your head a chance to regroup."

"I really am better. I don't feel dizzy anymore."

"Is that what happened?" He braced his arm on the back of the sofa.

With a nod, she explained, "I suddenly got nauseous and I couldn't focus on anything."

"Did you fall and hit your head?"

"No, but I almost lost my balance."

"How long were you like that?"

"Only a few minutes. I was finished in the house and checked the time. I saw that I was going to be late and left immediately. I got as far as this side of the hedge and couldn't go any further. That's when you found me."

"Were you disoriented?"

She slowly shook her head.

"How about pain?"

"Nothing more than a bad headache. It's gone now."

"Has this happened before?"

"No, never."

"How have you felt lately?"

He was beginning to sound like a doctor, watching her with a discerning eye, prodding for answers that a physician would be entitled to. Only he wasn't a doctor and his point-blank questioning and unwavering gaze had her wanting to squirm.

"I'm okay. Honestly, except for feeling extremely foolish." She had a mental image of him carrying her through the woods and laying her down on his sofa. Compared to the business-like way in which they had treated each other so far, his actions bordered on something more private.

She didn't know if she liked that, or the fact that she was so much the focus of his attention. It made her uncomfortable knowing that he had held her close. He was overwhelmingly masculine, and seated the way he was, rather intimidating. With his hard thigh pressed into her hip, and his arm stretched over her to the back of the sofa, his body surrounded hers in a manner she found abruptly and disturbingly intimate.

"I . . . I'd like to sit up now." And she didn't care that her voice sounded as vulnerable as she felt. She had just become excruciatingly aware of Jacob Quaide; the size and heat of him, the broad width of his shoulders and his unmovable presence. It was becoming increasingly more difficult to ignore the utter maleness of him.

And there he sat, watching her like a hawk watches its prey, his sapphire gaze sharp, piercing, returning her study, stare for stare.

Jake kept the smile from his face, but it was a struggle. She was suddenly uneasy with her position and wanted up. Badly. He half-expected to see her jaw take on that arrogant tilt in a silent demand for him to move out of her way. Disappointingly, no challenge was issued, which reminded him that she wasn't feeling one hundred percent yet.

That was a shame. He liked the idea of proving to Savannah Davis that he could keep her on her back if he wanted to. In a quick-silver flash, the private picture grew to include himself, his body covering hers, pressing her back into the cushions.

Deep in his gut, his body reacted to the thought.

"Take it slow." He helped her into a sitting position, letting his hands linger gently at her shoulders, but he was annoyed with his body's unexpected reaction. "Okay?"

Savannah didn't trust her voice. The move brought their heads so close her forehead nearly touched his chin. Instead she nodded and then mentally kicked herself when her skin lightly brushed over his.

Jacob felt the shiver that raced over her. "Savannah? Are you all right?"

"Yes," she said a little too quickly, too brightly. She used the moment to scoot backward and realized for the first time that her jeans had been unbuttoned, the zipper lowered completely. Her gaze flew to his.

"I did that," he told her. "You needed to be as comfortable as possible."

It was a perfectly reasonable explanation, stated in a mature, adult manner. Then why, she asked herself, did she feel like a virgin who had been thoroughly exposed? "Thanks, I think." She closed up her jeans, missing the concentrated hunger in Jacob's eyes.

That desire was not there by choice. Jacob even went so far as to tell himself that it was inappropriate given the circumstances. And yet, desire was what he felt, tugging unmercifully when it wasn't in his nature to get aroused by a woman he didn't know well enough to like.

He hadn't come to any conclusions about Savannah Davis yet, but that didn't stop him from appreciating the taut flatness of her belly, or the way the small triangle of her navy blue panties lay against her skin. In the few seconds before she zipped up, he savored the inherent sensuality of woman and lace, and then expanded on the theme.

Savannah Davis in lacy, sexy little bits of nothing. It was a dynamite image that dragged at everything that was male within him.

"I'm sorry about all of this," she muttered, finishing at last with the stubborn button. She felt off center and didn't like it. It was time to put things back on their normal track, beginning with the angry accusations he had hurled at her.

Shoulders straight, she faced him dead on, her chin finally angled upward. "I'm not certain what happened about the time earlier. My watch must need a new battery, but that wasn't any reason for you to call me a liar."

"Would you like something to drink?"

She blinked. And blinked again. "Did you hear what I said?" she demanded to know.

"Yes."

"Don't you have anything to say?"

"No."

"You can't just ignore the matter."

A one sided smile stretched the firm line of his mouth. "Yes, I can, especially when the discussion involved would be a waste of time."

"A waste of time?" Her eyes rounded in a mixture of hot indignation and cold disbelief. "If that isn't the most—"

He ran a hand down the length of her arm. "Take it easy, Savannah. I made a mistake. I apologize. End of discussion." Coming to his feet, he headed for the doorway. "I'll be right back."

She sat there stunned. Their discussion was *not* ended. "How dare you?" she muttered to the empty room, aiming her words at him. In a move similar to his, she rose and made her way from the den. Unlike Jacob Quaide's easy stride down the hall, however, hers was marked by a temper on the verge of igniting.

"You're a real piece of work, Q Man," she announced the second she entered the kitchen. She didn't even wait for him to turn from the refrigerator, but launched right in, only remembering distantly why she had tread so carefully with him up to that point.

"I resent your attitude. You accuse me of being an irresponsible liar and then shrug the whole thing away as if it were nothing at all." She took her stand in the middle of the kitchen, ignoring his cool, appraising expression. "You've reduced my feelings to a 'waste of time,' like I didn't have an ounce of sense, or worse, that I really am a thoughtless, deceitful person."

Unknowingly, her hands clenched into fists. Her temper was fraying rapidly, which made her all the more angry. She normally kept a lid on her temper, but there was something about this man that could reach past all her restraint and politeness and make her want to throw things—big heavy things—at his head.

"Who died and made you king? Where do you get off treating people this way, or am I the only recipient of your high and mighty arrogance? Well, if this is what I have to put up with, then I'll leave my car at the county road from now on. Having to endure your ideas of manners just isn't worth the trouble. It's too demeaning and hurtful."

She was shaking with her last word. He was the most difficult man with which she had ever had to deal and she wanted to leave. Spinning for the hall, she shoved a hand into one of her pockets for her car keys, and silently fumed at him. Then at herself when she couldn't find the damn keys.

"Looking for these?" he asked in succinctly modulated tones.

His tight, low voice whirled her around to face him again. Dangling from one long index finger were her keys.

"What are you doing with those? Give them back."

"No." Instead, he gave her a smile as thin as shaved ice, and slowly advanced on her.

Savannah's entire spine straightened, and she hastily stepped back. He looked dangerous, predatory, like some hunter stalking his prey.

"Stop it," she whispered, the feral gleam in his eyes sending her pulse racing. Again, she moved back, again, he advanced.

"I haven't done anything," came his silky reply.

Whatever she would have said, got caught in the middle of a gasp when she bumped up against the counter. In the next instant, he towered over her, reducing her field of vision to the broad plane of his chest.

Her thoughts became a chaotic mess. He was too close . . . he was angry . . . she was angry. She didn't fear him physically, not in terms of rape or assault, but he threatened her in other ways, on other levels.

She felt trapped, and dazedly admitted that it was a trap of her own making. The last time she had gotten angry with him, she had left before he had had a chance to respond. Apparently, she was about to find out how he took to being told off.

"What do you think you're doing?" she demanded, striving to keep her voice level.

Jake didn't bother with an answer, at least not the one he literally had to chew back. Although why he chose not to verbally take her apart was beyond him. She certainly deserved to reap the rewards for her little discourse on his behavior. With any other woman, he wouldn't be debating the matter. He wouldn't have even given it a second thought.

He could chalk up his restraint to some latent, throw-back impulse left over from a more chivalrous time, where temperamental, fainting women were coddled by strong, tolerant men. But that was bullshit. The real reason he didn't make mincemeat of her was because Savannah Davis was the most unique woman he had ever met. Damnably, he couldn't pinpoint the exact reasons why.

He hadn't pegged her yet, not the way he normally got an instant fix on a personality. Miss Davis was proving to be more complex, more multilayered than other women. Peeling back those layers would take time, and he suspected that the more he learned, the more he would find that his assessment about her uniqueness was correct.

That as yet indefinable quality showed up in her photos. It was why he had agreed to help her out. It was why he couldn't flay her verbally.

"That's some temper you've got there. I suggest you keep a lid on it." Her head came up, her eyes snapped wide. One of his black brows quirked up at the offended, indignant expression she wore and he waited for her to explode.

She didn't and he was equally pleased and disappointed.

"Smart move. Not so smart is your habit of flying off the handle the way you've done twice now."

"It's not a habit," she snapped in her own defense.

"Oh?"

"The only reason I've gotten angry is because you've pushed me to do so."

"So, it's my fault."

"Yes."

He shook his head slowly, wondering about the workings of the female mind . . . and the foolish courage of this woman. "Miss Davis, if you'll remember, I apologized to you. I said I had made a mistake. I meant what I said." He bent low to drill his gaze into hers. "What more do you want?"

She glared right back. "It isn't as simple as that. Among other things, it's not what you say, it's how you say it."

"Exactly which of the subtle nuances do you think I missed?" he asked, his patience running thin.

"Diplomacy."

"Saying I'm sorry wasn't diplomatic enough?"

"You were tactful and courteous, but then you ruined it by assuming you had the right to make up my mind for me."

"How did I do that?"

"By putting an end to the entire matter." She jammed her hands onto her waist, amazed that she had to spell this out for him. Forgotten were their positions, his body so close she could feel his heat, his face near enough she could see the various hues of blue in his eyes. "Didn't it occur to you that I might want to discuss the situation with you?"

"Of course, but I thought I had gotten right to the heart of the matter." Sarcasm infiltrated his voice. "Obviously, I was wrong. Again. Well, I'm listening, talk. What more do you have to say?"

She opened her mouth . . . and nothing came out. For

several long, tense seconds, she tried to scrape together her thoughts, and then realized that all had been said.

"Nothing," she finally muttered with remarkable dignity. "I've said everything I wanted to say."

"So have I. Are we done arguing?"

Again, she was held mute. They had beat the issue to death and what remained, awkwardly enough, was the bare-bones truth. They had come full circle; he had apologized, end of discussion.

"I suppose." Heaving a huge sigh, she massaged her temples.

"Shit," he muttered. "Sit down."

Her indignation flared to life again. "Don't you know how to talk to people without giving orders?"

He narrowed his eyes at her tone. "I give orders when the situation warrants it. Around you, that seems to be all the time. Now, are you going to sit down or are you going to keel over right there?"

There was enough appeal in his words to satisfy her sense of outrage. Taking a seat at the round oak table, she shut her eyes and scrubbed her fingertips over her forehead. A dull headache was centered behind her eyes.

"I think you should stay put for a while."

His remark surprised her. She would have thought he'd be ready to toss her out. "I'm just tired." How true that was. Nothing with this man was easy. They had yet to have a discussion that wasn't filled with tension and outright anger. She felt completely drained.

"Here, drink this," Jacob ordered quietly.

Savannah looked up to find a glass of orange juice on the table in front of her and chose to ignore his tone of command. Gratefully, she took a healthy sip.

"Thank you." Until that moment, she hadn't realized how hungry she was. The juice helped clear the pangs from her stomach and the fog from her head.

"Better?" he asked, leaning back against the counter to openly stare at her.

"Yes." With his arms folded over his chest and one ankle crossed in front of the other, he looked completely at ease, very unlike the intense man of moments ago.

On second glance, she noted that most of the fire had been doused from his eyes. The tense lines that had creased his face were gone. His mouth was curved in what couldn't truly be called a smile, but neither was it the grim slash she was accustomed to seeing. She found that encouraging.

A tiny smile rooted in total absurdity pulled at her lips. Calmly, ruefully, she admitted, "It would help in the future if you realize that I don't like being told what to do."

"So I've noticed," he replied, studying the slight upward curve of her mouth.

"I suppose it's some perverse streak in my personality. Usually, if asked, I'll do anything I can to help anyone if it's at all possible."

"As long as they don't make it an order."

"Right."

Jacob gave vent to a single spurt of dry humor. "Then you should know that I spent sixteen years in the Air Force, a good many of those years in command, issuing orders and expecting them to be followed. To the letter."

"Oh, lovely. What a pair we make." She fingered the cool surface of her glass. "It would probably be best if we stayed out of each other's way."

"Not good enough. You'll be coming and going. We're bound to bump into each other."

"Then what do we do?"

"I'll try to remember that you don't take orders worth a damn and you'll have to remember that if you push me, I'll push back with greater force." A slow grin stretched the line of his mouth as he added, "It must be a perverse streak in my personality."

His smile was full and genuine and . . . divinely wicked.

It reminded her of just how sensual he could be. With that photographic eye the critics had hailed, she unthinkingly, reflexively let her gaze skip along the length of him.

The soft white turtleneck he wore under his navy sweater hugged his neck and provided a perfect contrast for the sharp edge of his jaw. Hands that were are at rest, were finely boned, yet lightly calloused. Shadows and highlights on the snug, faded jeans delineated the solid muscle tone of the long legs beneath.

He was a prime example of man at his physical best. In a flash, she mentally had him stripped; the possibilities for a classic, nude photographic study endless . . . and arousing.

"Looking for anything in particular?" Jacob's faintly amused voice cut into her thoughts.

Caught staring, Savannah struggled with embarrassment. It was part of her nature, her job, to study people. She did so all the time, but never, *never* on a sexual level.

"I'm sorry, it's an occupational hazard," she offered in a rush, asking herself what in the world had come over her. "I didn't mean to scrutinize, but I tend to view things in . . . in terms of photographic possibilities."

Jake's smile shifted to one side. "Is that so?"

"Yes."

"Care to explain?"

No, not really. She felt as if she was digging herself into a hole. While she knew she would tell him part of the truth, she also knew it was going to come out sounding like a bunch of excuses.

"Well, where most people see trees, I see overlapping values of green. Others look at a portrait and . . . and see an assortment of features. I focus in on the translucence of the skin, or the difference in the shape of each eye, or the network of the age lines. When I looked at you, I saw . . ."

A face and body that are so appealing, my mouth goes dry.

". . . I saw the faded color of your jeans in contrast to the rich blue of your sweater."

"Interesting." Slowly, never once breaking eye contact, he straightened and, just as slowly, crossed the room to stand directly before her. "But do you know what is even more interesting?"

She was almost afraid to ask. "What?"

"Not only do you not take orders worth a damn . . ." He planted a hand on the chair's arms on either side of her and bent low. "You don't lie worth a damn, either."

He gave her an unflinching, knowing look. And then he kissed her.

Five

He kissed me!

For the umpteenth time, Savannah asked herself why Jacob Quaide had done that. No matter how often she posed the question, though, she couldn't find an answer. The ride home from his house, the long silent night and the new Saturday morning brought her no clues. By the time she finished showering, she was ready to grab hold of her wet hair and pull.

Staring at herself in the bathroom mirror, she didn't see her reflection. Her mind's eye was resolutely fixed on the day before. Every detail of the Q Man's kitchen was clear. Every sensation she had felt at the touch of his mouth on hers was sharp.

Her stomach braided itself into a nervous twist and her eyes drifted shut. She could still feel the hard, warm pressure of his lips molding themselves to hers, forcing her lips to part. His tongue had swept over hers in a powerful caress that had been insolent, commanding and wholly sensual.

For the first time in her life, she truly understood what it meant to be breathless. Her body, certainly her lungs and heart, had gone useless on her. Pulse pounding, she had helplessly clung to his taut arms as if her life had depended on it, as captivated as she had been shocked by his move.

She opened her eyes. Even now, in her steamy bathroom, miles and hours removed, she felt the same surge of desire she had felt then. Rubbing a hand over her stomach didn't alleviate the jabs of hungry sensations that shot straight downward.

A low sound halfway between a moan and a sigh accompanied her grimace. She had never responded to a man the way she had to Jacob Quaide and it had nothing to do with the fact that it had been a long time, four years, since she had been with a man. What he made her feel had nothing to do with suppressed lust or a frustrated libido out of control. A single, staggeringly hot kiss had proven that.

His mouth had snatched her mind and turned her body to mush. Worse, that single kiss had left her wanting more. More than she was used to thinking about these days, more than was wise for her to need from Jacob Quaide.

He was dangerous to her peace of mind. He could annoy her at the drop of a hat. Desire was the absolute last thing she wanted to feel about him. She had assumed he felt similarly about her.

Then why had he kissed her?

"Get a grip, Savannah," she told herself. She was thinking herself in circles and the only conclusions she had drawn were that Jacob Quaide was the quintessence of the sexual male, and that she didn't seem to have any defenses against him.

She didn't like her confession one bit. Hair dryer in hand, she bent her head to her knees and sent a blast of hot air into action. All the while she concentrated on not concentrating on kisses, desire, or Jacob Quaide.

By the time she was dressed for a day of shopping, she was feeling better—not entirely free of her memories, but at least satisfied that she had talked herself into not asking *why*. When her sister arrived shortly before nine, she had Jacob Quaide's actions relegated to a fragile prison corner of her mind.

"Hey, Banana," Leanne Lawson greeted with a hug.

Savannah laughed at the childhood nickname and returned the embrace with all the mutual love that had always existed between her and her older sister. "Hello, General."

Leanne stepped back, tossed her purse onto the living room couch, then gave her sibling a quick inspection. "Rough week?"

Savannah let several seconds pass before answering. "I've had better."

"Uh oh. Trouble in paradise?"

"I haven't been to paradise this week. It's been a little bit closer to hell."

Leanne's wide hazel eyes rounded in real concern. "What happened?"

"Too much." Heading for the kitchen, Savannah asked, "I've got water boiling. Want some tea, or are you in a hurry to be gone?"

"Tea first. The stores don't open for another hour. Besides, I don't want to be driving when I hear what's going on with you.

Savannah sent her a grinning glance over her shoulder, oddly comforted by the familiar sight of Leanne. Some said they could pass for twins. Savannah couldn't see that degree of resemblance.

Although Leanne was an inch shorter than Savannah's own five feet six, they shared the same physical build, and the same shaped mouth. That was where Savannah thought the similarities ended.

Lee's eyes were more round than almond shaped, her jaw more squared than oval. Her hair was a lighter shade of brown and the bone structure most people thought she shared with her sister was actually filled with so many subtle differences that Savannah wondered if people really knew how to make accurate observations.

"I thought you were an expert at driving under pressure."

"You mean the kids?" Leanne laughed, her smile a carbon copy of Savannah's. "I've learned to tune them out."

"What are they up to today with their mom gone?"

"Oh, big stuff," Leanne sighed in high drama. "John's taking them to the park this morning, McDonald's for lunch, and to his mother's this afternoon."

Knowing how rambunctious her five-year-old nephew and three-year-old niece could be, Savannah mentally saluted her brother-in-law's stamina. But then, John dearly loved his children, as did Leanne. Neither ever minded the time and effort required to raise well-adjusted, well-mannered, loving, happy children. It was exactly the kind of attention Savannah knew she would devote to her own children if she were ever lucky enough to have any.

Much to her surprise, she felt a tiny spurt of wistfulness, the feeling catching her so off-guard she fumbled with the sugar bowl.

What was the matter with her today? First desire and then a yearning for babies. Since Eric had died, having her own children didn't seem to hold much interest for her and only in her more vulnerable moments did she ever think about desire or marriage.

Painful memories wanted to crowd forward. She ruthlessly shoved them back. "You and John are great parents," she said.

"We try hard."

"You're succeeding."

Although Leanne couldn't hide her pride, she protested, "You're a little biased."

"No, I'm not. You've raised your children to have values, to know the difference between right and wrong. They're honest and compassionate." She turned with two cups of tea. "And besides, they give the best hugs and kisses."

"They miss you."

"I miss them, too."

"Christy wants to know when she's going to see her favorite aunt? It's been over a month. To a three-year-old, that's forever."

As Savannah took a seat in the living room, the stress

of the last few days settled on her shoulders. "Tell her I'll try to get up to Richmond next week."

A frown creased Leanne's forehead at the sound of weariness in her sister's voice. Sitting beside Savannah on the sofa, she noted, "You look tired. What's happened?"

Savannah exhaled deeply. "Well, to start with, I passed out yesterday afternoon."

"What?" Leanne grabbed hold of one of Savannah's hands, her eyes sharpening with worry. "Are you okay?"

"I am now."

"Tell me."

"I was going through that house I told you about last week."

"Oakwood, right?"

Nodding, Savannah continued. "It's great; *I* was feeling great until I was leaving. Then I got dizzy and nauseous."

"What did you do?"

"I stayed conscious long enough not to throw up and then blacked out. Thankfully, the brother of the owner of the place was there. He carried me back to his house."

"Oh, my God, he had to carry you?" Leanne demanded to know, nearly coming off the seat. "You mean you were that out of it that you couldn't walk?"

"Afraid so. It was pretty embarrassing."

"Forget embarrassing. You could have fallen and hit your head."

"Don't worry, I didn't. Like I said, Mr. Quaide was there."

"Thank goodness. Lord only knows what would have happened if he hadn't been. Did he call the doctor or 911?"

Savannah took a sip of tea before going on. "No, he had everything under control." Too much so.

"How about now? Are you all right?"

"I feel as if nothing happened."

"Do you think you need to see Dr. Walker?"

"My gynecologist?!"

"Don't look so shocked. You could be PMS-ing to the max, or something."

"I am not. I'm sure it was a combination of things. Stress and a lack of food. It was going on dinner time and my blood sugar level probably dropped into the minus-zone."

"What stress?" Leanne asked, ignoring the latter of the reasons and zooming in on the first.

Savannah dragged a fingertip over an eyebrow. "Ooohhhh." She stretched the word out into a sound of irritation. "I've had to deal with Jacob Quaide all week, and it hasn't been pleasant."

"The same Mr. Quaide that picked you up and carried you to his house?"

"Yes, the arrogant beast."

A lively spark of interest lit Leanne's face. "What did he do that makes him a beast?"

"The list is endless." Hitting all the major points, Savannah described every encounter she'd had with Jacob in the last few days. Beginning with her initial call to his attorney and ending with his yelling at her just before she fainted, she slowly worked herself into a stew.

"You're right, he is a beast," Leanne agreed, but with a smile Savannah found suspicious.

"Why are you grinning, Lee?"

With a look of pure innocence, Leanne said, "Because it's been a long time since I've seen you so steamed up over a man."

"I'm not steamed up." That earned her a look that said, *who are you trying to kid?* "All right, maybe I am, but I swear, Lee, he makes me so angry at times. Everything is a contest of wills with him."

"He sounds interesting."

Savannah wouldn't have described him in those terms. Coming to her feet, she made her way to the kitchen. "He's interesting if you're into overbearing men."

"What's he look like?" Leanne asked from three steps behind.

"What does that have to do with anything?"

"Nothing. I'm curious, is all."

Rinsing out her cup, Savannah replied, "Tall, great bod, nice eyes."

"Mmmm, sounds yummy."

Savannah faced her sister squarely to continue. "Yes, but he's also arrogant, opinionated and domineering."

"An aggressive man. I like this."

"You would. You believe you'd like to have lived two hundred years ago 'when men were men and knew what to do with women'."

"Don't criticize," Leanne protested mildly. "There's a lot to be said for being swept off your feet. It's very romantic."

"Tell it to John. Personally, I like to know when I'm going to be kissed."

"He kissed you?!" Reaching out, Leanne grabbed Savannah's arm, excitement suffusing her face.

"Yes."

"When, where, why?"

Savannah rolled her eyes. "Last night, in his kitchen, and I really don't know why."

"You have to know."

"Believe me, I don't. We had been arguing, as usual; the discussion levelled out and the next thing I knew, he kissed me." At the memory, her traitor of a heart flipped over in her chest.

"This is great," Leanne exclaimed, her joy continuing to shine. "Are you going to see him again?"

"Of course, but not the way you mean. I'll be on the man's property. I'll be sure to bump into him at times."

Leanne wiggled her eyebrows. "There's bumping and then there's bumping."

"Oh, for Heaven's sake." Savannah threw her hands up

and walked off. From her bedroom, she called back, "Give it a rest, Lee."

"I don't know what you mean," Leanne asserted from the kitchen.

Savannah tugged on a denim blazer. "You're playing matchmaker."

"So?"

"So, stop it."

"I'm simply speculating."

Adjusting the strap of her purse over her shoulder, Savannah entered the kitchen with a warning look in her eyes. "I know what you're thinking: that I've got a new man in my life."

"Is that so bad?"

"Yes, because it isn't true."

"It doesn't sound that way to me."

"Only because it's what you want to believe."

Leanne's brow drew into a deep frown. "Can you blame me? It's been four years, Savannah. You haven't dated anyone in all that time."

"Yes, I have."

"Not seriously," Leanne scoffed, and then caught herself. She had obviously heard the censure in her own tone and gentled her voice. "The minute someone starts getting too close, you stop seeing him."

Savannah studied the ceiling. It was a lot easier doing that than facing Leanne's truths. "I really don't want to talk about this."

Leanne sighed, her eyes softening. "I know you don't, Banana, but you can't go on living in this void you've created for yourself." Before Savannah could say anything, she said, "Eric is dead. Let him rest in peace."

Inwardly, Savannah flinched. It was difficult enough thinking about Eric without having to talk about him.

"You have to let the past go," Leanne coaxed.

"I do." Savannah shrugged. "Most of the time."

"And the rest of the time, you blame yourself for Eric's death."

"No. Not anymore." Through the years, her guilt had been strained down to minute, elemental questions. What would have happened if she and Eric hadn't argued? Would he have still gotten into his car and raced off? Would he still have wrapped that car around a telephone pole?

And what if he had lived? Would she have loved him the way he wanted her to? The way he had professed to have loved her?

"I'm sorry," Leanne whispered, "I didn't mean to make you cry."

Until that second, Savannah hadn't realized she was crying. She brushed at the tears on her cheeks and gave her sister a wobbly smile. "It still hurts."

"I know. I forget, though."

"It's not your fault. There are times when the memories swamp me."

"It's to be expected, Savannah. You and Eric were close. He wanted to marry you. What kind of a person would you be if you didn't feel anything?" Leanne draped an arm around her sister's shoulders. "I shouldn't have pressed so hard. It's just that I love you and I hate to see you stuck in the past. What happened wasn't your fault."

"I know." The therapist had made her realize that. "I'll try to do better. Give me time."

The issue of time was one that Leanne appeared to want to debate. She didn't though and instead, made a blatant effort to lighten the mood. Shaking back her mane of hair, she declared, "We've got all the time in the world. Why don't we go spend some of it? And some money, too!"

Savannah regarded the woman who had always been her closest confidante, her toughest critic, her best friend, and felt the bonds of sisterly love as never before. "Sounds good."

"But I'm driving. You've had a bad enough week without having to put up with the interstate."

"I won't argue." The idea of sitting idly and watching the landscape go past was very appealing at the moment. "You drive, I'll navigate."

Leanne laughed. "You bet you will or who knows where we'll end up."

The humor behind the statement brought a smile to Savannah's face. Leanne could get lost backing the car out of the garage. "Don't worry, Lee, when you grow up, you'll be able to read a map just like all the other big girls."

"I'm still working on figuring out the difference between north and west."

The long-standing joke between them went far in extinguishing more of Savannah's upset. By the time she and Leanne were headed north, she felt better than she had in days.

"Remind me to get a new battery for my watch."

"I'm supposed to remind you?" Leanne choked out. "I'm the person who needs a shopping list for one item, remember?"

Savannah's response was another laugh, one that quickly set the tone for the day of milling through sale racks, trying on shoes, and testing out the latest chocolate chip cookies at the bakery. Spending time with Lee never failed to supply a steady source of humor and good-natured gossip. Savannah appreciated the shared camaraderie to its fullest. It was the perfect distraction she needed and only once during the afternoon did her thoughts become pensive.

Four hours later when Leanne pulled up in front of the charming little cottage, Savannah felt as if her cheeks were permanently stuck in the smile position.

"Every time we go shopping, Lee, I promise myself I won't let you talk me into buying things I don't need."

Leanne blinked like a woman falsely accused of murder. "I didn't force you to buy anything."

Savannah gave a cry of laughing disbelief as she got out of the car. From the back seat, she collected several bags, one of which bore the name of an exclusive French lingerie store. "I have an abused checking account that says differently."

"Shopping is good for the soul. And I'm right. You look a zillion percent better than you did this morning."

Tipping her head to one side, Savannah confessed, "I feel a lot better. Thanks for making my day."

"No problem." Leanne checked the clock on the dashboard. "I've got to scoot. I promised John I'd be home by five."

"Tell him I said 'hi.' "

"I will. Take care of yourself."

"I'll call you this week." Savannah stepped back from the car then remembered to add, "Don't say anything to Mom about my fainting yesterday. I don't want her to worry."

Pure skepticism lined Leanne's face. "She won't hear of it from me, but you know how she is."

Yes, Savannah knew, and that was what bothered her. Their mother had the uncanny, almost spooky ability to sense whether either of her daughters was in trouble or not feeling well. It was a "talent" Savannah had often rued from her earliest childhood.

There had been that time in the third grade when she had broken her arm. Her mother had called the school at the same time the school nurse had been calling her. According to Mom, she had had the strangest feeling that something was wrong.

Then there was that time when Savannah was a freshman in college and a fire had broken out in the elevator shaft of her dorm. Savannah and her roommate hadn't been back in their room more than a half-hour when Mom had called, wanting to know if everything was all right.

That kind of occurrence was more the norm than not for Savannah and Lee and their mother, so much so, that Savannah believed that the three of them were somehow "linked." It wasn't anything she could explain. She simply accepted the situation as being one of the mysterious, leaning-toward-the-psychic incidents that happened in life.

So it didn't surprise her when the phone rang later that evening and it was her mother calling.

"Hi, Mom."

"Hello, Anna. How are you, dear?"

"Okay. How about you?"

They went through their routine conversation; her mother asking her if she had taken her vitamins, she, checking to see if her mother's arthritis was acting up. Savannah found a comfortable spot on the bedroom floor and leaned back against the bed.

"Lee and I went shopping today," she said, hoping to keep the discussion away from her health.

"Were you up to it?"

"Sure." She nibbled at her lower lip. "Why wouldn't I be?"

"You've been working so hard lately. I worry about you."

She laughed. "You always worry about me, Mom. It's what you do best. But I promise, I'm doing fine." She was beginning to sound like a broken record.

"Are you sure?"

"Yes."

"Anna . . . ?"

It was the tone of voice that never failed to get to Savannah: worried uncertainty laced with a mega-dose of determination. She had never had any defense against it. She didn't now.

Sighing, she propped her elbow on her bent knee and scrubbed her hand over the back of her neck. "I don't know how you do this," she muttered in defeat and then recounted the events of the day before.

Her mother's response was similar to Lee's, her questions following the same lines which eventually led to Jacob Quaide. Again, Savannah was forced to discuss the man when she would have preferred to not even have thought about him at all.

"Yes, he was very kind to help me out," she replied, confirming her mother's comment.

"I'm glad he'll be near by looking out for you."

"Mom, he isn't my keeper."

"Oh, I know dear, but it makes me feel better knowing that you won't be out in the middle of nowhere all by yourself."

It was a contention of long standing between them. They had had this conversation many times. "Mom, I don't want you worrying."

"Of course you don't."

"But that won't stop you, right?"

"You know me so well, Anna."

Savannah had to grin at the humor in her mother's voice. "I don't know how you managed when I worked for the magazine."

"I didn't get very much sleep, that's for sure. But at least you're only an hour away. And this nice Mr. Quaide is there."

"Mom," Savannah sighed in a light warning. "I told you, Mr. Quaide is—"

"I have a good feeling about him, dear."

Savannah's invisible armor erected itself in an instant. She had learned long ago never to take her mother's "feelings" for granted. Call them intuition, motherly wisdom, or pure psychic foresight, Savannah didn't care. Mom's "feelings" were almost always right.

"What?"

"You heard me. I get this light, warm feeling at the thought of him."

"That's because you haven't met him."

"That doesn't change how I feel. Trust me, there's something special about this Mr. Quaide."

Savannah didn't want to believe it. Somehow, though, she didn't think she had a choice.

Six

It had been a bitch of a day. As Jacob drove up to his house, he decided that as Mondays went, this one sucked. All he wanted was a quick five mile run, followed by a cold drink, a hot shower, and the silence of his den with the evening news on TV thrown in for the hell of it.

The day had started with a conference call that had grown ridiculously tedious after ten minutes. The day had ended with the decision that he would have to go to Washington D.C. tomorrow after all. In both cases, he had had to deal with men who were as egotistical as they were asinine.

He had little patience for idiocy and absolutely none for inflated egos. Consequently, his supply of patience for one day was gone, and mentally he turned on the answering machine to his phone. He damned anyone stupid enough to bother him at home tonight. He decided he wanted to be left alone . . . until he spotted Savannah's car parked off to the side of his house.

Instantly, he readjusted his thoughts, his mind closing in on the other night, specifically Savannah's mouth. God, the feel and taste of her lips had been two-hundred proof lust. Like fire and ice combined, like hunger and pleasure blended to excruciating perfection. The rousing effects had hounded him all weekend.

Getting out of the car, he loosened his tie and glanced toward the trees. Five minutes ago, he had craved solitude. Now, he gave into a craving of another kind; the urge to analyze Savannah Davis—to probe her mind and understand what made her tick.

He was excellent at reading people, but from Savannah he kept receiving conflicting impressions. She was incredibly strong-willed, but she possessed a core of rare sensitivity that was plastered all over her photos. Outwardly, she wore the polite, self-assured shell of a world-class photographer, accustomed to viewing the hard realities of political turmoil. And yet, that same woman had become unbelievably self-conscious at finding her jeans unzipped.

This same woman had also looked at him like a lover, stroking his body with her gaze. And she hadn't been the least bit adept at hiding that fact from him.

Knowing that Savannah had been sexually aware of him had been a wild turn on. The second his mind had felt the allure, his body had reacted as if he were some hormone-crazed teenager.

"Who are you, Savannah Davis?" The dossier he had compiled on her hadn't given him clues to the kinds of questions he wanted answered.

From around the corner of the house, Ares advanced at a full run, barking as if in response to Jacob's query.

"Hey, boy."

Ares stood at Jake's feet, shamelessly pleased to have his neck scratched and thumped.

"Catch anything worthwhile today?"

The dog gave a single bark which Jake interpreted to his own satisfaction.

"Yeah, I know. *She's* here again, traipsing all over your territory. Did you let her know who's boss?"

Ares whined and grinned.

"Well, go easy on the lady. She's going to be here for a while."

Savannah had pricked his interest big time, not only because of his own response to the kiss he'd given her, but because of her response. They had shared the heat. He had felt it and he knew that she had, too. But the second he had released her mouth and stood back to give her breathing room, she had bolted from the kitchen and out of the house.

That had been three days ago and no matter how many times he considered the situation, he hadn't come to any conclusions as to why she had run.

"Go find the lady, Ares," he ordered with a grin.

The Airedale cocked his head from one side to the other, his brown eyes intent.

"Go see what she's up to."

It was the most perfect afternoon of Savannah's life. Mother Nature, often known for her bitchiness, had been in a wonderfully good mood. The temperature hovered in the low sixties, not a gust of wind anywhere, and the tang of falling leaves scented the air. But mostly there was plenty of "sweet light" to shine down on the beauty of Oakwood's mansion.

Bending low over her tripod, she focused her camera on one of the chimneys. As never before, she appreciated the afternoon light preferred by most photographers for outdoor shoots. What the waning sun did for the house was indescribable, highlighting the intricacy of the brickwork, accenting bold contours and delicate details.

Unfortunately, the light was fleeting, and she had used up the several hours worth with regret. With a sigh, she capped her lens and called it a day, surrendering to dusk.

She knew she could use artificial light. She chose not to. The natural beauty of the forest so complimented the structure of the house that she couldn't bring herself to flip on the lights she had brought with her.

Perhaps for special effects, she mused, and most definitely with parts of the interior. Other than that, she would rely on the sun, regardless of its unreliability. The house was a marvel, worth any amount of time and effort it demanded.

Once again, she was reminded of the history saturating the structure. Old things always had a way of touching her heart, but as she let her gaze travel the full length of the house, she felt more than her usual amount of interest.

There was something different about Oakwood, something . . . profound. As never before, she was aware of the people, the lives, the souls that had made the house their home. In her mind, she tried to picture the generations living out their lives with the normal human sorrows and joys, tears, and laughter.

Without warning, sound receded and she felt a sinking sensation in the center of her chest. As if she were on an elevator that descended too quickly, her insides seemed to lodge in her shoulders. Automatically, she sucked in a breath and moaned in queasy discomfort.

"I must have a touch of the flu," she muttered. "First passing out and now this." Maybe Leanne was right. Maybe she did need to see a doctor.

It wasn't a tempting notion. Going to the doctor was on the very bottom of her list of things she liked to do. On the other hand, she couldn't afford to be sick, at least not now, not when her work on the book was nearly completed.

Determinedly, she took another deep breath and thankfully felt better. The mild queasiness vanished as suddenly as it had come, the usual forest noises returned with unexpected clarity. So much so, she felt as if she had just emerged from a vacuum.

"You're tired," she told herself. "It's been an intense day. Just go home and call it quits."

She gathered up the equipment she had left on the front steps and carefully packed cameras, lenses, and note pads into her backpack. A hot bath and dinner were waiting with great appeal.

Hefting the pack onto her right shoulder, she gave the

house a last look . . . and then did a double take. Her gaze riveted to one of the windows, seeing what looked like curtains and panes of glass.

The hollow feeling returned, slamming into the center of her chest, forcing her to blink repeatedly. When she focused clearly on the window again, all looked as it had. An empty hole—no draperies, no warped glass.

And her center of gravity was exactly where it was supposed to be.

"Go home, Savannah. Your mind is working overtime." Imagination was a wonderful thing. In this case, however, it was running amok.

Taking as firm a grip on her resolve as she had on her sack, she ducked through the hedge only to literally come nose to nose with Ares. In one move, she straightened and backed up, instinctively giving the dog a wide berth.

"You damn dog."

The Airedale stood his ground, his upper lip quivering on the verge of baring teeth.

"I need you like I need a hole in the head."

Ares' response was to bark right back.

Gritting her teeth, Savannah mentally skewered Jacob Quaide. She could understand why he was as protective of the old house as he was, but she didn't appreciate being held hostage against a row of shrubbery by this canine programmed to seek and destroy.

"I have permission to be here," she explained, and then wondered why she was trying to reason with a dog. "Your master and I are going to discuss this." That was, if she ever managed to get back to her car. Ares, god of war that he was, didn't look like he was going to let her go anywhere until he was good and ready.

"Fine." She threw her hands into the air, tired and disgusted. She'd survived some of the toughest places on earth; war-torn countries, rioting inner cities, only to be cowed by a dog. Ruefully, she admitted, she had survived because she'd had the good sense to know when to back off.

"Okay, we'll wait right here. Sooner or later, you'll get bored, or the Q Man will call you home. But you're not taking a chunk out of me."

She slid her pack to the ground, intending to follow it and make herself comfortable while she waited. But again, the nerves in her chest seemed to want to shift upward with that empty feeling, and she sighed heavily.

Ares stopped barking in the same instant.

"Thank you, at least, for that."

The dog cocked his head from one side to the other, looking as if he were about to screw it off his neck. From deep in his throat emerged whining yaps. Savannah had the distinct impression he was trying to comprehend some deep, dark mystery.

"Let me make it simple for you," she told him with light sarcasm. "I'm tired. I just want to go home."

To her surprise, Ares backed up a step, his brown eyes staring at her with a remarkably human expression of confusion. His yaps dwindled to quivering whimpers.

"Ares?"

He retreated another step.

Savannah shook her head in disbelief. His behavior was so startling, she forgot her annoyance. Something was definitely bothering the dog to the point that his naturally aggressive inclinations were gone.

"What is it?" She was tempted to reach out a hand in comfort. "What's wrong?"

From the direction of Jacob's house came the muted sound of a shrill whistle. Ares turned and raced away, leaving Savannah alone and puzzled.

"Goofy dog," she whispered as she gathered up her things. "There's a place for you at Disney Studios."

The goofy dog—and his master—were waiting for her,

sitting on the front steps of Jake's house. She eyed them both suspiciously.

"I'm glad to see you made it back," Jake said around an innocent smile. "It's beginning to get dark."

"I would have been here sooner, only I was detained." She gave Ares a meaningful look. The dog stared back, looking his normal self.

"He found you, did he?"

She crossed her arms over her chest. "Wasn't he supposed to?"

Instead of answering, Jake lifted a long-necked bottle of beer, took a sip, then handed it her way.

She declined with a raised hand. "No, I better not. I haven't eaten since breakfast. It'll go right to my knees."

"Your knees?"

"Alcohol affects me that way. My knees are the first to go, and then my head. Not a good combination when I have to drive."

"Does food help?"

"Oh, sure, but I'll never be a heavy drinker."

He skimmed the contours of her figure with an assessing, blue gaze. "Considering your body weight, I wouldn't think so."

The force of his look scrambled Savannah's composure. "What's . . . what's wrong with my weight?" she asked, looking down at her legs, mentally kicking herself at being so easily flustered.

"Nothing that I can see," he drawled. "Everything looks pretty good. Actually, better than good."

At the directness of his statement, her eyes jerked up to meet his, and her heart lurched. His stare was intent, relentless and powerful, sending messages that reached her on a purely feminine level and made her think of sex, hot and wild.

"Are you hungry?" He posed the lazy question as he lifted the bottle to his lips, his stare fixed, unwavering.

Savannah had to wonder if he intended the innuendo in his query, or if she was letting her imagination get the better of her again. The latter was easy enough to do with him sitting there looking sexy as all get-out.

Did the man know what a pair of jeans did for his legs? Did he know that the denim shirt he wore accented the width of his shoulders and chest?

Deciding it would be better not to read any hidden meanings into his words, she answered with straightforward, albeit wobbly, honesty. "Yes, as a matter of fact, I'm on my way home to eat."

"Have dinner with me."

"Dinner?" She had heard him, she just didn't know what else to say.

"I have a taste for seafood tonight, and there's this great place right on the water that serves the best fresh fish and oysters anywhere."

Her mind finally clicked in. He was inviting her to have dinner with him. Dinner, as in sitting across from each other, conversing over drinks and salad. Or seafood.

"I'm not really dressed for anything." Jeans, a stylish flannel shirt and her Reeboks wouldn't do for a restaurant.

That was as good an excuse as any. The truth was, he confused her. He had from the very beginning. With every passing day, she found him increasingly fascinating, but she didn't understand him or her own reaction to him.

"Don't worry, the place I have in mind is real low-key." The corners of his eyes crinkled with his smile. "You might even be overdressed." Obviously seeing her indecision, he added, "You said yourself you haven't eaten since breakfast."

She *was* hungry. Suddenly the idea of having dinner with Jacob Quaide took on a charm she couldn't resist, banishing any fatigue she might have felt.

"All right," she said, running a hand over her hair. "But I'd like to wash up a bit first. I'm a mess."

Jake reserved his opinion on that as he came to his feet. Savannah Davis looked exactly like what she was; a woman who had spent the day outdoors, totally captivated by her work. In a word, she looked great. Alive. Sexy.

That was three words, but what the hell. Her hair was a tousled frame of silky dark brown, surrounding a face that had been lightly kissed by the sun. And even though he could see hesitation in her eyes, there was also an inner radiance in the brown orbs that was impossible to miss.

A half-hour later, sitting across the table from her in a corner booth of *Bubba's*, he considered the luminous light in her eyes.

"You look like you've had a good day," he commented easily as he forked a raw oyster out of its shell.

"I have." Her smile came readily, the glow in her eyes increased. From the jukebox on the side wall, a country-western ballad mourned the loss of the love of a good woman. Ever so slightly, Savannah swayed to the beat of the music, the movement enhancing her radiant aura. "The house is unbelievable. Everywhere I looked, I saw something exciting, something I didn't expect to see."

"Such as?"

"The caps on the chimneys, the detail work on the molding, the scroll pattern carved into the steps. None of that should be there, not after all this time. It's like finding a chest full of treasures." She laughed as she snapped a crab claw in half. "It's going to be difficult choosing which pictures to use for the collection."

Leaning back in the fake, black leather seat, he observed, "You must be something else at Christmas."

She looked up quickly, her grin turned lopsided. "Why do you say that?"

"You should see your face. You look like a kid with a huge present."

The edges of her humor gave way to a self-conscious

bearing, the subtle swaying of her body stilled. "I sometimes get carried away."

"Don't apologize. It's refreshing to see someone as enthusiastic as you are." He paused for a sip of beer, taking his time as he studied her. "Why did you become a photographer?"

She shrugged with her brows. "From the time I was a kid, it was something I had always wanted to do."

"No wavering or changing your mind through high school?"

"No. My parents bought me my first camera when I was nine, and from that moment on, I was hooked."

"It's an unusual profession."

"As opposed to what?"

"Teaching, medicine, business."

"I suppose, but being a photographer is all I ever wanted to be."

"Why?"

She didn't even hesitate to think about it. "Because artistically it's very satisfying."

"So is painting or sculpting."

"Not to me."

"You sound positive. Obviously you've given this a great deal of thought."

"Yes. To both."

"What about the downside? Every job has its downside."

She gave a pensive sigh before answering, her brow puckering slightly. "I suppose there were a few bad times when I was first starting out. I used to work for *World News Magazine.*"

He already knew that. He also knew that she would be royally pissed if she knew of the check he had run on her. "Didn't you like it?"

"Most of the time. There was a lot of traveling involved. That wasn't always easy."

"World News is usually on top of whatever is breaking. You must have been in some tight places."

"A few."

"Why did you give it up?"

The spark of life that had glimmered in her eyes slowly died. Just as slowly, she replied, "I was in one tight place too many. I finally realized I didn't like being shot at."

She spoke without guilt or shame. Nonetheless, she paused to lift her glass of iced tea. When she looked at him again, her expression was completely composed. "I'm not tough enough to be surrounded by violence . . . to watch people die right in front of me."

He had seen war, he knew how overwhelming the reality of brutal death could be. Imagining Savannah in such circumstances tightened his stomach. "I think you made the right choice."

"I know I did," she concurred. "I'm much happier doing what I do now."

"How did you make the transition from one job to the other?"

"Believe it or not, it was remarkably easy. One of the editors at the magazine had a friend at one of the publishing houses. A few calls, a portfolio of my work, and presto, a new avenue in my career."

"I would say your reputation preceded you."

"It did. That was a help."

"It must make it easier on the men in your life having you around on a more regular basis."

In the process of buttering a roll, Savannah's hands stilled. "There are no men in my life."

"Why not?"

Savannah choked on an incredulous laugh and stammered, "You . . . you're the most direct man I have ever met."

Unfazed, Jake met her gaze. "I don't believe in beating

around the bush. If I want to know something, I ask. I wanted to know if—"

"If I'm seeing anyone."

He drilled his gaze into hers. "Are you?"

"I could ask the same of you."

"I'm not into men. I'm strictly heterosexual."

"That's not what I meant, and you know it."

He paused to run his tongue around the inside of his cheek. "Savannah, if I was seeing someone else, I wouldn't be here having dinner with you."

She leaned forward and angled her chin slightly to one side. "Neither would I."

He had to give her credit. She stood her ground and made her point. But she hadn't answered his question, and he wanted to know more than what he had read on her. He already knew she hadn't been involved with anyone steadily for the last few years. Before that, there seemed to have been an on-again, off-again situation with another photographer that ended with the man's death.

"So why *isn't* there a man in your life?" he asked, pressing for the response most pertinent in his mind.

"I don't know," she muttered, sitting back in a blatantly unconscious retreat from the topic—and him.

"Was there ever a man in your life?"

Savannah tucked her chin. Jacob Quaide was quite possibly the most annoyingly persistent person, male or female, that she had ever met. Despite that, and much to her surprise, she had been enjoying herself tremendously. She hated to have that change by delving into personal matters, but a single glance at Jacob's powerfully hewn features told her he was set on having his answers and there would be no distracting him.

Part of her dearly resented his intrusion into her private life. What made him think he had the right to do so? One dinner, great conversation, a single kiss . . . the fact that he had carried her in his arms . . . held her close . . . knew what her underwear looked like . . . ?

She squirmed deep within. An intimacy had sprung up between them. As unexpected as that was, she couldn't deny it. Their relationship may have started out on combative grounds, but it had mellowed and matured into something else in a very short time. She wasn't exactly sure what that was, but she knew it demanded nothing less than complete honesty with herself as well as with Jake.

"There was a man. Once." Leftover memories swamped her as they usually did whenever she thought of Eric. She fought them, but at the cost of her appetite. "He died." The somber words out, she glanced away, doing her best to regroup.

It wasn't the facts that Jacob had sought. It was Savannah's reactions he had been interested in. Those told him more than her words ever could. "I'm sorry, Savannah. I didn't mean to upset you."

The deep tones of Jacob's voice were low, compassionate and drew her attention as nothing else could. He was genuinely sorry, and for reasons she couldn't begin to understand, that helped ease her discomfort.

Relaxing a little, she explained, "It's a touchy subject."

Quietly, soberly, he asked, "Is it anything you want to talk about?"

His offer brought her up short, mainly, she admitted, because she hadn't gotten completely past her first impressions of him. However, he wasn't the harsh, angry man now. She realized that his powerful, hard exterior shielded a streak of remarkable sensitivity.

He would listen. And she could probably bring herself to tell him everything. Still, she shook her head. She didn't want to talk about Eric. Not now, not tonight when she had been having such a good time, better than she had had with any man in a long while. Not when she had discovered that she liked Jacob Quaide.

"Maybe some other time. Talking about Eric can be depressing. But thank you for offering."

He let it go at that, for which she was grateful. With an ease and skill she appreciated, he directed their conversation onto a more light-hearted track. By the time they left the restaurant and stood on the warped wooden dock, they were laughing over the glory of their respective college days.

"What did you do after you graduated from the Air Force Academy?" she asked.

"I gave my time to Uncle Sam. That's part of the deal."

"I know, but for sixteen years? What did you do?"

"I flew."

Savannah's eyes rounded. "You were a pilot?"

Nodding, he braced his elbows on the wooden rail, stared out at the darkened river and drank in its tangy scent.

"What did you fly?"

"The F-15."

"Really?"

"Really."

Her enthusiasm was back full force, complete with a delighted laugh. "That explains a lot."

His gaze returned to her. "What does that mean?"

Rolling her eyes at his slightly stung tone, she quipped, "Everyone knows that fighter pilots are a breed unto themselves. You're a classic."

"I'm no longer a pilot."

"Minor point. The personality traits that enabled you to do what you did haven't changed. You're basically still the same person."

Shifting to face her, he braced his weight on one forearm. "What exactly am I?"

By the light of a full moon, she smiled up into his face and teased, "Are you sure you want to know?" The look he gave her said "yes". "All right, but remember, you asked."

"You sound as if you're going to insult me."

"Not at all. I'm going to give you the facts. It's up to you to deal with them."

"Savannah," he warned at her continued sparring.

"All right. Pilots are known to be more aggressive than most men, more determined. They see things in terms of black and white. They're opinionated—" She arched a single brow at him "—they like to be in control, and on a moment's notice, they can detach emotionally."

"Where did you learn all of this?"

"Books, magazines."

"Then this could be nothing but some author's bravo sierra opinion."

"Bravo sierra?"

"B.S. Bullshit."

"Oh, no. What I'm telling you is verifiable. There have been studies and statistics to back all of this up." Warming to her subject, she asked a touch smugly, "Did you know that pilots, for all of their high profiles, are charmingly modest about what they do?"

"I'll agree with that."

"Ah, but did you know that most male pilots marry women who are as strong-willed as themselves?"

"You're a regular fountain of information, aren't you?"

"You bet." Caught up in her teasing, she missed the deliberate, lingering assessment he gave her smiling features. "One of my first assignments at *World News* was to photograph a squadron of naval aviators. Believe me, I did my research before I stepped foot on that aircraft carrier."

"I can just imagine." His gaze dropped from the curves of her lips to the curves of her breasts.

This time, Savannah caught the seductive speculation in his manner and stilled, instantly aware of him on an entirely different level, a level where the essence of his masculinity touched the basic spirit of her femininity. Such cognizance was emotional and sexual. Dizzying in its intensity.

Feeling as if her mind was rushing to "catch up" in a game she hadn't been aware of playing, she struggled to understand why things had shifted between them. As far as she knew, she hadn't said or done anything to put *that* look in his eyes.

Trying to sound as if her pulse wasn't pounding or her brain wasn't quickly turning to cooked oatmeal, she asked, "So . . . so what was y . . . your call name?"

He stepped closer and gave her the same words she had given him earlier. "Are you sure you want to know?"

Where her phrasing of the question had been humorous and light, his was a study in seduction. It danced on her nerve endings, forcing her to melt or gather her senses and reply calmly, rationally.

But oh, it was difficult to do the latter when the upward lift of one corner of his mouth made him appear nothing short of carnal. And the way he stared down at her made her mentally scramble to remember what he had asked her.

"Uhm, yes," she managed to get out. "I'd like to know what name you flew under . . ." His hand slid along her waist. Her words faded to a whisper. "What did you go by?"

His smile grew. "Stud."

Her lips formed the word. No sound emerged. Silently, she asked herself how he had derived the name, but there was no way on earth she was going to ask him.

He didn't give her the chance.

Seven

He claimed her. There was no other way for Savannah to describe the exhilarating sensation of Jacob kissing her. Like the 'alpha-man' he was, he simply lay claim to her mouth . . . and then with frightening speed, her senses and her body. Both were rendered useless by the feel of his tongue thrusting past her lips and his arms circling her with stunning force.

Any modest thought that they barely knew each other, that they had been at serious odds with each other, was demolished the second his lips took possession of hers. Then thoughts of any kind ceased as her instincts urged her to tip her head back, cling to his shoulders, and return the kiss wholeheartedly.

She did. It was like releasing the floodgates of a powerful storm. A hot wave of excitement raced through her. Her legs shook, her breath fluttered in her chest, and low and inside, she felt the wild onslaught of a rush of desire.

Helplessly, she released a sweet moan. She wasn't prepared . . . could not begin to grasp the reality of such intense passion flaring to life. She struggled to hold onto reason. It wasn't possible. She responded to him with the ache of long-suppressed need.

And the well-being of familiarity.

There was no logic to that. She barely knew him. And yet, *everything* inside her contradicted that argument. In some indefinable way, his kissing her was perfect and right.

Stunned, she jerked her head back, dragging in one strained breath after another. Staring at him in awe, her mind recalled the very first instant she had seen him. Instantaneous recognition. Now, as then, she sensed the most uncanny awareness of him.

"Jacob."

Ruthlessly he brought his mouth over hers again, cutting off anything else she might have said. He was past words, past talking. Listening to her laughter, watching her body and spirit come alive with her teasing had seduced him like the most potent aphrodisiac.

He drew her closer and his gut clenched at the feel of her breasts against his chest. Her body was supple and soft, luring his hands to her hips to press her into greater contact, greater intimacy with his body.

"I knew it would be like this," he whispered, kissing the underside of her jaw. "Intense, raw. Powerful." He trailed the tip of his tongue along her throat to nuzzle aside the collar of her shirt. "I felt it the last time I kissed you. I wanted you then, but you ran."

Eyes closed, head tipped to one side, she heard him as though from a distance. "I . . . wasn't prepared. I usually don't do this."

He didn't need for her to tell him that. Her body told him all. The quivering in her limbs and the mad beating of her pulse spoke of her unfamiliarity with passion. The way she held on to his shoulders, the way she rested so bonelessly against him, proclaimed other things entirely.

She might not be well versed. Maybe she was even downright innocent, but she wanted him.

God Almighty, what that did to him.

He bent his head and caught her mouth with his again, giving her just a taste of the desire that ripped at his insides. Driven by the kind of need he had *never* felt before, he closed his hand over her breast and was rewarded by the instant arching of her body.

"Jake . . ." She whispered his name on a high keening sigh. His fingers found the hard crest of her nipple. Her sigh turned into a moan of pure pleasure as hot sensation raced straight down and collected between her legs.

"Tell me you like that," he ordered roughly, pressing his mouth to her forehead, his thighs into hers.

Unable to get the words out, she nodded.

"Tell me not to stop."

She didn't want him to. The admission stunned her, snapping her eyes wide. She normally didn't let this kind of thing happen. She normally kept men at a distance, not wanting to get herself entangled emotionally or physically.

It was a protective reflex brought on by Eric's death. She understood and accepted that. Consequently, viewing the male of the species as friends, and nothing more, had become second nature. To suddenly have that instinct breached by Jacob Quaide was unsettling.

Suddenly self-conscious and confused, she tried to withdraw.

"No." He felt her retreat and held her more securely. He didn't want to let her go. The feel of her was too good, the taste of her a rare pleasure that had him forgetting that her experience might be limited. "Just let me hold you."

"Oh, God, Jake, what am I doing?"

"Letting me get close."

"I know," she whispered.

"Does that bother you?"

"I don't know what to think. We didn't start out very well. I didn't expect that I . . . that you . . ."

"Would want to make love to you?"

She tipped her head back to stare intently into his dark eyes. "That's what you want."

It was both a question and a statement. In answer he urged his hips forward. A long, lazy grin creased his face and one of his hands circled from behind to cup her breast. "What do you think?"

Her breath came in sharply and stayed, forcing her voice up an octave. "I . . . can't think of anything when you do that."

"That's the way it should be." He flicked a glance to the sky, his voice deepening. "You're like one of those stars up there. Bright, hot, pulsing. You get to me fast and hard and deep, making me want to discover just how bright and hot you really are." He circled her nipple with his thumb. "Yeah, I want to make love to you. I want to be inside you so deep you can feel me clear to your soul."

He was talking out of her league, making her feel things she hadn't ever thought to feel. His heated murmurs dragged on her emotions, combining with his seeking touch to tempt her spirit. All the while, spirals of pleasure radiated out from where his hand stroked her so insistently. The tension, centered deep within her, tightened and she felt herself melt from the inside out. "Jake, you have to stop."

"I know, because you're not ready, are you?"

Shaken, aroused, she shook her head. "No." She had come a long way in a few short hours, but she was still in first gear while he was well into Mach One.

"But you do want me."

He brought his fingers into play, plucking at her turgid flesh. It was all she could do to stand, let alone, speak.

Against her parted lips, he murmured darkly, "Tell me."

"Oh, Jake, I'm not usually . . ."

"Tell me, Savannah."

She felt completely defenseless, helpless against the combined forces of his determination and her own sense of honesty. "Yes, I want you. I've never felt this way before."

Nothing she said could have pleased him more. Satisfaction expanded in his muscles, filling him with a bone-deep pleasure. Smiling, he drew a long breath even though his body was making serious demands. For Savannah, he would wait. It wouldn't be easy, but he wanted her ready. As ready for him as he was for her.

God, he hoped that wouldn't take too long.

"Come on. Let's get out of here."

The ride back to Oakwood passed in an exhilarated contentment for Savannah. A cocoon of emotion swathed her whole being in both euphoria and a tense, uneasy eagerness that left her excruciatingly aware of herself. Emotionally, she was coming down off a roller coaster of mixed feelings. Physically, her body felt empty.

She shifted in the fine leather seat and wished she could pull it all together. She didn't like feeling separate from herself, her body knowing what it wanted, her mind a jumble of uncertainty. Until tonight, both had been in sync, free of discord, satisfied to exist in a passionless domain.

Jacob had changed all that. He had her thinking about desire and making love when, for years, she had taken for granted that both would be absent from her life. Yet there she sat, feeling the remnants of a passion she had never felt, not even with Eric, her only lover.

Out of the corner of her eye, she watched Jacob handle the car with the sure expertise of a man comfortable with a high-powered machine. What was it about this man that enabled him to upset her entire existence? With a word, a look, and most definitely a kiss, he took her orderly, grounded life and shook the daylights out of it.

"Photographic possibilities?" he asked, taking his eyes from the road long enough to glance her way.

Her brows arched. "Pardon?"

"You're staring again. Are you designing photos in your mind?"

She laughed a bit nervously. "No. I was thinking about you, actually."

"I like the sound of that. Something good, I hope."

"You're very much in charge. You have a forceful nature. I can well imagine you in the cockpit of a jet."

"Don't imagine too hard," he scoffed. "My jet jockeying days are over."

"Do you miss them?"

His eyes narrowed. "I miss the sheer joy of flying. Of taking my plane through her paces. I miss the fraternity of the squadron."

"I sense a 'but' coming."

He grinned that one-sided grin that did such devilish things to his expression. "But I don't miss the rest of the crap that comes along with the job. The paperwork, the internal workings of the military."

"Is that why you got out?"

"Partly. Mostly it was because I knew from the start I wasn't a *career man*. Being a fighter pilot was one of the things I wanted to do with my life. When I accomplished that goal to my satisfaction, I decided to move on."

"Did you know you wanted to own an investigative agency?"

He downshifted smoothly to take a sharp bend in the road. "I knew I wanted to work for myself. I knew I wanted to utilize all the schooling and training I'd received to the fullest. The kind of agency we run does that."

"We?"

"I have a partner, Phil Stewart."

"Was he in the Air Force, too?"

"No, Phil is former FBI."

"A fed?" she asked, tantalized by the idea.

"In the flesh."

"This sounds serious. Two former government employees snooping out—" She sent him a narrowed gaze. "What *do* you investigate?"

"This and that."

"Meaning you can't say?"

"Meaning we're hired to collect hard-to-come-by information. Which reminds me. I'll be in Washington for the next few days. I'd like to see you when I get back."

Her heart did a little flip flop in her chest. *He wanted to see her again.* After the way he kissed her on the dock, she shouldn't have been surprised, and yet she was.

"Savannah?" He sent her a questioning look.

She was getting in deep here and she knew it. With any other man, this is where she would politely but firmly put a halt to their involvement. But Jacob wasn't any other man. The idea of not seeing him again was horribly disappointing.

She could have rolled her eyes. As if she needed one more feeling to add to the growing list of raw emotions bombarding her tonight. "Um, I'm sorry. It's been some time since I've been part of the whole dating thing. This is all happening so fast. I feel a little out of it."

"No problem. We can keep it simple." He drew his chin to his chest with a prolonged inhale. "So, are you free Thursday night?"

"Yes, but I thought you were going to be in D.C."

"I'll be back sometime in the afternoon." He slowed the car as he entered the long rutted drive leading to his house. "How does dinner sound?"

It sounded terrific . . . and frightening. The easy way out would be for her to cling to the security of old habits. But no matter how many self-doubts she harbored, she couldn't lie to herself about wanting to see Jake again.

"Dinner sounds wonderful."

"Good, I'll pick you up around seven."

"Are you sure you want to do that? If you're going to be traveling all day, wouldn't it be easier if I fix dinner for us?"

He turned fully to look at her, pleasure mingling openly with mild doubt. "You wouldn't mind?"

"No." She smiled, pleased by his obvious delight. "I love to cook."

Turning his attention back to the drive, he grinned. "All right. I'll bring the wine."

It was strange how his easy grin seemed to reach across

the space and soothe her frayed nerves. There was nothing noteworthy about this particular curving of lips and yet Savannah felt touched by its very simplicity. Its honesty and directness personified Jake himself which above all else, disarmed her.

Yes, she was very glad she was going to see him again.

"I really enjoyed myself tonight," she murmured moments later, standing at her opened car door.

Jacob slid a hand up her arm to cup her shoulder. "So did I." He gave the interior of her car a quick visual once over. "Are you going to be all right driving home?"

"Oh, sure. I'm only fifteen minutes away."

"Be careful on these back roads. Without streetlights it can be tricky in places."

"I'll take it slow."

He reached into his back pocket for his wallet and removed a business card. "Call me when you get in."

"Why?" she asked, taking the card.

"So I'll know you got home safely."

That this formidable, dynamic man would concern himself for her sake warmed her heart deeply. She nodded and then felt ridiculously awkward. She didn't know what more to say or how to end the evening, especially since she really didn't want to leave.

He took the matter out of her hands. Leaning forward he brushed his lips over hers. Once. Twice. Mere whispers of a kiss that tempted her body, burnished her spirit, and left her feeling nourished for the entire ride back to the cottage.

She called him the minute she got in. "Hi."

"Hi, yourself." The deep tones of his voice sounded more mellow than usual. "Everything go all right?"

"Yes."

"Sleep tight, then."

"I will. You, too. And have a good trip."

"No sweat. I'll see you in a couple of days . . . Oh, and Savannah?"

"Yes."

"Think about me while I'm gone."

It was impossible for her to do anything else. For the next two days, she did her best to concentrate on her work, but Jacob was always there in her mind. A sweet distraction if there ever was one.

Her emotions swung from the highs of excitement to the lows of dread. By getting involved with Jacob, she was leaving herself wide open for getting hurt. On a philosophical note, she told herself that no one escaped the human condition without some pain. On the defensive, she debated that she'd had her share of grief and didn't want any more.

In the end, she borrowed a bottom-line attitude from Jacob himself and decided that there were some things in life worth taking risks for. There was something unique about her relationship with Jake. She couldn't explain why, but she would never forgive herself if she didn't give them a chance regardless of the emotional risks involved.

He was different from the men she usually dated. No man had ever managed to break through the barriers she had erected in the aftermath of Eric's death. She had never allowed a man to do so. She was glad that Jacob had, because he was the single most appealing male she'd ever met. Even more than Eric.

She wasn't being disloyal. She knew—had always known—that what she felt for Eric had been based on a deep, abiding friendship, and the basic need of one human being for another. For her, emotion stronger than that had never existed. With Eric or any man.

Until now. Until Jacob. He had her thinking and feeling everything from humor to lust.

Repeatedly, she recalled his expressions, the sound of his laughter, the way the blue of his eyes darkened with emotion. And of course, the way he had kissed her. That memory alone was enough to make her ruin more than one photo and question again and again where they were headed.

It took her until noon on Wednesday before she was truly focused. Once she had control of her attention, however, her work progressed smoothly and with what she hoped would be satisfying results. She wouldn't know for sure until she was in her dark room.

The interior of the house proved to be as interesting and challenging as the outside. So much so, that Savannah lost track of the time. Again. It was the noisy rumbling of her stomach that interrupted her concentration several hours later. In the unrelieved silence of the master bedroom on the second floor, the hungry gurgles sounded ridiculously loud.

Camera hanging from its strap around her neck, she looked about, only then realizing just how thick the silence was. She couldn't hear anything beyond herself. No chirping from the birds in the trees that surrounded the house, no creaking of old wood setting and complaining, not even the ever-present scratching of the mice in the walls.

Nothing. It was like being in a vacuum with all the sound sucked away. She'd never realized how disorienting that could be and strained her ears to catch a hint of any sound.

Again, nothing.

Instinctively, she snapped her fingers. The reassuring little pop brought a lopsided grin to her face . . . a grin that slowly, sickeningly gave way to the hollow sensation she had experienced the day before. Her equilibrium said she was sinking; her body, however, remained stationary.

She squeezed her eyes shut, and silently cursed her luck. It was time to see the doctor. If this was an early case of the flu, she wanted it over and done with as soon as possible. She wasn't fond of hypodermic needles, but this couldn't go on.

Breathing in a steady, paced rhythm, she opened her eyes, and instantly wished she hadn't. The room around her seemed to quiver. She squinted, pressing her fingers into her temples, but the effort didn't help. Everything in her vision appeared distorted, as if she were looking through heat waves emanating from a long stretch of super heated highway.

She was really sick this time and Jacob wasn't there to catch her if she passed out now. Acting on reflex alone, she sank to her knees. The second she did, the room . . . changed.

The quivering distortion gave way to shapes that gradually took form. Between the two windows, a nebulous mass of brown came into view and mutated into a diaphanous dry sink. A semi-transparent bed appeared on the right wall. Two chairs flanked the fireplace to the left.

Savannah wheezed in harsh, grating breaths. Stunned, frightened, she knelt unable to move; heart pounding, mouth dry, her entire body shaking.

What was happening? What was she seeing? Was she hallucinating or had she stepped into some kind of a time warp? She didn't believe in time warps . . . had never given them serious thought. A minute ago, the room had been empty. Now, it was filled with strangely thin antique furniture pieces. *Was she losing her mind?*

No! She could see everything clearly. The paintings on the walls, the rugs on the floor, even the canopy over the bed. All were right there in front of her, all were in full; albeit, transparent color.

Automatically, she grabbed her camera. Her fingers fumbled for endless seconds and then finally triggered the automatic drive. Tense, endless moments elapsed as she focused on each shape, entire walls, the floor.

Struggling to keep her hands steady, she photographed everything she saw, dying a little inside, wishing she'd had time to set up one of the tripods; praying the camera would catch the images, praying for safety from the unknown until she used up every bit of film.

Then she scrambled to her feet, tore down the stairs, and drove straight back to her apartment in Richmond.

Eight

"Savannah," Leanne exclaimed happily, opening the front door of her house. "What are you doing here? Come on in."

Savannah didn't attempt a smile or an immediate reply. She wanted merely to soak up the reassuring, rational environment of her sister's home.

"I didn't know you were going to be in Richmond," Leanne said with a smile. "But I'm glad you are."

Words didn't want to come for Savannah. The past hours had stripped away most of her inner reserve. "Are the kids asleep?" she finally asked, for several very good reasons. She loved her niece and nephew, but she was not up to laughing and teasing just then. And too, what she needed to discuss with Leanne was best not overheard by two impressionable children.

"John's tucking them in right now. Seven-thirty, and it's lights out for those two munchkins."

In a gesture completely foreign to Savannah she scrubbed and twisted her hands, not knowing how else to combat the awful tension still roiling inside her.

Leanne studied her closely. "Savannah? Are you all right?"

Frowning, eyes dark, troubled and tinged with helplessness, Savannah shook her head. "No. I'm not."

Leanne took hold of her hands, her face lining with concern. "What is it?"

Where to begin? Savannah stared at her sister feeling as if she were walking through a dream that had no end. "Could we sit down?"

"Of course." Leanne's frown deepened as she led the way down the hall to the family room at the back of the house. "You're scaring me," she declared, sinking slowly onto the blue plaid sofa.

"I don't mean to." Savannah literally slumped into a thick cushioned chair at a right angle to her sister.

"Savannah, what's wrong? Have you passed out again?"

"I wish I could say 'yes'." She pressed the heels of her hands into her eyes. From beneath her palms, she muttered, "Oh, God, Lee, I don't even know where to start."

Leanne was off the sofa in the next heartbeat, kneeling in front of Savannah, taking her gently by the arms. "Tell me no one is dead," she demanded in the slow, calm tones of someone trying to gain information from a hysteric.

"No, it's nothing like that." Savannah dropped her hands, realizing as much from her sister's voice as from the anxious look on her face that Leanne's imagination was in full flight. "I'm sorry, I don't mean to worry you. No one is dead, I haven't been in an accident, I'm not sick."

"Then what is it?"

Savannah's lips parted. She remained mute for far too long, having no idea of how to continue. She had to though. This wasn't something she could keep to herself. "I . . . something happened at the old house today," she finally whispered in a rush.

"The old house at Oakwood?"

"Yes. I . . . I was upstairs and . . . and . . ." She rolled her eyes toward the ceiling, exhaling a single short breath.

"Just take it easy, Sav. Start at the beginning."

From the doorway, Savannah heard John ask, "What's going on?"

Looking up, she found her brother-in-law, just entering the room, and somehow managed a quick greeting. "Hi."

John folded his lanky frame onto the sofa. "Geez, you look like hell, Savannah. What's wrong?"

"I'm trying to get her to tell me," Leanne replied.

Savannah let her gaze rest on John for a moment. With his boyishly handsome face and thinning blond hair, he was as welcoming a sight as Leanne was. From them both, she flat-out stole some fortitude. "You're both going to think I'm crazy."

Obviously believing levity would help, John teased, "We've always thought that, Sav."

"Well, now you're going to have proof." As if waving her right hand would free up some of her inner tension, she gestured a little frantically "I . . . I was photographing the old Oakwood mansion today. Things were going well. It was around three o'clock . . . I was working in black and white . . . no problems until . . . until the room b . . . be . . . gan . . . damn . . ." Confessing this aloud was almost impossible. "Furniture started to appear out of nowhere!"

Leanne blinked and angled one ear slightly forward. "What?"

Striving to maintain her breathing, Savannah repeated, *"Things, furniture filled the room."* Suddenly sitting there became unbearable. She shot to her feet and paced to the stone fireplace. When she turned, she found Leanne seated beside John; the two of them staring at her confused and disbelieving.

"I told you, you'd think I was crazy," she declared. *"I* think I'm crazy."

"We don't think that," John soothed.

"Tell me what you do think."

Leanne turned to John, both her brows and her shoulders elevating into shrugs. "John?"

He kneaded his forehead. "What exactly did you see, Savannah?"

"Too much." In the ensuing minutes, she related in exacting detail everything that had occurred earlier.

"Was the furniture real?" Leanne queried, her voice two octaves higher than normal, her eyes as rounded as Savannah had ever seen them. "Did anything actually solidify into . . . you know, *real objects?*"

"I didn't wait around to find out."

"What did you do when you left?"

"I drove straight back to my apartment and developed the film. That's where I've been for the past two hours." She paled to a ghastly white. "Everything on the roll developed," she whispered, "except the frames I shot when the room changed."

"There was no furniture?" John asked.

"No, you don't understand. There was *nothing*. No room, no furniture. The film was black, as if I had taken the pictures inside a closed closet with no light at all."

"Was there any chance you left the lens cap on?"

Savannah adamantly denied the possibility with a shake of her head. "None. I was halfway home before I remembered that the cap was in my pocket. I dug it out when I had to stop at a light."

He tried for another explanation. "Maybe something was wrong with the film or one of your development solutions."

"If that were the case, nothing on the roll would have developed."

"Is this the first time this has happened?"

She started to nod but stopped, recalling the incident from two days before. Incredulous, attention focused inward, she confessed, "Monday, I felt that awful empty sensation, like I had just stepped off a roller coaster. I wasn't quite dizzy, but neither did I feel like I had both feet planted firmly on the ground.

"After I finally got my head settled, I looked back at the house, and thought I saw curtains and glass in one of the windows. I thought it was my imagination." Sinking onto the raised hearth, she lifted haunted eyes to her sister. "Oh God, what's happening? Am I losing it?"

"No," Leanne declared in immediate defense. Crossing the room to sit beside Savannah, she put her arm around her shoulders and hugged her close. "You're not going crazy."

"I feel like I am," Savannah cried, panic creeping into her tone. "I know what I saw . . . what I felt. I can't explain it."

"Maybe there is no other rationale."

Coming to his feet, John scoffed, "That's no answer, Leanne."

She sent him an insulted stare. "Well, what do you think?"

"I don't know."

Into the tense silence, Savannah asked, "Do you believe me, John? Do you believe I'm not imagining all of this?"

His expression somber, John shoved his hands into his back pockets. "I believe *you* believe you saw something."

Leanne wasn't as cautious or tactful. "Well, I think the place is haunted."

Savannah's eyes snapped wide. "Haunted?"

"It would make sense."

"Sure, if I believed in ghosts."

Leanne went on unperturbed. "There are too many unexplained phenomena in this world for us to pooh-pooh this as a trick of light or a flight of fancy."

Savannah had always prided herself on having an incredibly open mind when it came to the unexplained. She wasn't one to discount anything just for lack of evidence. But this kind of thing happened to other people, not to her. She wasn't psychic or telepathic. All she could claim was a certain sensitivity to life in general.

"I don't know, Lee. A haunted house? Aren't ghosts or spirits usually involved in that?"

"I couldn't say. Maybe haunted isn't the correct term, but something *is* going on in that place."

Feeling as if her life were spinning out of her control, Savannah gripped her head. "This is so illogical."

"That's the point, Savannah, there isn't any logic when you're dealing with the supernatural."

John spread both hands wide. "Leanne, don't you think you're jumping the gun a little here?"

"No, not at all. And for three very good reasons."

"Which are?"

"One, Savannah isn't one to make up tales. She's too grounded for that."

"I agree."

"Two, we have a mother who *routinely* checks into the clairvoyant zone. You can't deny Mom's abilities, John. She's been spot on more often than not when it comes to me and Savannah."

"All right, I'll grant you that your mother has a megadose of motherly intuition."

"It's more than that."

"So make your point."

"Given Mom's abilities, I think that makes Savannah very susceptible to anything metaphysical."

John heaved a sigh, plainly sorry he had entered into the debate. "What's your third reason?"

Leanne gave a smug smile. "Savannah's watch."

Savannah rubbed at her aching temples, not even trying to decipher the last of her sister's clues. "What?"

Leanne took hold of Savannah's wrist and tapped the flat face of the wrist watch. "I noticed the time on your watch. The hands are stopped at 3:07."

A chill settled in the depths of Savannah's spine. It had been shortly after three when she had encountered whatever it was at Oakwood. "I had a new battery put in on Saturday," she breathed in dismayed awe.

"Exactly," Leanne confirmed. "Because several days before that, you had been in the old house and you—"

"I felt strange, lost track of time—"

"And finally fainted. *And your watch went dead.*"

"Oh, my God." Savannah dropped her head onto her knees. She didn't know what was happening, but it stretched the limits of reality. At least the commonly accepted version of reality. That most definitely did not include stopped time and rooms changing before her eyes.

"Take it easy, you two," John coaxed, but even he took a seat, his face suffused with astonishment.

Leanne continued. "Stuff like ESP goes on all the time. The papers are full of accounts of people connecting with other dimensions, the spirit world, that sort of thing. More and more, psychics are helping police with investigations that are dead ended."

"But I'm not psychic!" Savannah exclaimed into her knees.

"How do you know? Maybe you're a late bloomer."

Savannah sat straight and gave her sister a jaundiced look. "Get real."

Leanne took the slight reprimand in stride. Leaning back against the fireplace screen, she folded her arms across her chest and goaded, "You asked what I thought. I told you. Do you have a better explanation?"

Savannah didn't, and that had her exhaling in pure frustration. She surged to her feet and made her way to one of the windows. There she stared out into the darkness of night. Indistinct shadows played with the more solid forms of trees, a swing set, a fence. In her present state of mind, the scene appeared sinister.

Wrapping her arms about herself, she tried to ward off the tremors that threatened. It would be easy to give into tears, if for no other reason than she was too tired to do anything else. As it was, her whole life had been turned inside out and she had no idea of how to continue.

The most lonely, vulnerable sensation gripped her. Surprisingly, instinctively, her mind called out to Jacob. Whether it was foolish or not, she longed to have his arms around her. She needed to feel his strength and warmth.

"Could I stay here tonight?" she whispered, still searching through the grays of the back yard.

"Of course." Leanne's voice was just as hushed. "Stay as long as you like."

There was an element of hiding out in that option that didn't sit well with Savannah. She wasn't one to run from life. That had never been her way no matter what she had had to face. She wasn't going to start now.

But for tonight, she desperately needed to fortify. She wouldn't be able to do that in the emptiness of her apartment or the cottage. Tomorrow, she would face what came, including going back into the old house.

"Thanks. Please don't say anything to anyone about this."

"I wouldn't think of it," Leanne said.

"We don't know what's going on. There's no point in getting people stirred up, especially if it doesn't happen again."

Leanne's jaw dropped. "You're planning on going back?"

Savannah faced her squarely. "I don't have a choice. With the exception of the one camera I brought with me, I left all my equipment on the second floor of the old mansion. I have to go back."

The next afternoon, the master bedroom of Oakwood was as normal as any empty, three-hundred year old room could possibly be. In fact, Savannah found entering the second floor room to be anticlimactic. The walls remained stable, no shimmering waves clouded her field of vision, and sound was in full volume.

From that she gained back some of her spirit. Nonetheless, she didn't linger. She dredged up the old mind-set from her days with the magazine. Get in, get the job done, get out, and don't stop to think or question things too closely. Quickly, cautiously, not wanting to tempt the fates, she collected her equipment and returned to the cottage. The phone was ringing even as she opened the front door.

"Hello," she said, breathless from her dash down the hall and into the bedroom.

"Savannah, it's me, Leanne sighed in blatant relief. "Are you all right?"

"Perfect."

"Did anything happen?"

"No. Although I half-expected to see an armoire or a chair materialize out of thin air."

"I never should have let you go back alone."

Savannah settled onto the bed and smiled patiently at her sister's protective nature. "We discussed that at breakfast. Don't worry, I made it in and out in one piece."

"I can't believe you actually went back in."

"I've been in tighter spots." A conclusion she had reached in the shower that morning. A sleepless night hadn't helped her headache, but it had set her on track again. That track had her facing the issue head on. "And besides, what was I supposed to do? Leave my cameras? Not in this lifetime."

"You and your damn cameras," Leanne groused. "You'd think you were joined at the hip."

"Stop grumbling at me. Everything went fine."

"Thank goodness for small favors. You sound okay."

"Lee, I haven't turned into the monster from the Lost Lagoon."

"How can you joke at a time like this?"

"I'm not, but I can't shrivel up and die over this whole thing. Something happened. I have to accept that."

"I should tell you," Leanne warned, "Mom called. She couldn't reach you, so she tried me."

"What did she want?"

"You have to ask?!"

From the incredulity in Leanne's voice, Savannah knew that their mother had 'connected' again. "What did you tell her?"

"I didn't want her worrying, so I lied, sort of. I told her that you were probably off somewhere working hard."

"Thanks. I'll call her later and tell her I've been to La La Land."

"Please don't joke about this, Banana. You don't know what you're dealing with. That house could be a portal to another time or a collecting point for astral energy."

Savannah choked on a startled gasp. "Where do you get these ideas of yours?"

"They're not mine exclusively. And if I remember right, up until now, you've been very accepting of this kind of thing."

"On a purely theoretical basis. It's a whole other matter to actually experience it, whatever *it* is."

"I would think that having lived through it, you'd be a firm believer, not a skeptic."

"Having lived through it, I don't want to peg it like some episode of *Unsolved Mysteries.* We both agree something is happening in the house."

"That's putting it mildly."

"Until I know what, I'd prefer not to blow this out of proportion."

"You're being way too logical about this," Leanne complained. "How do you explain the whole thing with your watch and time? And what about your getting sick?"

Through the endless hours of the night, Savannah had thought and rethought the entire situation and hit upon one very startling realization. Whenever she had gone in or near the house, something had happened to either her or to the state of time.

She tried not to shudder at the admission, but the facts couldn't be ignored. The first time she had been in the mansion, she had been quite certain about how long she had explored those rooms. And she had checked her watch and found herself late by only fifteen minutes. It wasn't until later that she discovered her watch had stopped, and an hour had lapsed without her being aware of it.

How had she misplaced an entire hour? Ten, fifteen minutes was understandable, but not sixty. Nothing like that had ever happened to her, not even during some of those harrowing times in Bosnia when her life had been in doubt and when time had become relative.

"I can't explain either," she told her sister.

Leanne remained silent for a long moment before asking, "Savannah, do you think the physical symptoms you experienced happened because time in Oakwood is in some way skewed?"

Instinctively, Savannah denied the possibility. Then she recalled her memories and uttered a broken curse. "I don't know."

"It is possible."

Savannah wasn't ready to admit what was possible and what wasn't. Oh, she didn't expect the boogey man to loom up out of the old walls and drag her into the unknown. That occurred only in Hollywood.

No, the truth was, she didn't know what had happened or what to expect. And until she did, she was caught somewhere in between fright and a powerful curiosity that bordered on obsession. Part of her warned that she have nothing more to do with Oakwood. Another part insisted that she embrace the incident and explore it to the max. Still, another part remained doubtful of her sanity.

"Savannah?" Lee's voice pulled her back to the present. "I'm here."

"What are you going to do now?"

"I haven't decided."

"Are you going to tell Jacob?"

His image shot into Savannah's mind, giving her world

true focus for the first time in nearly a day. The tension that had gripped her inside melted enough so she was able to take an unfettered breath.

Lord only knew what he would make of all of this. She didn't know him very well, but she strongly suspected that he and Leanne would be worlds—light years—apart in their thinking.

She checked the clock. In less than three hours, he'd be there for dinner.

"I don't think telling him is a good idea."

"Why not?"

"Leanne, think. How . . . what do I say? 'I hope you like chicken cacciatore, Jacob, and oh, by the way, the old house is haunted. More wine?' *If* he doesn't believe me nuts, and *if* he doesn't laugh his way out the door, it will be a miracle. More likely, he'll chew me up and spit me out in little pieces before he gets on the phone, calls his brother and tells him that I'm certifiable."

"You don't know he'll react that way."

"You don't know the man. He'll do exactly that." No, she wouldn't, couldn't tell him. If she did, she ran the risk of his interfering with her work.

The thought jerked her body straight. Until that very second, she hadn't decided whether to continue shooting the house or not. But the idea of walking away from this particular subject was suddenly unthinkable.

Despite everything, the old house held a fascination for her that she couldn't explain. It lured her with its history as well as its presence. She couldn't abandon it.

A crooked grin pulled at her lips, and she bowed her head in rueful defeat. Of all the conclusions she could have come to, this wasn't the one she would have banked on. And yet her instincts told her she was right to go back, to finish what she had begun.

Her instincts had never failed her before. She prayed they wouldn't now.

Nine

"Am I early?" Jake smiled down into Savannah's up-turned face with his question. It had been three days since he had last seen her. She looked better than ever.

"No. You're right on time." She held open her front door and waved him into the cottage; her lips lifting tentatively into a smile. "How was your trip?"

He contained his more rude opinion of his time spent with the good congressman in Washington and released only a laughing scoff. "I'm glad to be back." Stepping into the living room, he scanned the length of Savannah and silently amended his sentiments.

It was better than good to be back. It was great and he didn't even try to tame his wandering gaze. He had repeatedly pictured her in his mind while he had been gone, but his imagination hadn't done justice to the reality of Savannah as she was now.

She wore a lightweight tunic sweater that was just heavy enough to drape her breasts to perfection. And while the curve of her waist and upper thighs was completely hidden by the burgundy knit, the length and shape of her legs were definitely not. Her ankle-length skirt was made of a gauzy, slightly transparent, flowered material that revealed the sweet shape of her legs encased in dark leggings.

Damn, she looked terrific. He had never considered himself a leg man, but the shadows and teasing hints within her skirt had his entire system on stand-by. All too easily, he pictured those legs of hers wrapped about his hips while he fused his body with hers.

"Hi." He stretched the word into a soft, low rumble, then lowered his head and brushed his mouth over hers. "I missed you."

The vibrations of his words danced on Savannah's lips, making her insides knot with a pleasurable ache. That he had thought about her enough to miss her, added to the pleasure and relieved some of her tension.

Remnants of her experience in the old house lingered in her system. Being with Jacob eased her mind and settled her nerves. She tipped her mouth up to his, welcoming the feel of him, welcoming *him*. "I missed you, too."

Jacob made no move to lift his head, perfectly content for them to remain as they were, absorbing each other's heat as their lips stroked and caressed ever so slightly. The taste, feel and scent of her were spectacular.

He wanted her, it was that simple. But unless something had happened while he had been away, she wasn't ready to take a flying leap into the bedroom. And that was where his body was beginning to urge him to go.

Swallowing a grunt of frustration, he straightened to his full height. "What have you been doing while I've been gone?"

Her answer was a quick, almost nervous chuckle. She tucked her chin and stepped back. "The usual. I'll take your jacket, if you like."

"Did you have any problems at the house while I was away?"

It was a casual question. Savannah was sure he intended no underlying meaning. Still, she was glad her back was facing him as she hung his leather jacket in the closet. She hated lying to him. He deserved better than dishonesty from her. And yet, how could she tell him the truth? She wasn't convinced she knew what that was.

Turning, she said, "Actually, I didn't get as much work

done as I would have liked. I . . . I ended up going back to Richmond. I spent last night at my sister's." She was glad for the truth of that statement and managed a smile, then dropped her gaze to the bottle of wine he held. "Do I need to chill that?"

"No, room temperature is fine."

She preceded him into the kitchen with its bank of windows overlooking the river. From the oven, the aroma of chicken, garlic and tomato filled the air.

"Something smells good," he commented.

"An old family recipe," she explained as she hunted a corkscrew from one of the drawers. "I hope you like Italian."

"My favorite." Leaning back against one of the counters, he noted, "You're Italian?"

"On my mother's side."

"How'd you end up with a name like Savannah then?"

Corkscrew in hand, Savannah faced him and had to laugh. "My father was a died-in-the-wool, born and bred Virginian. He had a remarkable loyalty to the South." Eyes filled with tender, amusing memories, she added, "He also had a wonderful sense of humor."

"Don't tell me. You were born in Savannah."

"Close. I was conceived there." She set the bottle on the table in the dining alcove and efficiently set the corkscrew.

"What's your sister's name? Charlotte?"

"No, Leanne, Lee for short." Laughter lit her eyes. "As in General Robert E."

Jake gave an appreciative laugh. "You're right about your Dad's sense of humor. Must have made things interesting for your mother. Didn't she have a say in what her children were named?"

Savannah scoffed lightly. "If you knew my mother, you wouldn't have to ask."

"Determined woman?"

"That's putting it mildly." With a sure tug, she pulled the cork from the bottle, never missing a beat in the conversation. "Mom's a walking study in resolve and tenacity. If she hadn't liked our names, my sister and I would be signing different signatures today."

"That explains a great deal."

Savannah tilted her head to one side. "I don't follow you."

Lifting one broad shoulder into a negligent shrug, Jacob explained, "You're definitely your mother's daughter. You're one of the most determined people I've ever met."

"Am I?"

"That can't come as a surprise."

She considered that for a moment. "To some extent it does. I've always just done what needed to be done."

He gave her a pointed look. "Like I said, determined."

"You make it sound like a disease," she returned in mock offense.

"Not at all. I happen to like determined people." More to the point, he liked Savannah. Watching her move about the kitchen, he was struck by her honest grace and style. Both reflected a competent, unpretentious manner he found unbelievably sexy.

Hell, everything about Savannah was sexy. The way her lips pursed when she was deep in thought, the way her eyes rounded with indignation when he challenged her, the way she laughed that low, lazy laugh of hers.

And then there was her body. It was bad enough that her wit and intelligence and charm had a potent effect on him. To have all those attributes contained in slender curves and lush roundness, was pure eroticism. Through the course of dinner, it had him clenching his stomach muscles more than once. By the time they finished dessert and settled on the love seat in the living room, he was alternately damning his principles and applauding the finer points of anticipation.

"Where did you learn to cook so well?" he asked in sated contentment. Positioned in the corner of the two-seat sofa, he faced her with one arm resting along the back of the cushions, his fingers grazing the curve of her shoulder.

"From my mom."

"Well, thank her for me. It's been a long time since I've had a home-cooked meal to compare with tonight's."

"Spoken like the proverbial bachelor."

"Spoken like a man who appreciates fine cuisine."

She sent him a teasing grin. "Don't tell me you're a microwave-dinner-man."

"Most of the time. When I'm feeling ambitious, I'm good for pasta or a steak on the grill."

"Well, there you go. You aren't completely helpless. You're probably a better cook than you know."

"My ex-wife wouldn't agree."

The comment sent a small shock wave through Savannah. Oddly enough, she found the idea of Jacob having been married strangely disappointing. She had no right to feel that way. He had a past—and a present and future—when it came right down to it, but her gut reaction leaned heavily toward . . . well, hurt.

She conquered the emotion at once. "I didn't know you had been married."

"It was a long time ago. We parted amiably enough."

"You're lucky. I have several friends whose divorces were extremely bitter."

One side of Jacob's mouth quirked. "That would have required too much energy from Catherine. She wasn't one to expend herself emotionally. When she wanted out of our marriage, she got out. For her it was as simple as that."

She peered steadily into his eyes, hearing what he had left unsaid. Her heart constricted. "But it wasn't as simple for you."

Jacob didn't respond at once. His fingers trailed the line of her upper arm, his expression one of deep contemplation. "From the very start, I wanted different things from our marriage. Kids, home and hearth."

"And your wife didn't want that?"

"I thought she did. It turned out she got off on the idea of being married to a fighter pilot. She had some half-baked notion that marrying me would be glamorous and exciting, an endless round of parties and living a life that was as fast as the speeds I flew. Unfortunately, she couldn't live with reality."

"Which was?"

"That I was no different from any other working man. When I climbed into my car at five every night, I tried to leave my job at the 'office'. Sure, there were plenty of times when we partied, got good and rowdy, but that's never defined my lifestyle.

"I wanted to come home from work, catch up on her day, maybe go out for pizza, take in a good movie . . . you know, the mundane, every day things that most couples do."

"Like haggling over who's going to empty the dishwasher."

"Exactly."

Personally, Savannah thought spending the evening curled up in Jacob's arms while they watched reruns on TV sounded nice. And as for exciting, just being with the man gave the word new meaning. The force of his personality precluded boredom of any kind. To her way of thinking, that made him as unlike "any other working man" as one could get.

"She must have had other priorities in life."

"That became apparent six months after we were married. That's when things began to fall apart. We divorced eighteen months later."

"I'm sorry."

"Don't be. I'm fine with it."

She could see that he truly was. "I'm glad."

"Are you?"

Nodding, she explained, "I don't like to see people hurt."

Jacob cupped the ball of her shoulder in one hand and

openly studied her. It wasn't often that he discussed his marriage. He had no emotional hang ups about his few years with Catherine, still it was a private matter. One which he felt entirely comfortable confiding to Savannah.

She sat facing him, her legs curled up on the cushions, her knees touching his. In the low light of the room, he saw her as the personification of woman, all softness and curiosity, sensitivity balanced with indomitable female strength.

His hand skimmed along her collarbone to the warm column of her neck. Against his fingertips, he felt her pulse leap.

"Do I make you nervous?"

The light, stroking pressure of his fingers was distracting. "No. Why?"

He looked at her with a gaze that matched the sensuousness of his touch. "Your heart is racing."

She bit her lower lip. "Is it?"

"Yeah."

"You . . . you tend to have that effect on me."

Her honesty made him smile. He repeated the words she had given him. "I'm glad."

"Are you?"

He nodded. "You don't normally react to men this way, do you?"

She managed to shake her head.

"You don't even let most men get this close to you."

Again, she moved her head in a tiny negative motion that was abruptly cut off when his hand slid down her arm to take gentle, indomitable hold of her wrist. With carefully controlled strength, he pulled her from her seated position until she found herself stretched across his body. Chest to chest, faces only inches apart, she stared into his eyes and saw blatant masculine arousal.

"I've wanted to do this from the minute I walked in here tonight," he muttered.

He slanted his mouth over hers and thrust his tongue past her lips in a carnal rhythm that left no illusions as to what he really wanted to do. The hand that held her wrist tugged her closer while his other arm circled her back and bound her to him.

For a brief moment, Savannah considered the wisdom of what she was doing. And then he deepened the kiss and being sensible was the last thing she could think about. His kisses were urgent and explicitly sensual, banked by a hard-driving desire suddenly released. He demanded a response. Helplessly, she clung to his shoulders and gave him what he sought.

Conscious thought slipped away; years of personal reservations vanished. Even haunted houses melted into nothing. She wanted to be in Jacob's arms. Out of habit alone, surprise and wonder registered distantly, but not enough to dissuade her. She accepted the feeling and kissed him back, entwining her tongue with his.

A low groan worked its way up his throat. He captured her breast in his palm, sending shivers of pleasure into her stomach, out to her fingertips, and straight to her loins. Her whole body became boneless and she melted against him in the same manner she had when he had kissed her days earlier on the dock beneath the stars.

Her response then had been intense and heated. It was no less so now. She wrapped her hands about his neck and drew him closer, not even aware that she was panting in small erratic breaths, or that Jacob had shifted their positions so that she lay on her back and he loomed over her.

She welcomed his weight; her body instinctively accepting his strength and heat as naturally as if his form had been sculpted specifically for her. The satisfaction in that was heady stuff that fueled her desire.

Through the layers of his clothing and hers, the muscles of his chest caressed her breasts. The taut plane of his stomach embraced the hollow of hers. Rejoicing in their harmony, she slipped her hands up his back and held onto him tightly.

His hips moved, parting her legs, then he settled himself intimately between her thighs. Pleasure burst like a thousand rockets at the contact of his rigid flesh rocking against her softness. And still, his mouth never left hers. His tongue surged into her mouth, making her dizzy with a longing that doubled and redoubled when his hand slipped under her sweater sliding it upward.

The lace of her bra was no barrier. His fingers released the center catch, and he finally lifted his head, only to lower it again, this time to the pouting crests of her breasts. With his lips and tongue, he worked a magic that had her clinging to his head, holding onto him as her entire body arched.

"Jacob." She struggled to say his name. Not that she was capable of actually telling him anything. Her senses were winging free; her heart pounding so hard her chest ached.

Jake spared her a quick glance, only to assure himself that it was passion he heard in her voice. Her enthralled expression confirmed what he already knew, that Savannah was on fire.

He was on fire. Indescribable need had literally erupted through his every muscle and nerve, obliterating reason and common sense. He hadn't come here tonight intending to make love to her, but she was making a shambles of his self control, and for the first time in his life, he didn't care.

He wanted her. Now. Hard and fast and deep. He wanted to wring every drop of passion from her, he wanted to hear her cry his name again and again when he buried himself in her body, he wanted to stare straight into her eyes when she convulsed around him in orgasm.

"Savannah," he growled. Shoving her skirt out of his way, he lay claim to the intimate heat between her legs.

She curled into his touch, pulling into herself, a little frantic at the power he wielded over her. But he wouldn't allow her even that small retreat. He ground his mouth on hers, forcing her to meet the turbulence of his passion. All the while, his fingers branded her with a bold possession.

She belonged to him. His message couldn't have been any clearer if he had stood up and shouted it for all to hear.

Oh, God, he was going too fast, taking her to emotional planes that were beyond her experience. His desire buffeted her, overwhelmed her with its intensity, and made her feel things that she had never, ever felt before.

Like a marauding lion who had been released from captivity, he gave into his primal instincts. In a sudden thought, she realized just how much control he had exerted on himself until now. But no longer. Everything about him declared that he was single-minded. He was going to have her.

In a flash, she pictured their naked bodies twisting on her bed, bathed in sweat, and knew she wasn't ready. Her body might be quivering with need, but her heart wasn't prepared.

Instinctively, she stiffened, hating herself even as she tried to lever her legs together. She wasn't a tease. She hadn't meant for this to happen.

"Jacob."

The rigidity of her body registered on his senses instantly. He jerked his head up and glared down into her uncertain face. Her refusal stared back at him.

"Shit." He pushed himself up and off her in one fluid movement. Standing with his back to her, he jammed his fists onto his waist and ground his eyes shut. Behind him, he could hear her shifting on the sofa, sitting up and rearranging her skirt.

"Jacob, I'm sorry."

At her whisper, he whirled on her with narrowed, turbulent blue eyes, grimacing in an effort to alleviate the discomfort in his crotch. *"What the hell happened?"*

Savannah took the brunt of his fury as best she could. However, she wrapped up in her arms and felt only marginally better. "I . . . I think things got out of hand. I shouldn't have let it go this far."

"Babe, I've got a hard-on that says you weren't thinking at all."

Inside, she flinched at his crude remark. Outwardly, her frayed nerves bristled. "I said I was sorry, but it seems to me that you weren't thinking either."

"You were so hot for me, you made thinking impossible."

She came to her feet and met his accusation head on, ignoring the fierceness of his expression. "I hope that's frustration talking."

"It sure as hell isn't satisfaction."

Her shoulders stiffened and her chin angled upward. "I said I was sorry. I truly mean it, but you have to understand, I'm not ready to go to bed with you."

"You could have fooled me. I was between your legs, for Christ's sake."

As long as he took that arrogant attitude of his, she wasn't about to try to explain that she had been helpless to keep him from getting between her legs.

Anger surged up hot and red, replacing all and any desire she felt. He was deliberately being unreasonable. She had to wonder if this was the first time he had ever been denied.

"If this is how you're going to act, then it's time you left."

His mouth thinned to a hard slash. "Oh, no. You can't call it quits on this relationship that easily."

"What relationship?"

He lowered his face to hers, grinding his words, "The one we're trying to build."

That snatched the wind from her sails. The brown of her eyes softened with confusion and uncertainty. "Is that what we're doing?"

Seeing her vulnerability, Jacob lost most of his temper. "Yeah." Mentally, he kicked himself for being an ass, but for the life of him, no woman had ever tied him in the kind of knots Savannah had.

Swearing under his breath, he crossed to the front window and ran a hand along the back of his neck. Silently, he got a grip on his self-control and contemplated the reasons for his actions.

He had been involved with enough women through the years to know that what he felt for them and what he felt for Savannah were worlds apart. No other woman had ever incited his spirit the way she had; no other made him feel so alive. It was little wonder that he had never wanted a woman the way he wanted Savannah, past reason or caution.

"I'm sorry," he said, turning to face her with his apology. "You're right, neither one of us was thinking."

Savannah hadn't gotten past his declaration about a relationship. Mutual interest was as far as she had gone in defining what they shared. It would seem that as always, in his own high-handed, issue-an-order-way, Jacob was miles ahead of her in his assumptions. Giving into complete bewilderment, she sank back to the love seat.

"Are you all right?" he asked.

"I don't know."

"You look a little shaky."

"That's how I feel. I didn't realize where we . . . were going, that you were getting serious."

"I didn't expect it either, but that's the bottom line. Couldn't you tell?"

She was only now becoming comfortable with the idea of their seeing each other. Anything more than that, she expected would take time. Apparently, they were on two different time tables. "I know that I turn you on."

"Babe, you've got a great bod, but that's not what turns me on." He clarified that instantly. "Well, it does, but only because my mind is involved."

"Really?" Her lips parted on a quivering smile that began in her heart.

"Really. You should have known that."

She gestured to the cushions before lifting a hand to him. "This doesn't happen to me every day."

She had said as much before. By her own admission, she kept men at a safe distance, but he didn't want to be kept at any distance at all. He had no intentions of letting her do that to him, to them both.

He let his gaze roam over her features, and not for the first time, asked himself what it was about this particular woman that got to him as she did. He could rationalize her sensitivity, her delicate beauty and her intellect until the cows came home, but it went deeper than that. In ways that he was only beginning to understand, she touched him.

Something within her called to him, a unique quality that made her special. Yet try as he may, he couldn't define it past summing it up as the whole of her personality. All and everything about her appealed to him, and the more he came to know her, the stronger that feeling became.

He wanted to know everything there was to know about Savannah Davis. The dossier he had had compiled on her had given him the basic, sometimes sketchy, facts, but it hadn't explained why she could kiss him like hell on fire one minute, and then freeze up the very next. And it didn't tell him what, or who, was responsible for that uncertain look in her eyes. From everything he had learned about her, he suspected he knew.

"Why is that, Savannah?" His voice emerged as a velvet caress. "Why haven't there been any men in your life? Does it have anything to do with Eric?" He recalled the name and the anguish he had seen on her face when she had spoken of the man's death. "Tell me what happened."

Something inside Savannah stilled. As vulnerable as she was right then, she had no defenses against all the old memories that crowded forward. With all her heart, she wished not to have this discussion, especially on the tail-end of the argument they had just had. There were only so many emotions she could handle in one night.

Scrubbing her hands over her knees, she quietly protested, "I really would rather not talk about Eric."

"We have to." He crossed back to her and sat on his heels, his spread legs encompassing her thighs. "If you and I are ever going to go anywhere, you have to get over the past."

She massaged the ache in her forehead. It didn't lessen the tension twisting behind her eyes, or the naked truth that Jacob was right. Any chance for them was doomed unless she was honest with herself and Jacob.

Honesty, in this case, was that she wanted a relationship with Jacob. More honesty; she had to screw her courage to the wall to proceed. After years of placid nothingness, getting seriously involved with Jake meant tramping through all the hurt left over from Eric.

She heaved a defeated sigh, not sure where to start. "Eric is . . . he's dead." Somehow beginning at the end made the telling easier.

"You told me." He watched her with steady, intent eyes. "Who was he?"

"A man I dated. We were close."

"Lovers?"

She nodded, her brows elevating before she frowned at the memories. "If you could call it that. We both worked for the magazine. Our schedules kept us apart more often than not, but when we both managed to be home at the same time, we were together."

"Were you in love with him?"

The intense query brought her eyes to his. It would have been easy to look away at that point, and in doing so, give into the guilt that had hounded her for years. Instead, she kept her gaze level with his. "No. I cared very deeply for him. We were good friends, we had our jobs and interests in common, but I didn't love him. Not the way he deserved."

"How did he die?"

His words speared straight into her and she shivered. "You don't mince words, do you, Q Man?"

The nickname struck some of the intensity from his face. "You should know that by now." He came to his feet, gathered her in his arms, turned and sat; pulling her on to his lap. "Tell me all of it, Savannah."

Whether it was because of the command behind his request or the reassurance she gained from his embrace, Savannah found the words.

"We had a strange relationship. We were both committed to jobs that took us into some hairy places. Danger was part of our lives; we accepted it. I think most of what we found in each other was someone to cling to."

She hoped she was making sense. Now that she had begun, she so wanted him to understand. "There were times when he would come back from outer nowhere, torn up inside from what he had seen, and he would need someone to hold him; someone to get him through the night and make him feel human again. I was that person for him."

"As he was for you?"

"Yes. After my first time to eastern Europe, I didn't think I'd ever be able to sleep in the dark again for seeing the dead bodies I had photographed. It was Eric who held me when I'd wake up crying and sweating."

The words ripped at Jacob's heart. He didn't want to think of her in shock, so frightened that she couldn't make it through the night. His arms tightened about her, a reflexive move meant to protect her from past hurts. It also helped to assuage the aching need within him. If anyone's arms and body had soothed her fears, it should have been his.

"That was the way things were for us," she continued. "Nothing else seemed feasible with me going off to one part of the world, him to another. We never discussed marriage or a future, until he dropped the whole issue in my lap." She exhaled in remembered disbelief. "One day, out of the blue, he announced that he loved me, that he wanted to marry me. I didn't know what to say then or even months later when he demanded an answer."

Her voice dried up. "It was June of '91, we were on vacation together, although it was anything but relaxing. He was just back from Japan, I had come straight from what was left of the Soviet Union. We were tired and drained. We spent most of our time arguing."

"About getting married?"

Savannah nodded. "He kept pressing me, I kept asking him to give us more time, although both of us knew that wouldn't have helped."

"Why do you say that?"

"Because no amount of time would have changed how I felt. Our relationship had been built on anything but normal grounds. All of our emotions were tangled up in adrenaline highs, the aftermath of shock, a few stolen moments here or there. We felt many things for each, but our bond had always been based on need not love. For me, that wasn't enough for marriage."

"He didn't agree."

Her shoulders rose in a rickety shrug. The breath she drew was as shaky. "I don't know what was going on with Eric. He wouldn't listen, no matter what I said. On the last day of our vacation, he finally snapped. He stormed out of the beach cottage we were renting and drove off. Two miles from home, he lost control of his car and drove straight into a telephone pole. He died instantly."

She didn't continue. In the thick silence, Savannah sat limply, her forehead snuggled into the curve of Jake's neck. Utterly spent, she shut her eyes and for one blessed moment ceased to feel or think.

Jacob felt her exhaustion acutely and did the only thing he could; he held her securely and gave her as much of his own strength as she was capable of taking. He doubted that was very much. His gut instinct told him that she didn't tell many people what she had just told him. He would bet anything that only a handful, those closest to Savannah, knew all the details. Her confiding such a private matter to him must have been doubly exhausting.

"Thank you," he murmured.

She shifted her head to one side. "For what?"

"For trusting me enough to tell me."

"You deserved to know."

"There aren't many who do know, are there?"

"No." Drawing a deep breath, she let herself absorb the wonderful sensation of being held by Jacob. He surrounded her with warmth and muscle. And understanding. "If I was still seeing my therapist, she would be pleased as all get-out."

He tipped his head to try and catch her expression. "Why?"

"She would have believed that I had just made great progress and muttered something about this syndrome or that and coming to terms."

"Have you come to terms with it?"

She thought about that. "Yes. For a long time I carried a lot of guilt for Eric's death."

Jacob cupped her face between his palms, his dark brows angled low. "It wasn't your fault."

"I know that. Just as I know I wasn't responsible for what was going on in Eric's mind those last months. Just as I wasn't to blame for his impatience, or his not listening to reason, or his driving forty miles over the speed limit when he died. Those were his choices. Realistically, logically, I knew that." Tears gathered, but she gazed steadily into the fierce depths of his eyes. "But my heart never accepted it until this very second."

Which was why, Jacob rued, there hadn't been any men in her life. Until him.

"Oh, God, babe." He kissed her with tender fury, stunned to the core. He couldn't begin to describe what it did to him to know that he was the man to break through her emotional cocoon.

Savannah melted into his embrace, encompassed by the perfect, sublime sense of coming home. Once again, she felt the intimate impression of familiarity that she had experienced with Jake from the very start.

She gave up on trying to understand the sensation. Damn logic and inexplicable feelings . . . and a haunted house. Her heart, so long dormant, had finally been freed. It was firmly committed. She had no choice but to follow it.

Ten

The last person Jacob expected to see entering his office was his brother. Doug never made unannounced visits from his home in Norfolk . . . during a work week . . . first thing in the morning. To see the man when it was barely 9:00 AM Friday, brought Jacob to his feet with a curious grin.

"What brings you here, Counselor? I didn't think you gave yourself free time from your office except on Sundays."

Douglas Quaide stood just beyond Jacob's desk and faced his brother with a patent, mediocre attempt at humor. His normally comfortable smile was strained. "Can't I drive up to see my only brother?"

"It's fine by me, even if it is unexpected."

Doug cast a quick glance about, shifting his shoulders slightly beneath his gray suit jacket. "Mary Beth waved me in. I didn't catch you in the middle of something, did I?"

"Not anything that can't wait. Have a seat." Jacob gestured to one of the leather chairs opposite the desk. "So is it business or pleasure?"

"Is what business or pleasure?"

"Your reason for being here."

Doug exhaled slowly, his dark brows elevating just as gradually. "I wish I could say it was pleasure."

"At this time of the day? You're not good for anything even remotely resembling pleasure until noon." He gave his brother a searching look as he walked around from behind his desk. "What's wrong? Are Iris and the kids all right?"

"They're fine."

"Then what is it? You look like hell."

Not bothering to swallow his curse, Doug scoffed and squeezed his eyes shut for a second. "Is it that obvious?"

"I've seen you worse, but I don't remember when." And Jake wasn't joking. Doug usually carried his forty-one years with natural ease. That wasn't so this morning. Even sitting, his medium weight seemed too heavy for his lanky frame. His angular face was drawn, and in his blue eyes, Jacob saw fear and . . . defeat.

Jake's humor evaporated instantly. Doug was as solid and confident as they came, tackling problems both in and out of court with absolute expertise and skill. To see him subdued for whatever reason was sobering.

"Do you need a drink?"

Doug shook his head. "No. That's the last thing I need." His face contorted with blatant frustration. "And it isn't going to solve anything."

Jacob leaned back against the front of the desk and waited. This wasn't easy. He had never seen his older brother so shaken, for any reason. "Doug?"

For a long moment, Doug remained silent as if debating how to proceed. Finally, he surged to his feet and paced across the room to the wall unit of shelves. There, he toyed with a piece of petrified wood.

"Damn, this is hard."

Jake had no doubt that Doug was not referring to the stone-like branch. "Why don't you just say what you have to say?"

Doug's fingers stilled, his shoulders slumped. Abruptly, he set the wood piece down and turned. Any color his face had retained was gone. The blue of his eyes stood out in stark relief. "I'm in trouble, Jake."

Jacob straightened, his muscles tensing automatically. "What kind of trouble?"

"The worst kind for a man in my position; financial."

Jacob absorbed the statement, his mind examining the ramifications of that one qualifier. *Financial.* It struck at the heart of what a lot of men considered their self-worth. Doug was one of those men. "How bad is it?"

Doug swallowed heavily, twice, before he answered. "Bad. I've begun to liquidate every asset I can spare."

Jacob muttered an obscenity under his breath and shut the door to his office. Already, he was anticipating the conversation that was to follow. As he returned to his desk and picked up the phone, he eyed his brother with real concern.

"Mary Beth, hold all my calls. No exceptions." Quietly, he set the receiver in its cradle, his gaze never wavering from Doug's stiff features.

Doug returned the stare. "I suppose you want all the details."

"It would help."

That glint of defeat entered Doug's eyes again. "I don't know how it happened, I swear I don't." He studied the ceiling, speaking as much to himself as to Jacob. "Man, I had it all, great lifestyle, successful law practice, what I thought were sound investments." With a harsh laugh, he clenched and unclenched his hands. "That's what I get for thinking. I've really screwed it up." Staring straight into Jake's eyes, he confessed, "I'm broke."

"What do you mean you're broke?"

"I'm going to lose everything."

"Explain that."

"The bank's going to call my loan."

"On what?"

Sighing, Doug did nothing to hide the fact that he was worn out. He returned to the chair in front of the desk to explain. "You know that I bought into a hotel in California three years ago."

"Yeah, in San Diego." Jacob also knew that the hotel was just one of his brother's many dealings in real estate.

"At the time, it was a great investment. Until it went bad. Until the economy slumped, until people lost their jobs, until the tourist trade went belly up." The line of Doug's mouth thinned. "Hell, I don't know."

"How much do you owe?"

"Seven million." Seeing Jacob's narrowing gaze, Doug challenged harshly, "You can't tell me anything I haven't already told myself. It's a classic case of mismanagement that I was too stupid to catch. My only defense is that as long as the dividend checks kept coming in, I assumed everything was all right. Like I said, stupidity on my part that's cost me everything. Or close to it."

"Your house?"

"I think . . . I'll be able to hang onto it. That, and my practice, but that's about all." Cupping one hand in the other, Doug leaned forward to brace his elbows on his knees. "My banker called a month ago to tell me that 'in light of the hotel's poor showing' over the past twenty-four months, they've reexamined the loan and felt their money was 'at risk.' "

Jacob filled in the rest. "So the bank wants their money."

"In full. Which I don't have, except on paper."

Disgust and grief boiled hotly in Jacob. On the one hand, he wanted to grab Doug and beat the shit out of him for getting himself into such a fucking mess. On the other, he wanted to offer any kind of relief that would help.

"Whatever money I can spare is yours."

A lopsided grin of gratitude twisted Doug's face, but he waved the offer away. "Thanks. I appreciate it, but . . . I can't let you do it. I've already sold my stock, cashed in the insurance policies, annuities, bonds . . . I was lucky enough to find a buyer for the beach property in Carolina and the land in upstate New York . . . and . . ."

Doug seemed to shrink in his seat. The gaze he tried to

hold so steadily faltered, then slid away into the dead still-ness of the room, becoming a blank stare ironically rife with the full extent of the truth.

Realization hit Jacob with all the impact of a full-body blow. "And your half of Oakwood," he bit out into the silence.

The rough words drew Doug's head up. His face shriveled with his anguish. "I'm sorry, Jake."

The confirmation slammed into Jacob's system, numbing him with the kind of disbelief and rage that stripped him down to nothing but his soul, making it nearly impossible for him to listen to Doug any further.

"It's the only way, Jake. Unless I sell off my half of Oakwood I'll be lucky to scrape up three million. As it is, I've lucked into finding a buyer who's ready to purchase the entire two hundred and fifty acres at top dollar."

The instinct to reject the truth was overwhelming. Every one of Jacob's reflexes impelled him to strike back—to lash out in denial.

"Sonofabitch. Why the hell didn't you come to me first?"

Wearily, Doug rose. "It wouldn't have done any good unless you have a spare five million hanging around."

"I could have helped you out before it got this bad."

"I didn't *know* it was this bad until it was too late."

Dragging a hand through his hair, Jacob insisted, "Shit, I would have bought a portion of the property from you. I still can."

"It isn't possible."

"Why the hell not? Sell me the land the old house sits on and the surrounding fifty acres. You'd get the money you need, and part of the land will still remain in the Quaide family."

"That fifty acres is the prime selling factor, and you know it. Every developer between here and hell has been after that property for years. The tract sits on the water. It's precisely what the buyer wants, water-front property with

all the privacy in the world and a kick-ass view. If I can't
sell that, then I don't have a sale. The rest of the land is
window dressing."

Nothing about Oakwood was window dressing. Its history went back forever, back to the very heart of Jacob's
roots. And now, suddenly, hideously, half of it was gone.

He whirled to face the windows, eaten up with anger at
being so damned helpless. Again and again, part of his mind
demanded that he do something, anything, but the demand
was as futile as the entire situation. He couldn't refute
Doug's logic or disparage his need.

"You knew about this last week when I called," he grated.
His frozen gaze was fastened on the scene outside the window, but his memory heatedly recalled every vacillation and
awkward pause in Doug's voice when he had championed
Savannah's cause. *Hell, the old house isn't going to be there
forever.* "Why didn't you tell me?"

"Nothing was definite."

"When?"

"What?"

"When? How long before you close on the deal?"

Hearing the brutal savagery in Jake's tone, Doug's voice
lowered to a tragic vibration. "If all goes well, in a month."

By the middle of December. A time frame took the matter
from possibility into the realm of reality. Jacob fought the
desolate sense of loss and fury tearing at him. Somehow
he conquered a small portion of the rage, corralled it to a
frighteningly civil level. The loss . . . it would take more
than willpower and sheer guts to come to terms with that.

"I'm sorry, Jake."

He wished he didn't believe that, so he could smash his
fist into Doug's face, so he could verbally annihilate him
and make him feel worse than he already did. As it was,
Doug was in his own hell. All the wrath and bitterness in
the world wouldn't change one dammed thing.

Bracing himself against the hollow sensation making

hash of his insides, Jacob faced his brother, letting some subconscious part of his brain take over. It was the only way to cope, to detach until a nebulous later time. "At least you'll have all of this behind you before Christmas."

"Yeah, there is that."

Jacob nodded, shoved his hands into his pockets, nodded again. "How's Iris taking this?"

For the first time since he had entered the office, Doug managed a genuine smile. "She hasn't threatened to divorce me."

Again, Jacob nodded. "Do you need any money to get you through?"

"No," Doug insisted instantly, making a point of that with raised hands. And then his grin cracked and his eyes filled.

Jake's chest constricted around the pain that was already lodged there. Before he could say anything, Doug shifted disjointedly where he stood, and muttered, "I'll call."

With that, he made for the door, leaving Jacob with the feeling that a part of him had just been stolen.

Savannah made a point of taking off her spare watch and leaving it in her car. She decided it was the wisest thing to do. Because as she had driven up Oakwood's long drive, she felt instinctively that something was going to happen today. How she could be so certain was a mystery until she realized she was experiencing every physical symptom that had hounded her lately. Faintly, mildly, but the closer to the old house she got, the more intense the sensations became.

Making her way through the woods toward the mansion, she focused her attention on the tightened nerves along the back of her neck, the touch of queasiness curling in her stomach, and her slightly skewed balance. Backpack full of equipment, she stopped dead in her tracks and recognized the symptoms for what they were. A prelude.

"To what?" she asked herself. She only wished she knew.

She also wished she could talk herself out of going back into that old house. She had only so much courage, and it was normally directed at the tangible world. How was she supposed to deal with the supernatural, with whatever force lingered within those three-hundred-year-old walls?

"You're beginning to sound like a character out of a Gothic novel," she scolded herself. She pictured any number of book covers she'd seen with a frightened heroine running for her life; behind her, a dark, hulking, menacing mansion backlit by lightning.

Savannah inhaled sharply at the thought. That wasn't how she viewed Oakwood's mansion. From the start it had reached out to her with its history, seeming to tug at some responding core within her. She was still unable to ignore its pull or her reaction to it. Good or bad, come what may, she had to see this through.

Settling her equipment more comfortably on her shoulders, she continued on her way, not stopping until she stood in the once grand foyer, the scratching sound of mice in the walls slowly fading away.

"Okay, Savannah," she whispered into the unnatural hush that grew ever so subtly. "You wanted this." Actually, she was rather pleased with herself for being aware of the diminishing sound. Such awareness made her feel more in control; less a victim. And it reaffirmed her conviction to anticipate some occurrence. But from where?

She looked up the stairway for her answer.

Gripping the straps of her pack with one hand, she took the first two steps with ease. On the third step, a chill caressed her skin and she stopped, holding onto the banister a little more tightly.

A few more steps upward, slowly, carefully, expectancy raising the fine hair on the nape of her neck. Out of nowhere that descending elevator sensation grabbed her stomach and stuck it right in her throat.

"What am I doing?" she asked herself, breathing heavily

to right her center of gravity. But she didn't retreat. She placed one foot on the next step, literally gritted her teeth and dashed up the flight to the second floor.

For an instant of time she felt sublime relief. Crazy thoughts of not having been sucked into another dimension frolicked in her brain, bumping into those that were more fundamental. She was still in one piece and everything still looked the same. Relief. But only for that one brief moment.

In the next, her whole being felt as if a wave of cold air washed right through her. Not over her or around her, but through her. Into her back, piercing her bones and muscles, lungs and heart, and out via the front of her. She groaned low in her throat and sensed reality shifting.

Eyes rounding, she stared around her. Everything looked the same, but it didn't. The paint on the walls appeared less grayed, the wooden floor lost some of its dullness. And in the air, she detected the scent of honeysuckle.

"Oh, God, *what am I doing?*" She should turn and run . . . now. "Get out, Savannah."

She didn't. She couldn't. In contrast to the chill she had just felt, a warm, pulsing energy throbbed inside her, urging her to forsake what she knew to be real, urging her toward the master bedroom.

Fully aware of what she was doing, capable only of panting little breaths, she walked down the hall, entered the master bedroom and stopped . . . everything—feeling, thinking, breathing, even blinking.

The room wasn't empty. It had been transformed with what appeared to be real objects: solid tables, mirrors, and chests. The four-poster bed with its canopy of lace stood where she had seen it materialize days earlier and in the fireplace opposite, a stack of wood sat ready to be lit.

Savannah clapped her hands to her mouth and stared. Flowers were arranged in a vase on the secretary in the corner, several lamps contained oil, and fitted into the once empty windows were panes of glass.

How had this happened? When? *Why?* Was any of it real?! She squinted for a better view of the bed. It looked real, but only in the same way images on a movie screen look real. Three dimensional and yet flat.

What exactly was she seeing? A view into another dimension or time? Whatever the explanation, the room was right out of the nineteenth century. But where had it come from? It hadn't been there all along, so what was it doing here now?

Hastily, she backed into the hall, hoping for some kind of reassurance that regardless of what was happening, her time and space and physical presence hadn't been altered. The hall offered no clues and certainly no reassurances. The brightly lit passage was no longer stale and weathered. It appeared as cared for as the . . .

She peered back into the bedroom and horrifyingly, the door beside the fireplace opened and a woman entered.

Savannah cried out, jerking back against the wall in gut-level fright. The bulk of her equipment dug into her spine. She ignored the discomfort. All of her attention was fastened on the dark haired woman blithely going about the business of unfastening the row of buttons down the front of her crinolined gown.

Oh-my-God, oh-my-God, oh-my-God. "Are you real?" Savannah spoke without conscious thought. Her brain acted on its own, as if needing to do something to find a spark of logic in a world suddenly on the edge.

The woman didn't answer. In no way did she even acknowledge Savannah's presence. Her delicate features appeared composed, her actions uninhibited. She was completely unaware of being observed.

Heart hammering painfully, Savannah tried again. "Hello."

The woman tipped her head to one side before easing the pink-striped muslin from her shoulders.

"Can you hear me? Who . . . who are you?"

The dress drifted slowly to the floor and landed in a colorful puddle. Savannah stared at the draped fabric, mesmerized by the soft garment as it slowly began to change. The pink and white folds gradually blurred into a transparent shape and finally faded away into nothing.

The room lay bare once again.

The old scent of mustiness filled the air. Wood and plaster displayed the rotting deterioration of time. From somewhere miles away, the muffled sound of a car horn could be heard. All traces of the nineteenth century were gone, taking with them most of Savannah's energy.

Exhausted, she slid down the wall and sat in the cobwebs and grime. Only then did she become aware that she was shaking, her entire body trembling so badly her teeth vibrated against each other in audible little clicks.

She drew her knees up to her chest and held on with as much strength as she could summon. Still, the shakes went on and on and finally gave way to tears.

Savannah didn't try to control her response. She tucked her chin to her heaving chest and weathered the storm, knowing from experience that her body was handling the shock in the most elemental way there was. All she could do was wrap her arms about her head and yield.

Not until her breathing evened out and her muscles lay calm did she let herself think and question. What had happened? Was the house haunted? Had she actually seen a ghost?

The term dragged up unflattering impressions of evil spirits. That didn't sit well. She had sensed nothing sinister in what had occurred. In fact, other than her fright, she honestly had to admit that she had felt no sense of danger or harm. The entire encounter had been brief and nonthreatening.

She exhaled deeply in relief and strangely enough, an odd contentment permeated her being. Her thoughts were suddenly, serenely uncomplicated. For all the anxiety and irrationality of what had happened, she realized that it came down to a very simple matter. She either believed what she had seen or she didn't.

She did.

That didn't mean that she understood it. Acceptance and understanding were two entirely different things. She didn't pretend to believe that she could explain even a bit of what had happened. She still had questions coming out the yin yang, but for now, she was comfortable waiting for the answers.

Resting her head against the wall, she scanned the hallway without moving her head. Without a doubt, the last ten minutes had been the most extraordinary of her life—a life that would never again be the same, a life altered by fate. Destiny had stepped in and given her what she could consider a curse or a rare gift.

She decided it was a rare gift. Her choice now was whether to accept it or reject it.

"Okay, old house," she whispered, her gaze tender. "I don't understand why this is happening, but you win." She came to her feet and hitched her equipment into a comfortable position. "I'd appreciate it, though, if somewhere along the line, you fill me in on the reasons."

She arrived at Jacob's house with her brain functioning on automatic pilot. Out of habit alone, she locked her backpack in the trunk of her car before she realized that Jake's car was parked in the garage.

Dragging her fingertips over her lower lip, she considered what she should do. She dearly wanted to see him, but she was no more comfortable confiding in him about the house now than she had been last night. Seeing apparitions was not an everyday occurrence. It wasn't something one could readily confess to. And yet, by not telling him, she would in essence be lying to him.

Lying wasn't something she did. She wasn't going to start now. She had to tell him what was going on, and then hope for the best. There was the outside chance that he would believe her, that he wouldn't think she had a screw loose.

Clinging to that fragile optimism, she made her way to the front door. Her knock was instantly answered by Ares' barking followed closely by Jacob's muffled voice ordering the dog to silence. Seconds later, he swung the door open.

He stood tall and immovable in the doorway, his face expressionless except for the raw chill in his eyes. In the cloudy dusk light, the blue orbs shone with all the fiercely seething emotions that were absent from his face and manner.

Savannah's greeting got caught in her throat, held there momentarily by confusion. What in the world was wrong?

"Hi," she whispered cautiously. He gave no indication that he was going to invite her in. Worse, she had the distinct impression that she was intruding. He didn't want her there at all.

Stunned, hurt, she shifted gears, mentally backing up and out of the awkward situation. "I, uh, noticed you were home." Her body followed her mind's reflex, impelling her to step away. "I thought I'd stop by, but I can . . . I can see this is a bad time." It truly was. The longer she stood there, the more she wanted to be anywhere but in the direct line of his sight.

Feeling foolish and embarrassed, she mumbled something about calling him later as she turned. In her heart, she wanted to stay and help him with whatever was upsetting him, but she didn't think that was an option. In every way imaginable, he had barred her from his house, from him.

She gained the brick walkway, fumbling in her jacket pocket for her keys when a firm hand caught her elbow and spun her around. In the next instant, she was clutched to the warm expanse of Jacob's chest and held with a strength that threatened to crack her ribs.

"Jacob?" She wound her arms about his neck, offering to help in the only way she could. "What's wrong?"

In answer, he turned his head into her hair and breathed deeply, not telling her anything. His arms loosened their hold enough so that she could breathe fully, but he didn't release her. She was glad. If something had happened, she wanted to be there for him.

She leaned back as far as his arms would permit and searched his face. He returned her look and obviously read her concern and unspoken questions.

"Let's go inside," he told her.

Willingly, she followed him into his den, noting that while she sat, he paced away to stare out one of the windows.

"I'm sorry," he apologized without looking her way.

"Is it something you can tell me about?"

Her soft inquiry met with a harsh scoff and he finally faced her fully. "You're going to learn about this sooner or later. It might as well be now." He swore in a muttered breath. "My brother sold his half of the land."

Savannah gasped in disbelief. "He sold it? I . . . I don't understand."

Jacob thrust a hand to the back of his neck. "Yeah, well, it's pretty easy to figure out. He needed the money to pay off a substantial debt."

Savannah felt her heart break for Jacob. She crossed the room and took him in her arms. "I'm so sorry, Jake. I know how much the land means to you."

His arms remained at his sides. "Quaides have always owned this land. Through two wars, the Depression, shifting economics; it's always been ours, and now it's gone."

Clenching her eyes shut, she absorbed his pain. "Not all of it. You still have your half."

"It's only half."

She couldn't dispute that. Nor could she belittle how that must make him feel. It was like a doctor telling you that he had to cut off your leg, but only half of it. No matter how you might feel about the half you got to keep, in every way that counted, the second half still belonged to you. Separation wouldn't change the emotions involved.

"What can I do to help?" she asked, laying her hand along his clenched jaw.

He shook his head. "Nothing. It's over and done with."

His bitter words pierced her in a single sharp thrust. Everything inside her rejected the finality of his statement. It wasn't over and done with. As long as he grieved and fumed and hurt, it wasn't over.

"Do you want to talk about it?"

He turned away at her query. "Get real, Savannah. What good is there in talking? It won't restore the plantation."

"No, of course it won't," she said to the back of his head. "But it might make you feel better."

"It'll take a lot more than talking to do that."

"But keeping your anger inside won't help either."

He whirled to face her, a feral passion glinting in his eyes. "What would you have me say? That my heritage has been taken away from me and I can't see straight for the rage that's eating away at my gut? Is that what you want to hear or would you prefer that I tell you that the basis for my own personal history is gone and there isn't a damn thing I can do about it?"

His pain was shattering, overwhelming. Tears collected in Savannah's eyes. "Oh, Jake." She drew him into her arms again, fully expecting him to reject her again, although not on a personal level. In his anger, he was rejecting everything around him, most especially the truth, and the bitterness of helplessness.

She didn't say anything more. There was nothing more to be said. She simply held him close. Gradually, he accepted the comfort she offered and wrapped his arms about her.

Her eyelids drifted shut, and in the awful hush of the room, she knew an absolute certainty in her heart. The loss of half the plantation and whatever was happening at the old house were somehow linked. The timing was too fantastic to be coincidental.

The realization filled her with an utter peace she had no business feeling just then. She hurt for Jacob and yet she could not escape the feeling that she had hit upon a vital truth. It all made sense; her meeting Jake, her coming into his life only to be witness to a haunting. And now the sale of the land. Every one of her instincts told her she was right.

Was the spirit attempting to communicate with her for some reason, or did the old house retain an energy that was trying to make itself known, at this particular time for a specific purpose? She knew the answers were all there, waiting for her.

She inhaled quickly, wanting more than anything to explain her theory to Jake. A single look into the haunted depths of his eyes, however, cut her words off at the quick. Even in the most receptive of moods, it would be difficult for him to accept her story. She couldn't tell him now no matter how much she wanted to reassure him.

Pressing her head to his chest, she swallowed the truth, aching for him with all her heart. She would tell him eventually, but not now. She had nothing concrete to tell him. There were no conclusions that could be drawn.

All she had was a soul deep certainty that life was playing out a hand dealt by fate.

And that she and Jake were the pawns.

Eleven

The buzzing of the telephone jerked Savannah from a bottomless sleep. Buried under a mound of covers and two pillows, she groaned and rolled toward the side of the bed. One hand emerged from beneath the blankets and groped blindly for the phone.

It took several swipes in the general direction of the nightstand for her fingers to connect with the annoying instrument. On the seventh ring, she finally managed to grasp the receiver. Hauling it back to her ear, however, was another story.

She was never her best first thing in the morning. Today, she was worse than usual as she tried to shake off the opiate sensations leftover from the night. She had fallen into bed shortly before ten, tired down to the marrow of her bones. As far as she could tell, she hadn't woken once during the night, not even while she shifted positions. She would have gone on sleeping, too, if the damned phone hadn't intruded.

Grousing to herself, she rolled to her side and shifted the sheet down over her shoulder. Not bothering to open her eyes, she connected phone to ear.

"Yes . . . what . . . hello."

"Good morning to you, too."

Jake. He sounded wonderful. "What time is it?"

"Eight forty-five." He supplied the information with an undercurrent of droll indulgence. "I take it I woke you up."

She hummed her agreement. "What day is this?"

"Saturday."

The pieces were beginning to come together. "I knew that."

"Why don't I call you back later?"

"No. Give me a second." He was on the phone now and she didn't want to relinquish this small connection with him. And besides, it felt nice to wake up to his voice.

Bunching the pillows against the headboard, she made a comfortable nest for herself. "I'm up."

"Bad night?"

"No, just tired." No small wonder there. After her experience in the old mansion and then dealing with Jacob's bad news, she had been wiped out.

Memories from the old master bedroom crowded forward, but she willed them away, preferring to give into the Scarlet O'Hara syndrome; she'd think about it later. Jake's present state of mind was far more important.

"How are you today?"

"Practical."

"What do you mean by that?"

"I mean there isn't anything I can do about the land. I'm not going to wallow. I ran five miles this morning; that's helped get rid of some of the tension."

Like he said, practical, but Savannah knew that emotions didn't always go the way of practicality. Especially not in this instance. As emotionally involved with the plantation as Jake was, it would take time for him to heal. Apparently, he was going to do so behind a controlled facade.

"You're such a man," she told him.

"Nice of you to notice."

She noticed a great many things, like the fact that there was no tapping into his "feminine side" for Jacob Quaide. Hard, powerful, testosterone-driven, he most likely didn't possess a "feminine side." That didn't mean he wasn't hurting.

"I'm an observant woman."

"Are you a busy woman today?"

"I don't plan to work, but I do have to go to Richmond for a couple of hours this morning."

"Anything in particular waiting there?"

"My washer and dryer. And my mail. Mom's been collecting it for me. You know how it is. Bills arrive whether you're home or not."

"I'll drive you up."

As was his way, Jake posed a question in the form of a statement. "I'd like that. How good are you with fabric softener?"

"Mean. When will you be ready?"

Savannah eyed the clock. "Give me an hour."

Once she was truly up and on her feet, it was easy for Savannah to dispel her sluggishness. A hot shower and an even hotter cup of tea helped, although it took a conscious effort on her part not to dwell on ghosts and haunted rooms. By the time Jacob arrived, she had Oakwood tamed to a peripheral awareness. It wasn't something she consciously thought about, but it was a distant impression that was unshakeable.

For a Saturday morning, the roads to Richmond were remarkably congested. Sitting beside Jacob as he maneuvered the Jaguar through the heavy traffic, Savannah considered the man beside her. Dressed in a casual pair of tan slacks and the customary bomber jacket over a dark blue shirt, he exuded a rugged sophistication. She suspected that he had always possessed the trait. On him it was too natural to have been learned.

"You're doing it again," Jacob observed wryly, wondering what she was considering this time. Her habit of staring at him with that speculative gleam in her eyes took a little getting used to. Not because he minded her looking; hell, she could lay those brown eyes—and anything else of hers—on him all she wanted. No, he just wished he knew what she was thinking when she was doing all that looking. With Savannah he could never be sure.

"Do you mind?" she asked.

"That depends."

"Don't worry. I'm not looking for any deep dark secrets."

"What *are* you looking for?"

"Nothing. I was just visualizing you as a kid." More precisely, she thought, all that rugged sophistication in its raw state.

He scoffed. "I was an average kid."

Savannah scoffed right back. "I'd put money on it, Q Man, that nothing about you from day one was average."

"Got it all figured out, do you?"

She cocked him a jaunty smile. "You bet. If I had to give your childhood a title, it would read . . ." Lifting her hand, she marked off an imaginary marquee, ". . . 'Jacob Quaide, the Life And Times of a Holy Terror.' "

From his side of the car, Jacob shot her an amused glance. "You're pretty full of yourself this morning."

"It's the company I've been keeping lately."

"Are you complaining?"

"Nope. In fact, I wish I had met you years and years ago. I think I would have liked to have seen you running around the plantation."

The instant the words were out, she mentally cringed. So much for controlling her subconscious. She hadn't meant to blurt the subject out that way. Eyeing Jake closely, she searched for any indication that he found the topic intolerable.

He interpreted her probing gaze, simultaneously tamping down his spurt of annoyance. "It's okay," he admitted roughly. "I'm not going to crack up every time someone mentions Oakwood."

"I didn't think you would, but at the same time, I don't want to say anything that makes you uncomfortable."

"Savannah, it's all right." But his severe tone said differently; that despite his assurances that he wasn't going to "wallow", his emotions were suddenly fully engaged. "You can't go tiptoeing through our discussions. Say what you want."

"Even if it makes you tense, like right now?"

"I'm not tense."

"Yes, you are." And it was little wonder. He was trying to keep his thoughts and feelings bottled up, which was the absolute worst thing he could do. "You're glaring at the road."

He gripped the steering wheel and worked his jaw. "Look, I'm sorry. This whole thing with Doug and the plantation is a bit hard to take."

It was a heart-felt confession that made her ache for him again. Quietly, her brown eyes softening, she said, "I'm not going to insult you, Jake, by saying I understand. There's no way I can because Oakwood isn't mine. I don't know what it feels like to have a kinship with a glorious piece of history. But I am truly sorry. I'm sorry that this has happened."

"So am I." His eyes narrowed, his voice taking on a brittle edge. "I can't divorce myself from my past even if I wanted to. My brother and I were raised to respect and protect the plantation. That philosophy is inbred into who we are. I can't shut it off just because the title to the land is going to change hands."

"I don't expect you to shut it off. Your outlook about the property is far too unique."

"Maybe so."

She shifted about to face him. "There's no 'maybe' about this. Most people don't feel the way you do about a piece of property."

"Most people don't own a piece of property as unique as Oakwood."

"Did your parents feel that way?"

Jake sputtered out a grating laugh, hearing his father's

words in his head. "My father believed that the land was everything. All else would come and go, but not the land, not Oakwood. It was the legacy that endured when all else failed, when all else in life was the proverbial 'dust in the wind'."

Savannah's brow puckered. In the region of her heart, she felt a pang of regret that he had been raised under such an attitude. Jacob Quaide's father should have believed that his wife and sons were everything. "That's a sad commentary."

He took his eyes from the road long enough to ask, "Why do you say that?"

"Because land isn't everything. People are, people and family and love. No offense to your father, but he was wrong about what's enduring and what isn't."

"It was what he had been taught by his father and his father before that and his father before that."

"I have no doubt. That doesn't mean they were right."

"Or wrong," Jacob countered.

"Or wrong. I'll grant you that your ancestors were products of their times, caught up in the landed gentry way of thinking. Their entire privileged existences were intertwined with the soil."

"And that bothers you?"

"I can understand how that can happen. Personally, I can't tolerate the mentality that relegates people to a secondary position."

"It wasn't as bad as that, Savannah."

His easy acceptance of the old Southern way of thinking pricked her temper. Setting her shoulders, she dug in for the debate, ignoring completely all her good intentions in having prodded him into this conversation in the first place.

"Oh no? Tell me there was never a single slave on Oakwood. Tell me that not one of the old Quaide wives hadn't been used for the sole purpose of brood mare to insure another generation of Quaides to take care of the land."

She didn't wait for him to agree with or deny her charges. "You know it was like that, Jake."

"That was the way life was back then, but we're talking over a hundred years ago, for Christ's sake."

"Your father didn't live a hundred years ago, and that concept made up a good portion of the basis of his life."

He slanted her a disgusted frown. "What's your point?"

She turned her head and stabbed him with the full force of her flashing gaze. "My point is that it bothers me to think that you were taught this antiquated, single-minded lesson to revere the land, to value it above anything or anyone. It bothers me to think that you could pass the lesson down to your children."

Behind his sunglasses, Jake's eyes flared with anger. "Have I ever given you the impression that I would?"

"No, but . . ."

"Fuckin' A, no, I wouldn't," he interrupted furiously.

His swearing didn't help in the least. "All right, then," she grated, "What *would* you teach your children?"

"I never thought about it."

"Well, think about it now!"

Cursing under his breath, Jake flicked a glance to his rearview mirror, shifted gears and changed lanes. He left four cars behind before he let himself tackle the issue, starting with Savannah herself.

She was like a dog with a friggin' bone. Once she latched onto something, she didn't let go. Her bone today was his outlook on the land, *and* of all goddamned things, his philosophy of rearing children.

In tightly modulated tones, he said, "I'd want my children to respect Oakwood, to regard it as a special part of their personal history."

"But," she prompted when he didn't continue.

"But what?"

"But where would you want their focus to be? Certainly not on what amounts to acres and acres of dirt?"

He didn't like hearing the plantation referred to as "dirt" and he bristled hotly again. "There's more to this than soil, Savannah."

"I'm doing my best to understand that."

"Then why in the living hell are you making an issue out of hypothetical children?"

Because those hypothetical children were hers. And his.

A bolt of lightning striking her squarely between the eyes couldn't have stunned her more than her last thought. Shaken, overwhelmed, she jerked her gaze out her side window and wondered what was going on in her head.

Jiminy crickets, two weeks ago, a serious relationship had been the furthest thing from her mind. Now she was arguing with Jacob about the children she imagined the two of them having, children and all the implications. Such as marriage.

She squeezed her eyes shut for a second. Oh, God, she was falling hard. And fast. A single kiss, a couple of dates, a commitment to that nebulous thing called a relationship and pow, she was thinking about children.

"I don't mean to make an issue of this," she remembered to respond, her voice reduced to a perplexed murmur. "I happen to believe that how we raise children is important. It says a great deal about who we are as people."

The death of her ire extinguished his. Its absence left him at ease once more, but as curious as he had been riled. "I agree. And I also agree that children have to be brought up to appreciate ethics and morals and family ties."

"As well as Oakwood?"

"Yeah. Any children I have will be lucky in that they'll have a remarkable heritage. I'd want them to appreciate that, but it will only be a part of their lives. They should have a healthy balance between their history and their future."

Savannah had been holding her breath, unconsciously waiting for him to say the right thing. He had, and she released a relieved sigh that did not go unnoticed.

"Spit it out, Savannah," Jake ordered, finally giving his curiosity full reign.

"Spit what out?"

"Whatever this was really all about. Why did you pick this fight?"

Savannah stared at him for a long moment before she silently admitted that she had indeed picked a fight. She wasn't proud of herself. She had wanted him to talk about his feelings for the plantation and instead she had turned the discussion into something else entirely.

"I don't know why I did that," she replied awkwardly. But she did know. In her heart she knew what had happened. Smoothing the denim over one thigh, she confessed, "Maybe I wanted to be reassured."

"About what?"

"You, me. Us. You're upset about the plantation, and rightfully so. It was selfish of me, but I think I lost sight of where I stand in the grand scheme of things."

He glanced her way and then did a double take. "You're serious, aren't you?" But he could see that she was. "Shit." In less than five seconds, he maneuvered the car from the far left lane to the shoulder on the right side of the road.

"Jake?" Her expression was incredulous. "What are you doing?"

In answer, he reached out, hooked his hand behind her neck, hauled her across the seat and kissed her hard. "You're something else," he told her when he finally lifted his head.

"Why did you do that?" she stammered, all eyes and genuine wonder.

"To remind you of where you are in the 'grand scheme of things'. Remember that, the next time you fall back into your old insecurities." He stroked his thumb over her cheek. "You aren't alone any longer, babe. You've got me in your life, and whether you like it or not, you're dead center in mine."

He couldn't have made it any clearer as to how he felt about her. Emotion clogged her throat. When she did manage to swallow, the lump settled around her heart and warmed her all the way to her toes.

"What are you smiling about?" he asked, one side of his mouth cocking into a half-grin.

"You, Q Man." She whispered a kiss over his lips. "I'm smiling because of you."

Savoring the exhilaration that surged through her, she gave him directions into Richmond's Fan District, past the towering monuments of Stonewall Jackson and Robert E. Lee, to a three story building of rich red brick. Four doors down, Jake was lucky enough to find a parking space.

"This is nice," he observed, taking stock of the quiet, tree lined street. Carrying Savannah's sack of laundry, he noted the various architectural structures.

"Of all the places in Richmond, this is my favorite." Savannah ascended the building's steps and unlocked the front door. "And of all the houses in the District, this particular one has the most charm." Part of that charm being its age and history. She had been drawn to both at first sight.

"Antebellum, right?"

"Circa 1835. A doctor and his family lived here. He and three of his five sons died in the Civil War. In this town, that makes him a bonafide hero and this house a Confederate treasure." She paused to check her mailbox on the wall in the foyer.

"Which floor do you live on?"

"The second, and only half of it." She preceded him up the wooden stairway. "Each floor has been converted into two separate apartments. I have the half with the working fireplace."

"You make that sound like a major coup."

Stopping at her apartment door, she smiled at him over her shoulder. "It is. You have no idea how hard it is to find a fireplace in an apartment, let alone one that works."

"That wouldn't make a difference to most people."

"What can I say? I must be a throw back to another generation. I like the ambiance created by a fire in the grate."

Into her mind flashed an image of another fireplace, real and yet curiously flat, wood stacked and ready to be lit.

"Need any help?" Jacob asked from behind.

She blinked the mental picture of Oakwood away and worked the locks on the door. "No, got it." But she suspected that before too long, she was going to need help, only not the kind Jake was offering. She was only so good at keeping thoughts of the old house in their place.

Focusing in on the present, she stepped into her apartment. "Hi, apartment, I'm home," she called out, then turned in time to see the humorous disbelief on Jacob's face. "I always say hello."

He exhaled a short laugh and shook his head. "You're something else."

"You keep saying that," she quipped, her smile neon bright.

"I mean it."

Which was better than fine, with her. "Here." She took hold of her laundry sack. "Let me do something with this."

The sack only got as far as the closet in the kitchen, housing the washer and dryer. Jacob's wandering from the doorway to the kitchen, from the kitchen to the living/dining room distracted her to the point of self-consciousness. He openly studied her home, picking out each of the personal touches she had given the place.

"Well?" she prodded. As opinionated as Jake was, she was convinced that he had come to a long list of conclusions.

"This is great." Compact, snug, he liked the sense of contemporary that Savannah had blended with age. A comfy, creme-colored sofa faced two black leather and chrome chairs. Between them, was a low, Oriental table of teakwood. The dining table and chairs were unfinished pine and looked to be antique, and on the hardwood floors lay throw rugs woven in slashes of bold colors.

Nothing seemed to fit any one style and yet it all blended together perfectly; reflecting the variety and intricacies of Savannah's personality. Everywhere he looked, from the patchwork quilt on the back of the wing-back chair in the corner to the collection of brass candlesticks on the mantle, he was given a private, almost intimate peek at the woman, Savannah.

"How long have you lived here?" he inquired.

"Two years. When I left the magazine I came back to Richmond. I lucked out when I found this place. The kitchen is cramped, but I have a spare bedroom that I use as my darkroom. And of course, there is all the hot and cold running history a person could want."

"Ah, yes, the infamous fireplace." His laughing gaze returned briefly to the mantle, then settled relentlessly on the wall to his left. Photographs decorated the entire space from floor to ceiling. Surprisingly, none of them were taken by Savannah.

"These are all antiques," he observed, bending low to study a discolored tintype of a horse and carriage.

"I collect old photos." She stretched up on her toes to point to a tiny, yellowed, black and white picture of an old woman seated on her front porch, hunched over her knitting. "This one is of my great, great-grandmother. It was taken in Italy in 1884. I don't think . . ."

The opening of the front door cut off her words.

"Savannah?" Leanne broadcasted. "Is that you in here?"

Savannah laughed. "It better be or you're in big trouble." She beamed her smile up at Jake. "My sister, Leanne."

"Aun' Sanna!" a wee voice chimed.

"And her kids."

Leanne bustled into the room five steps behind her offspring. By the time she gained the living room, Savannah literally had her arms full of three-year-old Christy and five-year-old Mark.

"Oh, I've missed you two," Savannah groaned, pressing her face into Mark's sturdy little chest.

"What about me?" Christy demanded to know with a toss of her unruly dark curls.

"You?" Playing the moment to its fullest, Savannah proclaimed in her best melodramatic voice, "I don't think I would have lasted another minute unless I had my Chrissy-hug."

Christy melted into giggles as she wrapped her chubby arms about Savannah's head.

"Ease up, ya'll," Leanne warned lightly. "Give your aunt some breathing room. She's got company, which she seems to have forgotten." With a roll of her eyes and an extended hand, she introduced herself. "Hi, I'm Leanne Lawson, Savannah's sister."

"Jacob Quaide." He returned the handshake.

"It's nice to meet you. Savannah's mentioned you."

One of Jake's black brows arched up over teasing eyes. "I can just imagine what she's told you."

"No, you can't," Leanne contradicted in open glee. She scanned the length of him and somehow managed to turn the clothes-stripping survey into a compliment of the highest order.

"Leanne, please," Savannah cautioned, setting the children on their feet.

"I didn't say anything," Leanne disclaimed innocently, then changed the subject. "What are you doing here? I didn't expect you until Wednesday."

"The usual. What are *you* doing here?"

"Delivering packages." To Jacob, she clarified, "Savannah insists on ordering from catalogues. Trouble is, she's never home to accept her packages, so she has everything delivered to my house." To Savannah, she added, "I left one in the hall by the front door, but you have three others out in the car."

"I'll go out and get them for you," Jacob offered.

Leanne didn't do anything to hide the fact that she was charmed right down to the soles of her feet. Not hesitating for a second, she said, "That would be terrific. It's the blue mini-van with the purple ribbon on the antenna, across the street, five houses up. Thanks."

"No problem." Jake accepted the keys handed his way then made for the door.

Behind him, both women watched his departure.

"Whew," Leanne exclaimed as soon as the front door closed. "What a stud-muffin. You were right when you said he had a 'great bod'."

"You could have been a little less obvious."

"That would have spoiled all the fun. Besides, that man is used to being on the receiving end of women's glances. Talk about gorgeous."

Savannah had to agree. "He is that. Thank God he doesn't have an ego."

"What's an ego?" Mark wanted to know.

"Nothing but trouble," his mother assured him. "Come on, you two. Let's find you something on TV so Aunt Savannah and I can talk."

Saturday cartoons worked their magic in record time and Savannah and Leanne settled at the dining table. "So," Leanne wondered, "how's it going, or need I ask? He's here, so things must be working out."

"We're doing okay."

"Just okay?"

"I suppose better than that, but—"

"But you want to take it slow, I know."

Savannah wasn't ready to confide her feelings about Jacob just yet. They were too new, too tender. "Don't start on me, Lee. Besides, neither one of us has had what you'd call a smooth week." She explained about Douglas Quaide selling off his half of the plantation.

"That's awful," Leanne lamented. "How's Jacob handling it?"

Savannah sighed. "On the outside, he's a rock. On the inside? . . ." She shrugged. "He's upset."

"I don't blame him. From what you've told me, that old house is special." Leanne darted a furtive look to the door and lowered her voice. "Do you think he knows about, you know?"

"I don't think so. I haven't said anything." Savannah stopped to nibble on the inside of her cheek, her gaze telling.

"Uh, oh, what happened?" Leanne demanded, sitting straight.

Making sure her voice didn't travel as far as the children, Savannah quickly explained. "It was worse this time. Or better, I don't know. But I could tell before I even got to the house that I was going to see something."

"Did you?"

"Yes. The entire master bedroom was changed, and it wasn't transparent this time."

"Oh, damn."

From the sofa, Mark chastised, "Mom, I heard that."

"Watch your cartoons, Mark."

"And that's not all," Savannah added.

"I don't know if I want to hear this," Leanne whispered as if in pain.

"Too bad, because this time the room came complete with a ghost."

Leanne's mouth dropped open, her eyes popped wide. *"What?!"*

"A ghost, a spirit. A woman in a long pink and white gown, and crinolines and a corset."

"Oh, my God."

"That's about all I could think at the time, too."

"What did she do?" Leanne gripped the edge of the table with both hands. "I mean, did you talk to her, did she see you?"

"I was a spectator, she didn't even know I was there, and then everything vanished."

"Into thin air?"

"Exactly."

"How long did this last?"

"It's hard to tell. Time does tend to get screwed up in that place, but it felt like ten minutes at the most."

Leanne was temporarily stunned into silence. "This is unbelievable," she breathed at last. "And you haven't told Jake?"

Savannah's gaze traveled out the windows in the direction of the street below. "I was going to, but the timing was wrong."

"Are you going to tell him?"

"Absolutely, especially if it happens again."

"You're going back in?" Leanne's expression was as incredulous as her tone.

"Yes." There was no doubt in Savannah's mind that she had to. "I feel good about what's happening, Lee."

"But you don't know exactly what *is* happening."

"It doesn't matter. And besides, I have a book to finish. Ben may be a great editor, but he's a stickler about deadlines. All my photos have to be in New York by the first of February."

The knock at the door caused Savannah to start in her seat, and even over the background noise of the TV, it sounded deafening. "That's Jake." She came to her feet, but was stayed by Leanne's grip on her arm.

"Promise me, Savannah, that you won't do anything foolish."

"I promise."

Leanne exhaled sharply, her concern apparent. "I worry about you."

Savannah patted her sister's shoulder. "I know."

Jake's knock came again. Even though Savannah rushed to let him in, little Christy was there ahead of her, swinging the door wide.

"It's the stud-muffin," she announced, putting every bit of her three-year-old energy into the proclamation.

Jacob stared down at Christy's angelically innocent face before he lifted his gaze to her aunt. One black brow arched in dubious humor. "Interesting vocabulary," he drawled.

Savannah swallowed her laughter, but her smile could not be contained. Freeing Jake of one of the boxes, she quipped, "Talk to her mother."

Leanne scooped her daughter up. "It's a good thing you're cute. And it's a good thing Mr. Quaide has a sense of humor."

Mr. Quaide's humor was fully operational. Without being obvious, he kept a close eye on Savannah as Leanne went through the process of gathering up her children and saying goodbye. More than once, Savannah met his taunting gaze and it pleased him to no end to see her get flustered.

As soon as they were alone, she propped her hands on her hips and asked, "What are you staring at?"

"Was I staring?" he teased.

"You know darn well you were."

He stepped close to toy with a strand of her deep brown hair. "Stud-muffin?" His lips quirked with a daring smile. "What *were* you two discussing?" As if he didn't already know. He just wanted to hear her admit that while he had been out acting the gallant, she and her sister had been verbally dissecting him.

"All right." Savannah knew when to 'fess up'. "We talked about you," she admitted on the way to the cartons on the sofa. "Leanne can be a first-class snoop."

"Does that audacity of hers ever get her in trouble?"

"Just about always." She ripped the tape from the smallest of the boxes. "That's what you have to love about her."

Sitting in one of the leather chairs, Jacob gestured to the array of packages. "What is all of this?"

Savannah's face lit up. "Christmas presents." She withdrew a ballerina doll outfitted in a gauzy pale tutu, obviously intended for Christy. "With Thanksgiving this Thursday, Christmas is right around the corner."

"Is that what Leanne meant when she said she wasn't expecting you until Wednesday?"

It had been an offhanded statement that Savannah wouldn't have thought noteworthy. And yet it hadn't slipped past Jake's attention. Did anything ever?

"My family makes a huge deal about Thanksgiving. Aunts, uncles, cousins; everyone gathers at my Aunt Nell's house. I promised Leanne that I'd help her bake a few pies on Wednesday."

"A true slice of Americana, huh?"

Savannah considered that with a tilt of her head. "More like the melting pot with strong undercurrents of Italy." Fond memories of past holidays inundated her. Quickly she realized she was alone in her joy.

Cradling the doll in her lap, she sat on the low table so that her knees touched Jake's; her heart caressing his. Thanksgiving was, if nothing else, tradition. Hers were very much intact. She imagined that Jake's had been ripped apart.

"What about you, Q Man?" The nickname emerged as an endearment. "What do you usually do for Turkey Day?"

Jake leaned back, his expression somber. "I don't have a large family. Both of my parents are dead. In the past, my sister-in-law, Iris, cooked. Doug and I usually watched the game on TV."

"Is that what you'll be doing this year?"

"I don't know."

The thought of him having a grim Thanksgiving bothered her deeply, and she most certainly did not want him alone on what was, to most people, a special day. Even worse, however, was the idea of her being in one place and him in another. Everything inside her rebelled at that.

Mentally, she sighed in resignation. Yes, she was definitely falling hard. Actually, she had landed—flat on her emotions. The question now was, what was she going to do about it?

"Spend the day with me," she whispered. "That is, if you think you'd like to, if you don't have any other plans." She offered a hesitant grin. "If you wouldn't mind mingling with forty of my closest relatives."

Jacob's eyes narrowed ever so slightly as a frown took root across his forehead. "Why are you inviting me?"

"Not out of pity, if that's what you're thinking."

"Then why?"

She fell silent for a moment. She knew she could offer him a dozen reasons, but in the end there was only one that mattered. "I want you with me. I don't want to spend the holiday apart from you."

There it was, out in the open; a declaration of commitment if she'd ever heard one. She'd acted on blind trust alone, trusted in the relationship they were trying to build, trusted Jacob and his avowals that they were part of each other's lives.

She waited, for what felt like forever, for him to say or do something. Finally, her patience ended and she prompted, "Jake?"

In answer, he leaned forward in a smooth glide of muscle, not stopping until his face was within inches of hers. He paused only to give her a smile, and then he lowered his head and covered her mouth with his.

She couldn't resist the lure of him. She had never been able to. Everything about him on every level appealed to her, pulling at a fundamental cord that was intrinsic to her being.

Tilting her head to one side, she sought to increase the contact of their lips. It wasn't enough, and her hands began a slow ascent up his chest. The added contact was satisfying for a brief moment and then it, too, became insufficient.

She breathed deeply, taking his breath as her own. The intimacy of that satisfied the passion that was quickly swelling, but again, the relief was only fleeting. Her stomach knotted, her heart thudded, and between her legs a sweet ache bloomed, making her feel and sense, crave and need.

Heart and mind and body, she wanted Jacob Quaide.

Twelve

Savannah tried to control the sensations that pulsed through her, but it was hopeless. A coiling heat unfurled inside her, deep and low and explicit. All the hunger she had felt nights ago ignited as if they had never been doused. As if they had lain quietly seething just waiting to be released.

Days ago, she had shied away from the desire, unsure and therefore unwilling. Now . . . dear God in Heaven, now she couldn't get close enough to Jake to satisfy either her body or her mind. The former urged her to part her lips, to savor Jake to his fullest, to explore him and the longing he evoked within her. Her mind searched for the old hesitancy and found instead a delighted acceptance of a passion that was good and right.

Unfortunately, her mind also sent out a needling reminder.

Regret washed through her and she yanked her head back. Feeling torn apart, she stared into Jake's indigo eyes. "I'm not prepared for this to happen today. I want to, but I haven't been to the drug store."

Jake didn't waste his time wondering if he had heard her correctly. She had just told him that she wanted to make love and his mind and body conspired in the next flash of a second. There was no languid rise of his body heat, no leisurely increase in his pulse. Blood pounded fast and with pin-point accuracy. He was hard and swollen before he could take his next good breath.

That was how it was with them. Instantaneous combustion. Explosive, intense, hot and as rare as hell. And it was all due to Savannah. She was as rare and special as the passion they shared.

"Why would you need to go to the drug store?" he asked, his voice a raspy murmur.

"For protection."

"You'd handle that?"

"I have in the past."

"Is the lack of a rubber the only thing stopping you from making love right now?"

"Isn't that enough?" She scrubbed the heel of her hand across her forehead, the move doing nothing to knead away her slightly pained expression. "I mean, most responsible people date, get to know each other, discuss among other things their mutual sexual backgrounds, have their blood tests and *then* go to bed."

In one fluid, powerful movement, he stood, taking her up and into his arms as he went. Savannah's arms automatically looped about his shoulders.

"Jake?"

"We've dated," he whispered in a low growl. "I know you well, though not as intimately as I intend to. I've never had unprotected sex and I'm not carrying any infectious diseases."

Savannah tried to remember why she was being so cautious. "But what about—"

"Babe, I've been ready, and *prepared,* to make love to you since we stood on the dock at Bubba's." Riding the hunger digging at him, he kissed her deeply, thrusting his tongue past her parted lips until she gave him the moaning response he craved. Only then did he relinquish her mouth. "Anything else you want to know?"

She couldn't think of a thing. In fact, she really couldn't

think at all. Jake had that effect on her and she wanted nothing more than to give into her heart. Out of habit alone, she waited for rejection to rise up and erect the barriers that would keep him at a safe distance. What she felt was calm acceptance and heady anticipation. Twining her hands behind Jacob's head, she pulled him closer as she lifted her mouth.

His arms crushed her close, his kiss deepened. Shivering with pleasure, she kissed him back, holding on as if she would never let go, hardly aware that he carried her down the hall.

"Which one?" he grated out, cutting each of the three shut doors in the passage an impatient glance.

"There." She pointed with her chin to the door at the end of the hall.

He opened the door then kicked it shut before crossing to the bed. Laying her on the quilted surface, he followed her down so that his torso pressed hers into the bed.

She slipped her arms around him, welcoming the weight and heat of him. He was far too heavy for her. She didn't care. She wanted to feel him with every inch of her body, to know this man as she had never known another . . . to the ends of the universe and back again.

"Jacob."

His name escaped her lips on an urgent sigh. He took it into his mouth, captured it just as he captured her breast in his hand. His thumb sought her nipple, and through the thin knit of her sweater, he felt the delicate flesh hardened into a nub.

His entire body tightened in response. There was something about her breast swelling and filling his palm that touched off a host of primal male instincts to take her, to conquer, and in so doing, bind her to him, make her—this one specific woman—his, as no other woman ever had been, or would ever be.

With a low groan, he pressed his face into the curve of

her neck. He had never felt such possessiveness toward a woman before and it had nothing to do with lust. They were still fully clothed, they had barely kissed and yet his self-control was in serious doubt.

"God, what you do to me." In his mind, he had her stripped and writhing beneath him as he pounded his flesh into hers.

"I think it's . . . it's the same as what you do to me," Savannah breathed.

"What's that?" he asked, looking into her eyes.

"You make me want you until I feel like I'll die if you don't . . . if I can't have you inside of me."

He ground his eyes shut and absorbed the sweet shudders brought on by her words. When he gazed at her again, his face was drawn by the effort to master his desire.

"This isn't going to work if you keep saying things like that." He punctuated his statement with a hard, drugging kiss. "I want you so bad, I'm on the edge right now, but I'm trying to remember that it's been a long time for you."

His concern for her brought a sweet, tender ache to her insides. "Then let me make it easier for you." Her eyes softened to a luminous liquid brown. "Take me now. I feel as if I've waited my whole life for you. I don't want to wait another second."

The effect her words had on Jake was unmistakable. His body clenched and his breathing halted. Savannah smiled a purely feminine smile, heady with the knowledge that she could move him to such depths.

She met his kiss with abandon, giving herself with an unrestrained eagerness that matched Jacob's fierceness. Her hands clung to his back as he plundered her mouth, drawing a sweet moan from deep within her. Beneath her fingers, she felt his muscles flex and bunch. The single layer of the fabric of his shirt was annoyingly frustrating.

Movements impatient, she tugged his shirt out from his

pants and slid her hands up the bare expanse of his back. His skin was hot and smooth, inviting her fingertips to explore, but Jake didn't give her the chance. He pulled her sweater up and over her head and unfastened her bra. Then he lowered his mouth to her breast and drew strongly on her nipple.

Tormenting pleasure arched her off the bed. She caught her breath, the ache inside her tightening until all she could do was cling helplessly to his arms and utter his name in a broken sob.

"Oh, Jake."

He loomed up over her, eyes glittering, blood speeding through his veins. He slanted his mouth over hers again, his hand lowering to the waistband of her jeans. One deft move had the button slipped through its hole. Another and the zipper was lowered. He sought out the softness of her at once, slipping his hand under the silk of her panties and between her legs.

Everything inside Savannah stilled for an infinitesimal moment. Crazily, she thought that she had died. And then his probing fingers parted the swollen folds of her and life surged back with stunning force, surging into her chest and lungs, filling her with a raw pleasure that bordered on pain.

"That's it, babe," he growled near her ear. She was unbelievably sensitive, responding to his slightest touch as if every one of her nerve endings was exposed. Quivering and wet, she was ready for him, but he didn't want to end this now despite what either of their bodies was demanding. He wanted to prolong this first time, to make it last as long as he could.

He traced the delicacy of her, smiling when her legs parted to give him better access.

"Oh, Jake, please," she panted.

He brushed his mouth over hers. "Please what?" He wanted to hear her say it. He wanted her as hot and desperate as he was. When he brought her to climax, he wanted it to be the best thing she'd ever experienced.

"I don't think I . . . I . . ."

"Yes, you can." He came to his knees, yanked off his shirt and flung it away. "We haven't even begun."

Savannah might have panicked if she had truly heard him. After all, nothing in her experiences had prepared her for the kind of arousal she felt. But his words were a distant sound, struck meaningless by the sight of Jacob without his shirt.

The power evidenced in his broad shoulders was repeated in his arms and again in his chest. Staring in blatant admiration, she traced the steely contours of him, letting her eyes linger on the black curling hair that formed a wedge between small dark nipples. From there her gaze followed the thin line of hair that coursed down the corded muscles of his stomach past the flat of his belly and below. There, beneath his pants, she saw the unmistakable bulge of his arousal.

Her gaze jerked back to his and locked. He took her hand and pressed it to him.

At the first touch of her fingers, Jacob stiffened and groaned, flattening his palm over hers. His hips surged forward and a little desperately, he reconsidered just how much longer he would be able to last.

"Bad move," he muttered.

"Why?" Disappointment furrowed her brow. "Doesn't that feel good?"

"That's the problem. It feels too damned good. Like I said, bad move."

Savannah didn't think so. She liked touching him. She liked watching his face grow taut with restrained pleasure. Pushing his enveloping hand away from hers, she came to her knees and faced him. Having no idea what he liked, she surrendered to her instincts.

"Do you like this?" she asked, slipping her hand lower along the hard length of him.

"What do you think?" His eyes narrowing at the friction created by her hand and his clothes.

"I think you like it a lot." If possible, he seemed to have gotten even bigger. She slid her hand lower and cupped him, all the while watching emotions flash over his face.

He sucked in a short dose of air. "Does watching me turn you on?"

Her fingers worked back up the pulsing length of him. "Turning you on turns me on. I like to touch you."

If he could have smiled at that point he would have. "That makes us even." He tucked his hands inside her jeans and shoved them and her panties down her legs in a single move. On the return trip, his fingers trailed up her sleek thighs until they met at the curls shielding her delicate secrets.

The feel of his hands against her sent a small flare of vulnerability through Savannah. The heat of his fingers made her realize just how exposed she was. Emotionally, she didn't bare herself to many people, and even fewer physically. Not surprisingly, she almost gave into the quintessential female move to drape one arm over her breasts and lower her other hand to the juncture of her thighs. One look at the compelling light in Jake's eyes, however, told her that he wasn't about to allow her to do that. He wanted her as naked as she could possibly be.

"I like touching you, too." He matched actions to words and cupped the heat of her in the same manner that she had held him.

It was all Savannah could do to remain upright and her paltry insecurities splintered like shattering glass. Her insides melted, bone and muscle and blood all turning to hot liquid. Helplessly, she sagged against Jake, her head coming to rest on his chest. The subtle woodsy scent of his cologne mingled with the scent of man. She inhaled as deeply as she could only to exhale sharply when his fingers slipped inside of her.

"You're so hot," he whispered darkly, his fingers coaxing, teasing, impaling. "This is where I want to be." And he wasn't going to be able to wait any longer.

He lowered Savannah to her back then quickly rid her of her clothes. In mute wonder, she watched him strip out of his own until he was splendidly naked. In those few seconds before he lowered himself to her, she glimpsed him in his entirety and marveled at the wondrous perfection of him. She also felt a very real, very feminine moment of shock when she saw just how impressive he was.

"Oh, my . . ." She had to wonder if they could actually fit.

He parted her thighs and covered her body with his, resting his weight on his forearms. "It's all right, babe." He patiently soothed her with a gentle kiss, feeling anything but gentle or patient. He *had* to bury himself in her, now. Reaching for his pants, he removed the little foil packet.

Savannah lifted her arms in welcome, discarding any momentary doubts. She wanted this with Jacob, her heart as well as her body demanded it.

He positioned himself between her thighs and she raised her hips to meet his blunt probing. Then with one sure move, Jake slipped his hands under her buttocks, lifted, and thrust powerfully.

She arched upward with a choked cry, feeling every inch of him clear to her soul. Automatically, her body clamped around him and held him tight.

"Are you all right?" he demanded to know, levering himself to his hands in order to see her face clearly.

She rolled her head slowly from one side, unable to get the words out. Her whole being was focused on the incredible sense of being too full, of being stretched to accept the hard, invading length of him. She felt whole, and oddly enough, connected with the ages. Woman taking man into her body. It was a timeless act, elemental in its simplicity. And yet, for Savannah there was nothing simple about it. Jake had become a part of her. The reality of that was profound.

"Savannah?"

Her eyes opened to reveal irises glazed by dewy heat. "Yes. Oh, yes."

Her sighs broke the last of Jake's restraint. He stroked his body into hers, driven by a raging hunger unlike any he had ever experienced. She was soft and hot and so tight it was almost an agony of pleasure.

The tempo of his thrusts increased, his body driving harder and faster into hers. Savannah grasped his arms, her head thrown back, her thighs gripping his legs, her insides tightening and clenching in anticipation. Her breathing was reduced to gasps of half-sobs and muted, unintelligible pleas for release.

"Let go, babe," he coaxed in a dark, rasping voice. "Let it happen."

It did in the next instant. The coiling tension inside her broke, sweeping into her with wave after wave of unbearable pleasure. She held him tightly, her fingers biting into his biceps while her body shuddered and pulsed and edged Jake ever close to his own climax.

He drove into her again and again, as deeply as her body would allow. Grinding his teeth, he labored for breath as he lifted her into his every thrust, holding her to him, revelling in her tight, pliant heat until he exploded. His body arched like a tightly drawn bow, and he called her name, mindless to anything except the pleasure he had found in the woman beneath him.

In the aftermath, he collapsed on top of her, too tired and spent to move. With every breath, he drew in her fragrance; sweet flowers and musky, well-loved woman. His woman. Some dormant savage impulse left over from the beginning of time rose up hard and sure. Savannah was his.

He had just claimed her in the most basic and personal way a man could.

A fanciful notion, but hell, he wasn't a fool. He knew what sex felt like, and what they had shared had *not* been sex. This had been too powerful and intense.

Closing his arms around Savannah, he buried his face in the tangle of her hair and smiled when she draped her arms around his back.

That was all Savannah felt capable of doing. From the inside out, she was consumed by a languid contentment that made movement impossible. Taking a huge sigh, she smiled as her chest hardly moved under Jake's weight. He was lying on her as if he didn't own an ounce of strength. Mentally, she laughed when she thought of how strong he actually was and how he had used that steely power.

"I didn't know," she whispered, deciding that she liked his blanketing weight very much.

He roused at her words, levering himself up to study her intently. "Didn't know what?"

She toyed with the damp curls on his chest. "That's never happened to me before."

Jake's brows rose. "You mean you've never had an orgasm?"

"No."

A purely masculine grin slowly stretched over his face. "How was it?"

"Wonderful." Her hands lifted to circle his neck. "You're wonderful."

He ignored the compliment. "Did I hurt you? Was I too rough?"

"No."

"I should have taken it slower," he confessed, shaking his head, "but God Almighty, Savannah, I didn't think I could wait another second if my life depended on it."

"I'm glad." A little shyly, she asked, "Was it okay for you?"

"Hell, yes." He gave her an incredulous look. "I can't believe you had to ask."

"Well, I'm not the world's most experienced woman."

Leaning close, he nibbled at her lower lip and drawled, "We'll have to work on that." He kissed her fully then carefully disengaged their bodies. Savannah's wince did not go unnoticed. "Sore?"

She curled into his arms, laying her head on his shoulder. "A touch."

"You were as tight as a virgin."

"You're not exactly underendowed."

At her meaningful glare, he chuckled. "A warm bath would help."

"Maybe later." She wouldn't forego the moment for anything. "This is nice."

"What is?"

"Being close like this for the sake of being close."

Which was, Jake surmised, something that had obviously been lacking in her past relationship. Any holding that had gone on had had to do with fear and survival of the human spirit.

"You can hold me any time you want," he told her, pressing a kiss to her forehead.

She tipped her head back to peer at him. "Any time?"

"Especially through the night." He tucked a strand of hair behind her ear, the blue of his eyes becoming as dark as the ocean's depths. "I don't want you going back to the cottage tonight. Stay with me."

A teasing glint entered her eyes at his command-phrased query. "Are you asking me or telling me?"

"Both. Neither. I want you sleeping in my bed, but not if it makes you uncomfortable."

"Why would you think that it would?"

"You've spent the past five years alone. This is happening damn fast for you."

"That's an understatement." Propping herself up on his

chest, she folded her arms and rested her chin on her hands. "Then again, you're one of those fast, bad boys my mother used to warn me about." She grinned in sheer joy. "You've corrupted me."

"It was my pleasure."

"Mine too. Do you snore?"

"Absolutely not."

"What about Ares?"

Jake frowned in confusion. "He doesn't snore either."

"No, is he going to be in the same room with us?"

"Don't worry, he sleeps in the kitchen." He grasped her by the arms and hauled her closer, distracted by the lushness of her breasts crushed to his chest. "Besides, I'm not into spectator sports."

"Meaning we're going to do more than sleep."

"What do you think?"

Against his lips, she purred, "I think I'll spend the night with you."

Thirteen

She was in Jake's bed. Savannah was aware of that the second she woke up.

She opened her eyes to the muted light of morning feeling as content and tranquil as she could ever remember feeling. Drawing in a deep breath, she snuggled under the covers and turned her head to stare at Jake sleeping beside her.

Her immediate thought was that he was a large man. His king-sized bed only served to define his long solid frame and make her all the more aware of the differences between them. Personally, she liked the differences. In fact, she rejoiced in them.

She studied the shadow of his heavy beard then let her gaze drift downward to the mat of hair on his chest. It took no effort at all for her to remember the feel of his chest against hers. Her softness as opposed to his dense muscle; just another of those wonderful differences.

Mentally, she continued with the list, beginning with his incredible, earthy skill as a lover and her relative inexperience. She ended with the contrasts in their sleeping habits. Silently, she admitted it was a good thing he wasn't a restless sleeper because she was. More than several times during the night, she had roamed his way, jabbing him with a knee or cuffing him with an elbow. He had had to finally subdue her in the only way he could, with an arm about her waist and a thigh thrown over both of hers. She smiled at the memory of where that had led.

They had made love five times during the warm cozy hours of the night, and each time, it had gotten better. As impossible as that seemed, it was true. It still amazed her that she had met his demands with equal ardor. Up until now, she had known herself to be compassionate and loving, but she had never viewed herself as overly sexual. Jacob had disproved that belief.

Letting her gaze caress his features, she marveled at the fact that all that vital, potent strength lay contained, momentarily harnessed by nothing more than sleep. The contrast between the Jacob Quaide who blazed his way through life and the one beside her was disconcerting.

Unable to help herself, she threaded her fingers through his hair, telling herself she should let him be. She couldn't seem to help herself, though. In her wildest dreams, she had never thought a man such as Jake would come into her life. To have him close and not touch him, especially after the night that had just passed, was impossible.

Lying on his side, he stirred under her gentle touch. He opened one eye, shut it briefly then raised both lids.

"Hi," she whispered.

Not saying anything, he snaked an arm out and caught her around her waist. One tug and he pulled her flush to his body. Thigh to thigh, chest to chest, he kissed her languidly, taking his time to explore the soft interior of her mouth. When he finally lifted his head, Savannah was searching for breath.

"Good morning," he said. He came to his elbow and gave the clock on the nightstand a critical inspection. "It's only seven-thirty. What are you doing awake?"

"I couldn't sleep."

That earned her a devilish, one-sided grin. "Oh, no?" He rolled her to her back and made a place for himself on top of her, his knees nudging hers wide, his face level with her breasts. "I would have thought you'd have slept in this morning." Resting his weight on his forearms, he scrutinized the round curves and satiny textures before him with such serious intent that Savannah's eyes rounded.

"I wasn't tired," she explained, wondering what held him so fascinated. It wasn't as if he hadn't already seen and touched every inch of her, several times over.

"You didn't get much sleep." His stroke as light as a sunbeam, he traced the contours of her nipple and watched it pucker.

Ribbons of electric pleasure curled downward through Savannah. "And whose fault was it that I didn't sleep?" Not that she really cared. Her body was responding to his caresses with lightning speed. Already, she could feel her insides quickening.

"Bitch, bitch, bitch," he chuckled, his attention focused on her other nipple. It rose up to the demands of his mouth.

Savannah arched, revelling in the pleasure that simmered inside her. Not for a moment did she doubt where the caress would lead and she took as much joy in that knowledge as she did from the feel of Jake's strength under her hands.

She shut her eyes and savored the feel of their bodies touching. There was an utter rightness about it that she couldn't dismiss. She experienced it every time he kissed her, every time he was deep inside her. It was as if they joined not only physically, but emotionally and psychologically as well, caressing each other on levels that had nothing to do with sex and everything to do with love. Her heart wrapped itself around the thought, warming her from the inside while Jake heated her from the outside.

They made love slowly, time stretching out into a series of voluptuous moments, each filled with wonder and discovery. Need gave rise to hunger, and hunger to fulfillment. In the end, Savannah clung fiercely to Jake's shoulders and cried his name as he gave himself up to his own climax.

"God Almighty, woman, what you do to me," he rasped, breathing roughly.

"You started it," she managed to get out.

"Think again."

Against her shoulder, she could feel his mouth stretch with his grin. She didn't have to see it to know that it was wicked. "What did I do?" she asked, genuinely confused.

He raised his head and placed a smacking kiss on her mouth. "You woke me up to the feel of your hands in my hair."

"It was a simple touch, Jake."

"From you, that's all it takes." Another quick hard kiss and he levered himself away and off the bed. "Stay put. I'll be right back."

"Where are you going?"

"To let Ares out before he decides to pay us a visit."

Her insides still quivering, Savannah watched him stride from the room, sweeping the length of him with an appreciative eye. Even from behind, he was the epitome of indomitable power. Wide shoulders tapered to a narrow waist and taut buttocks in a clean line. His legs were long and as finely sculpted as his chest and arms with none of the overblown delineation seen on body builders. She liked the look of him, both aesthetically and from a purely feminine perspective. He was so unequivocally male.

Basking in the remnants of that masculinity, she let her gaze drift about the room. She hadn't had time to look around, the night before. By the time they had gotten back from Richmond, it had been close to eight o'clock. Jake had hurried her up the stairs and into his bed. The last thing on her mind had been studying his bedroom.

She surveyed it now and found it to be as masculine as Jake himself. It was a large room, done up in a subtle blend of forest green and burgundy. Unlike the hardwood floors downstairs, this room was carpeted from wall to wall with a plush dark green rug. Mini-blinds covered the windows on opposite ends of the room. On the connecting wall facing the bed was a brick fireplace.

It was definitely a man's room. Everything from the set of weights by the walk-in closet to the brass inlaid dresser and chests to the absence of curtains boldly proclaimed this to be a manful domain. Savannah half-expected to see a posted sign that read, *Woman, enter at your own risk.*

She had definitely done that, and she couldn't be happier.

"Is that smile for me?" Jake asked, coming through the doorway.

"You were involved with it," she said. Unable to prevent herself from doing so, she stared at the juncture of his legs and her stomach lurched against her lungs.

He stopped at the side of the bed and drawled, "See anything you like?"

Her gaze flew to his and one of her shoulders rose in a rickety shrug. "I'm sorry. I'm not used to seeing a naked man, let alone one that . . . that looks like you."

"Is there something wrong with the way I look?"

"Absolutely not," she sputtered. "Just the opposite." She couldn't imagine any man being put together any more wondrously than he.

"Well, look all you like, but be prepared to pay the consequences."

"What consequences?"

His eyes narrowed ever so slightly as he warned in a tone as dark and shadowy as the corners of the room, "You have a definite affect on me, Savannah."

His meaning sunk in. The line of her vision dropped. "Jake! We just made love. How can you . . . I mean, I haven't even touched you."

"Damnedest thing." Lowering himself beside her, he flipped back the top sheet and blanket, leaving her bared to his greedy gaze. "God, you're beautiful."

Savannah would have debated that, but his hands were already making reality disappear. "Again?" she whispered, her awareness narrowing in to where he circled one finger-tip around the damp flesh between her legs.

"Again," he vowed. "And again . . ."

Again and again and again. The litany frolicked in the back of Savannah's mind as she peered through the lense of her camera. Bent low over her tripod, she clicked off in rapid succession several shots of the western exterior wall of the old mansion.

A storm front was moving in, filling the sky with thick, turbulent clouds. Against that backdrop, the old structure appeared painfully stark. She wanted to capture that image in full color as well as black and white.

Racing to catch the harsh, momentary light, she shifted to raise one tripod and then the other. At her sudden move, the muscles in her lower back gripped her with just enough force to remind her of the last few days. She quickly adjusted her cameras, focused and shot frame after frame, all the while smiling a secret smile.

For all of five minutes, the wind and clouds played devil's advocate with the sun, tossing shadows and highlights about with little regard for logic. And then without warning, the stormy light dimmed and softened, taking with it its extraordinarily unique properties. Savannah sighed in pleasure, certain that she had at least one photo for the book.

She straightened carefully, pressing a hand into the small of her back. For good measure, she arched into the stance, and had to grin around her low groan. After all, she had come by her aches in a most pleasurable manner.

In looking back on the weekend, she was rather amazed that she was capable of walking, let alone standing. She and Jacob had spent most of Sunday making love. Her muscles, long-unaccustomed to the type of exercise in which she had engaged, still protested strongly, and it was now Tuesday morning.

Nonetheless, she wouldn't have traded a second of the day for anything. They had shut out the rest of the world and devoted themselves to each other. Deadlines, the sale of the land and even ghosts had been forgotten; gladly pushed aside in favor of the passion that seemed to deepen each time they made love.

If a gray dimming of Jake's eyes hinted that his thoughts had darkened, that his sorrow and helplessness over the plantation plagued him, then she was there to kiss his grief away and restore the light to his gaze. When the enormity of the haunting sent shivers up her spine, he devoted himself to renewing her smile.

Only the dawn of Monday morning, with all its inherent responsibilities, had been able to break the interlude in which they had so wholeheartedly submerged themselves. They had each gone off to their respective jobs, but Monday evening brought them into each other's arms once more. Savannah could count on one hand the number of hours sleep she had gotten last night. Time and time again, Jake had reached for her in the dark. Time and time again, she had joyously gone into his embrace.

As she packed up her equipment, she considered the intensity of their relationship. At times, she was caught off-guard by how quickly she had become involved. It still amazed her that after shielding her heart for so long, she could give of herself so effortlessly. Of course, with Jacob, no effort was required.

He was the most remarkable man; complex, multilayered. She was coming to realize that he enjoyed variety out of life in general, sex in particular. By turns, he could be suavely seductive or lecherously carnal depending on his mood. She never knew what to expect. Regardless, she was ultimately left sated and content. From his response to her, she knew he enjoyed the same.

Unaware that she did so, she rubbed at the chafed skin

on her chin, a token of Jake's beard stubble. When she realized what she was doing, she laughed.

"You're just going to have to shave more often, Q Man." Because she had no intentions of changing the way things were.

Her fingers gradually stilled at her cheek with a sudden realization. Without knowing his name or seeing his face, she had been waiting for Jake for a very long time. Seemingly forever.

"Oh, Savannah, you're in deep this time," she told herself.

Her words bounced off the brick walls and floated back to her. In the graying morning, her voice was the only sound she could hear.

She came to instant awareness, stiffening in defense, eyes scanning the area in expectation. Her balance was intact, her stomach settled. Holding her breath, she waited.

The rush of cold air came out of nowhere and whirled straight through her, choking her for a brief moment. When she could breathe again, she laid a hand on her chest, blinking to clear the tears from her eyes . . . and stared straight at the ghostly woman.

Instinctively, Savannah stepped back, then caught herself. The smiling spirit hurried right past her unaware of Savannah's presence.

"Ma'am?" Savannah couldn't resist the urge to communicate. "Can you hear me?"

The dark haired woman merely raised the skirt of her blue gown and ran into the house, looking as if she were happily out of breath. Savannah hurried after her, afraid only that the spirit would vanish.

She didn't. The woman made her way up the stairs. For several feet in all directions surrounding her, the air shimmered and waved, warping and bending as she progressed to the landing. There, she stopped and cast a capricious peek over her shoulder, her gaze focused, but not on Savannah.

"The bedroom again." Savannah had to wonder what was so special about that particular room? Frowning slightly, she followed in the wake of the spirit.

The master bedroom was exactly as she had last seen it, completely furnished as if someone actually lived there. The spirit, stands of dark hair curling about her pretty face, quickly moved about adjusting the curtains to block out the bright sunlight.

Savannah gave a wavering laugh. Outside should have been cloudy and yet sunlight was pouring through the windows. Mesmerized, she stood just inside the room as it was cast into cozy shadows.

"Emily Jane."

Savannah whirled at the sound of a commanding male voice coming from the hall. It came again.

"Wife, where are you?"

"In here."

Savannah's head whipped about, her stunned gaze riveting back to the spirit in the room. Her name was Emily Jane . . . and she had spoken. Savannah barely had time to digest that fact when a man entered the room. Adrenaline surging into her bloodstream, Savannah stumbled away, coming up against a wall.

"I swear, madam wife," he growled in a low warning, "you are the most elusive bit of fluff I have ever met."

Savannah's heart lurched into her throat. Her pulse stopped, then jumped frantically. Another spirit! She was just coming to terms with one, and now there was a second.

She scrutinized him from head to toe. He was a tall, handsome man—ghost?—with black hair and intensely blue eyes. Like Emily Jane, he was dressed in clothes that dated to the mid-nineteenth century.

"There's no need for you to take offense, husband,"

Emily Jane teased, her already flushed face gaining added color.

"I wouldn't take offense, *wife,* if you didn't insist on playing these games."

"Am I playing a game?"

"More coyly than is seemly." The man planted his fists on his hips and narrowed his eyes at his wife. "You play the coquette with too familiar a manner."

Emily Jane pouted prettily and tipped her head to a jaunty angle. "For your pleasure, Nathan."

"My pleasure would have been better served in the stable loft."

"Like some randy cock?"

At her smiling taunt, Nathan slowly advanced on his wife. "There are cocks, wife, and then there are cocks."

"I am no pullet, sir."

"Yes, but I like the way you lay."

Emily Jane tried to elude her husband's hands, but succeeded in going no further than a single step. "You beast," she laughed up into his face.

"First a cock and now a beast," he murmured against her temple. "Either way, you *will* spread your legs for me and I *will* have you." His movements deft and knowing, Nathan flipped up the yards of skirt and layers of petticoats.

Savannah watched the intimate scene unfold in growing shocked dismay, feeling like a Peeping Tom. This was no longer a case of her observing some restless spirit incapable of finding a final resting place. These two were going about the day to day business of life in as humanly a way as possible. And yet they weren't alive.

What was she witnessing? Had this very moment been played out in another century and she was now being given a supernatural instant replay? Or were these spirits still roaming freely in the present indulging in their sexual fantasies?

Before she could decide, Nathan tumbled his wife to the

bed and followed her down. Savannah's eyes popped wide. "Ohmygod." She couldn't stand there and watch. This wasn't a movie. These people were real, or they had been. In any event, the atmosphere was charged and personal. It demanded privacy.

She backed out of the room and headed for the stairs. As much as she wished to stay and find answers to her questions, she wasn't comfortable remaining under the present circumstances. Her answers would have to come later.

Hopefully, she'd be given another chance to see the spirits, and hopefully, she'd be able to physically withstand the stress to her body. Once outside again, she was seized by a case of the shakes.

Sitting on the front steps, she rode out the tremors, legs draw up to her chest and her arms wrapped about her knees. Thankfully, the withdrawal this time wasn't nearly as extreme as she had known it to be previously. She gained control fairly quickly, and in so doing, sensed that the spirits were gone. Physically, she was herself again, all tension and discomfort replaced by a bracing, invigorating vitality. She felt infused with life.

She had to tell Jake! This was too incredible not to share. Few people were fortunate enough to glimpse the past this way. Of course those who had, and made it publicly known, set themselves up for a bundle of criticism.

She pondered that sticky point for most of the afternoon. She wanted to tell Jacob . . . had to tell him. For all she knew, he might have seen Emily Jane and Nathan a hundred times over. Then again, this might be a once in a millennium thing, happening at this exact point in time, to her alone. Jake could very well think she was looney.

Back and forth, she debated the issue, until her nerves were frazzled. Jake's arrival at the cottage shortly before six that night didn't help either for she hadn't come to any decision on whether to tell him or not.

"Hi." She opened the door and he stepped in to place a

brushing kiss on her lips, but when he straightened, his brow was lined with a frown.

"What's wrong?"

"Nothing," she denied a little too quickly. "Why would anything be wrong?"

"You tell me. You look preoccupied. Did everything go all right today?"

"Absolutely." If seeing two ghosts about to make love qualified as "all right." She tried to shut out the mental images she had of Emily Jane and Nathan. "How about you? How was your day?"

Hooking an arm around her shoulders, Jacob made his way to the kitchen. "Better, now that I have you close."

The glance she sent him was loaded with questions. He leaned back against the counter to answer. "Doug called today to fill me in on the latest with the land."

"How's it going?" Savannah asked, pouring him a glass of wine.

"No hitches."

"Which is both good and bad."

"To some degree." His tone turned brittle, his gaze hard. "Part of me still hopes that another solution to Doug's problems will come along."

"This can't be easy for him. Is he hanging in there?"

"Yeah."

"Are you hanging in there?" Her gaze was soft, compassionate, and as sharply honed as a razor's edge.

"Doing my best."

"Which means you're angry as all get-out but you won't let it show."

Jacob accepted the glass of zinfandel, slipping his fingers over hers so she couldn't release the glass. "I'm dealing with it in the only way I can, babe. This whole thing sucks, but pissing and moaning won't change the facts."

"True. It might make you feel better, though."

"It won't."

She could see that. His features were set in lines that declared he was in control; anger and regret tamed, although not completely conquered.

Laying her hand along the hard edge of his jaw, she offered, "I'm here any time you need to vent."

"Thanks," he murmured, against her mouth.

"For what?"

"For worrying."

"Comes with the job description," she breathed, and then kissed him with tender passion. When he lifted his head, his smile was as natural as hers.

She moved away to pour herself a glass of wine. Behind her Jacob relaxed into his long-legged stance.

"I asked Doug to speak to the new owner on your behalf," he told her. "He said he didn't think there'd be any problem with your continuing with your work."

"I appreciate that. The house is so special." *Here's your chance. Tell him, tell him now.* With her back to him, she hinted, "I've never come across a house like Oakwood's. There must be quite a . . . a few legends and tales about the place."

"Enough to fill a book."

"Really?" She did her best to keep her tone level, but it was difficult. The stress that had been eating away at her nerves in one form or another all day burst into full bloom. "What kind of stories?"

"The usual, about who caused a particular scandal, who fell in love with whom, what happened to the house during the Civil War, that kind of thing."

As nonchalantly as she could, she asked, "Any mention of ghosts?"

"Hundreds." Savannah was about to exhale in pure relief when Jacob added, "If you believe in bullshit like that."

Her heart dropped, her defenses went up. "I take it you don't?"

"Hell no," he scoffed around a laugh.

His reaction was just what she feared it would be. For a few tense seconds, she debated whether she should continue. Slowly, she crossed the room and sat at the kitchen table.

"I like the idea of a haunted house. That's part of the charm of old buildings."

"Charming but unrealistic."

"Oh, I don't know," she mused, wanting him to accept the possibilities. "Who's to say what's real and what isn't? I think that's something each person decides for himself."

"You mean in the same way a person decides the meaning of a divine being?"

"Something like that. Everyone views life differently, and that's okay. I just don't think we can dismiss any options."

"What sort of options are we talking about?"

"The *un*-usual." She searched in her head for another way to broach the subject. "For instance, when a person dies, what happens to all of his electrical energy? It has to go somewhere, right?"

"I've never thought about it."

"I have." She nibbled on the inside of her cheek, knowing she was going to sound unhinged. "Maybe it's possible that buildings soak up a person's energy."

Jake sipped at his wine, his eyes sparkling with a touch of indulgent humor over the rim of the glass. "Is that why you say hello to your apartment when you go home?"

She rocked her head from side to side. "In a way. Real, vital people lived there. I like to think that some essence of them remains in the structure."

Jake crossed one ankle over the other and tucked one hand under the opposite arm. "Why all this sudden interest in metaphysics?"

"It isn't sudden. I've always harbored certain convictions when it comes to the supernatural."

"Like what?" He grinned widely, the curve underscored with more complacency than true interest.

Her temper flared. She was trying to delve into a delicate, impossibly difficult subject that had turned her life upside down. She needed his support and he was almost laughing at her.

"If you're going to be smug about this, then forget it. I'm sorry I even brought the matter up."

The acerbity of her tone earned her a puzzled look. Setting his glass aside, Jake spun one of the chairs around and straddled its seat to face her. "Don't get bent out of shape, Savannah."

"It's difficult not to with you smiling at me like I don't have both oars in the water."

"That's not the way I feel. You should know that."

"But . . . ?"

"But nothing. I don't share your views on this, that's all. Don't make a big deal out of it."

But it was a big deal. It was a humongously huge, great big deal. "I happen to feel strongly about this."

"I can see that." He reached out and stroked a finger over the lines creasing her forehead. "So we disagree. That doesn't mean it's the end of the world. You have a more romanticized view of life while I believe in life's tangibles."

Her gaze stopped a hair's breadth short of a glare. "Which tangibles?"

"One plus one equals two, the shortest distance between two points is a straight line, for every action there is an equal and opposite reaction. Those theories are real." He rapped his knuckles on the table. "The same way this table is real."

That was all well and good for him, but she knew he had made a mere surface scratch in reality. And she doubted she would be able to convince him otherwise. That, more than anything, upset her. "There's more to life than that," she snapped, her irritation plain.

"I didn't say there wasn't." Leaning back, he planted his

hands on his spread thighs and shook his head. "Lord, you're defensive tonight. Are you all right?"

No, she wasn't all right. She wanted him to know what was going on and his attitude prevented her from sharing this with him. "I'm . . . I don't know."

"Have you got your period?"

Savannah shot straight out of her chair and paced to the sink. There, she clenched her eyes shut and willed herself to hang on to her patience. *Why* did every man lay a woman's tensions on that door step?

"Savannah?"

"No, I don't have my period, and your asking was as chauvinistic as it gets." She whirled around to face him. "Look, I'm tired. Maybe we should drop the subject." It was definitely getting out of hand and going absolutely nowhere.

Jacob stood to his full height and shoved his hands on to his hips, his eyes taking on an unyielding cast. "No, you started this whole mess about ghosts and goblins, and you're damn well going to finish it. I want to know what's got you so riled."

Ghosts and goblins?! She mentally squared her shoulders. He didn't want to hear the truth? Fine, she wouldn't tell him. And that would be the end of it, because she sure as hell wasn't a glutton for punishment. There was no way she was going to open herself up to his ridicule and condescension.

"Nothing's got me riled," she declared.

"Don't give me that. Talk to me."

"About what?"

Getting increasingly more annoyed by the second, Jake aimed a lethal glare through the space separating them. "You're pissed at me and I want to know why."

It was there in the blue fire of his eyes and the command of his voice. The fighter pilot not backing down an inch from a perceived challenge. All he needed was his flight suit and helmet and he'd have been ready to attack at full throttle.

Savannah's chin angled slightly to one side, the gesture telling more eloquently than words what she thought of his aggressive arrogance. "Fine, I'll tell you why I'm angry. I'm angry because of your attitude."

"What's wrong with my attitude?"

"It's narrow-minded, insulting and arrogant. In a word, it stinks."

He was across the room in three strides. One arm snaked around her waist and hauled her up against his chest. Jaw fixed rigidly, eyes narrowed to heated sapphire slits, he growled, "I haven't noticed you complaining lately. All I've heard from you is a lot of satisfied purring."

Savannah threw her head back to look him squarely in the eye. "Don't you dare bring sex into this."

"Why not?" He cupped her behind and lifted her thighs into an intimate coupling with his. "I'm getting turned on right now."

His mouth came down on hers, cutting off her protests. Savannah shoved at his chest and found it as immovable as she knew it would be. "Let me go," she demanded, yanking her head back.

"No."

"I thought you wanted to talk."

"We're done talking," he told her in between strained, ragged breaths.

He kissed her again. The force of his passion emanated in all directions and then washed right straight through her, in exactly the same way the cold air in the old house penetrated her. Her knees buckled, her head swirled, but the arms holding her plastered to his body tightened, making her excruciatingly aware of the blood pounding through him.

His hips thrust against her in an untamed rhythm that matched the movement of his tongue over hers. The twin assaults were staggeringly carnal, overwhelming, in a single instant transforming the heat of her anger into heat of an entirely different kind. The shift hit her like a jolt out of the blue.

Literally against her will, she sagged in his arms, wondering how she could relent this way. She despised women who were slaves to passion. It implied weak wills, and fragile, insecure personalities. Didn't it?

She wasn't one of those women to let a man kiss her into senseless submission. And yet, she was clinging to him, kissing him, wanting him.

"Jake?"

"I love it when you get steamed." He bit at a delicate spot on her neck as he jerked at the fastening of her jeans. "It's so goddamned sexy."

She tipped her head to one side, loving the feel of his mouth. "I don't want to do this," she murmured. "I'm not done being angry with you."

"Save it for later." Teeth clenched, he impatiently thrust his hands under the silk of her underwear. The thin garment and her jeans were shoved past her thighs, down and off one leg. Urgently, he tore at the zipper of his own pants and freed himself from the confining fabric. Then, slanting his mouth over hers, he lifted her and plunged into her waiting warmth.

Savannah cried out, the sound unraveling into a thready whimper of pleasure and astonishment. She'd never before had an argument escalate into sex. She didn't know if she could handle the emotions involved; anger and lust. She'd always thought them worlds apart, yet they coalesced with stunning intensity the second Jacob began driving himself into her repeatedly.

And then it all seemed to make sense. It was pointless to hang on to her anger. This compelling need, the endless giving and taking of pleasure, the exchanging of trusts and bodies and hearts was what was truly important. When it came down to the question of what was real and what wasn't, the basis for their passion was absolute reality, transcending whatever differences they might have.

She wound her legs about his waist and gave herself up to the tempest of desire that surged, peaked and exploded with dizzying speed. When it was over, she felt more connected with Jacob than she ever had.

"God Almighty," he groaned, bracing her against the counter.

Savannah stirred in his arms. It took a supreme effort to lift her head from his shoulder. "I think my legs are useless."

Eyes shut, Jacob rubbed his chin against her forehead. "I hope we can end all our arguments this way." He stiffened suddenly and looked down into her flushed face. "Savannah, I didn't use anything."

"I know." Their lovemaking had been as natural as it had been wild. It was only fitting that it should have been as unguarded.

"How's the timing for you?"

She pressed a fingertip to his lips to stem his concerns. "Nothing to worry about. I'm nearly at the end of my cycle."

"You're sure?"

Her finger trailed the firm line of his lower lip. "Sure enough that I want you in bed with me this way tonight." And for all the nights to come.

For the first time, she realized she was falling in love with the man.

Fourteen

"Sonofabitch." Jacob's lips narrowed around the curse as he scanned the cars on either side of the road. He had circled the block around Savannah's apartment twice without any success of finding a parking space. How in the hell, he wondered, did she put up with this idiosyncrasy of urban life on a regular basis?

True, it was Thanksgiving Day and people normally at work were home. That justification for lack of parking, however, didn't alleviate his aggravation. He had missed Savannah last night, and he wasn't used to missing a woman.

Impatience hummed in his blood as he began to start around the block again. Luckily, a car up ahead pulled out and he was spared further irritation. Minutes later, compact duffel bag slung over his shoulder, he buzzed up to Savannah's apartment.

"Yes?" Her disembodied voice sounded thin over the little speaker.

"It's me."

"Hi, 'me'," came her laughing response. The door automatically opened.

Jacob smiled in return, not even pretending to misinterpret the causes for his good humor. He knew damn well he was behaving like a teenager with his first girl, anxious to hear her voice, eager to get into her pants. Damn, but that felt good.

She greeted him at her door with a hug and a "Happy Thanksgiving."

"Same to you," he said, prolonging the hug by slipping his hand to the small of her back and angling her hips up to his. "You feel good."

"So do you," she breathed, molding her body to his.

He tightened his arms and kissed her as if it had been months instead of a single day since he had last seen her. "I missed you, woman."

"Did you?" She looked up at him with a mixture of delight and amazement.

"Big-time."

"I missed you, too."

His hands stroked the curving softness of her hips. Anchored thigh to thigh, he walked her backward into the apartment. "What time are we expected at your aunt's?"

Savannah didn't miss the speculative gleam in his eyes. "In a little while, so don't get any ideas, Q Man."

His smile broadened. "I have ideas all the time."

"I know, but can you save them until later?"

"I suppose if I have to."

Jauntily, she sassed, "You have to."

"You're a hard woman, Savannah Davis." He released her and made himself comfortable on her couch while she retreated to her bedroom. "How was 'pie day'?" he called.

From down the hall he heard her muffled scoff. "A mess. We made six pies. Flour everywhere. If I never see another pecan or apple again, I'll die a happy woman."

He could just picture her, a smudge of flour on her chin, white handprints decorating the denim of her trim jeans. The mental image was decidedly domestic and it hit him in the gut with a surge of tenderness that was as satisfying and stimulating as the most erotic fantasies he had of her.

In rapid succession, his head filled with impressions of Savannah in all her facets: the self-assured photographer, the easy friend, the capricious lover, the determined woman. On top of that, his mind added, the loving mother.

The thought brought him to his feet and carried him to one of the long windows. Not that he wanted to escape the idea, but it was such a shock that he was left reacting to it physically. He hadn't considered any particular woman in that particular way since his early days with Catherine. And yet with stunning ease, he imagined Savannah filled with his baby.

His baby, snuggled within that glorious body of hers. God Almighty, what an impression. His breathing thickened just imagining it.

He turned to stare down the hall toward her bedroom, as if he needed to verify her existence. There wasn't anyone else like her, no one who touched him as deeply, no one who made him feel the way she did, as if they were part of each other.

That was how he had felt the night before last, when he had stood in her kitchen and slipped his body into hers, free of any barriers. That had been a first for him and not because he had been overcome by lust. His formidable control had been destroyed and he hadn't been able to think past their joining, then. And again and again throughout the night. Now, watching her come toward him, part of him regretted that her monthly timing had been so safe.

"I'm ready," she announced. Dressed in a short, navy blue suede skirt and a matching wool sweater, she looked impossibly beautiful.

He cupped her face in his palms and kissed her slowly, tenderly, drinking in her sweetness like a parched man.

"Jake?" she queried, giving him an odd look.

He didn't answer the unspoken question. "Come on," he urged, linking his arm around her shoulder. "Let's get going before we end up having Thanksgiving dinner here."

"That isn't very likely," she laughed. "My refrigerator is bare."

"I was thinking more in terms of our feasting off each

other." He waggled his eyebrows; a lecherous gesture he took great joy in repeating several more times during the trip to the outskirts of town.

"I have to warn you about my family," Savannah cautioned when they neared her Aunt Nell's house.

"Why?"

"Because if you're not used to a big, loud, demonstrative group, this could be a bit of a culture shock for you."

"Demonstrative?" Jake slanted her a quizzical glance.

Savannah nodded. "Lots of hugging and kissing."

"I can handle that."

"I hope so. I've never brought anyone home for any of the holidays, so my aunts are going to descend upon you. And my grandmother, too. Be prepared to spend the afternoon wiping lipstick off your cheeks."

"Never?"

Savannah returned his look. He had homed in on the one fact he found pertinent "No, you're the first."

"I like that."

Even if he hadn't said as much, she would have been able to tell. His face took on the appearance of a man completely satisfied with life. He was looking much the same way ten minutes later when they were surrounded by her relatives.

"And this is my grandmother." She slipped her arm around the back of the tiny, orange-haired woman and spoke over the din of happy voices emanating from every part of the sprawling split-level house. "Gran'ma, this is Jacob Quaide. Jake, my maternal grandmother, Lucia DiBastista."

"Ma'am." Towering over Lucia, Jacob nodded politely.

Lucia aimed a sparkling smile his way, but when she spoke it was to Savannah. "I didn't know," she admonished, her voice laced with remnants of a delicate Italian accent. "You didn't tell me."

Savannah had anticipated this. Her grandmother expected to be kept abreast of her social life, primarily in regard to any special man. "I've been busy, Gran'ma."

Lucia clucked her tongue in disapproval, her narrow chin wrinkling as she pursed her lips. "Not too busy to pick up the phone."

Savannah rolled her eyes in feigned exasperation. "Don't pout at me. And besides, you didn't tell me about your hair. What color is it this week?"

Lucia reached a gnarled, arthritic hand to the fine wisps of hair that changed color with remarkable frequency. "Passionate Pumpkin." Patently pleased with the results of her latest choice of color, she pressed for the compliment. "What do you think?"

"I like it much better than the yellow it used to be."

"Good. Me too, but your mother doesn't."

"Where is she?" Savannah craned her neck, trying to catch sight of her mother among the group in the living room.

Giving a quick shrug, Lucia spread her hands. "With your sister somewhere."

From the kitchen, someone called out, "Lucia, come taste this sauce."

Savannah's eyes rounded in expectation. "Did you make the sauce for the pasta?"

"Of course."

Jake tilted his head as if he hadn't heard correctly. "Pasta on Thanksgiving?"

"In this family," Savannah explained, "it's pasta with everything. But don't worry, we'll have turkey, too."

The impatient voice from the kitchen came again. "Lucia."

"I'm coming, I'm coming." But only, Savannah noted, in her own good time. Lucia reached up, way up, and patted Jacob's cheek. "You be good to my Savannah."

Jacob leaned into the elderly touch. "I intend to."

At his remark, an unholy light entered the aged eyes. To Savannah, Lucia issued a string of rapid-fire Italian.

"Gran'ma!" Savannah nearly choked in embarrassment. "Behave yourself." Shaking her head, she watched the eighty-five-year-old bundle of audacity make her way to the kitchen.

"What was that all about?" Jake asked.

Savannah didn't know whether to laugh or grit her teeth. "I'm not sure I should tell you."

He gave her one of those determined looks that said he'd get it out of her one way or another.

"Well, it loses a little something in the translation, but she said you're a big man, the . . . uh . . . implication being that you're big all over." She raked her bottom lip with her teeth. "And because of that I must be enjoying myself."

Incredulity flashed across Jake's face only to be replaced by a smugness that was wholly male.

"I suppose that makes you feel good to hear that," she accused lightly.

Looking for all the world like he was going to impart nothing more interesting than the weather, Jake casually leaned down so that his lips skimmed her ear and whispered, *"You* make me feel good, especially when I'm deep inside you and you make those soft whimpering sighs."

The fleeting touch of his lips combined with the low seductiveness of his words tripped her pulse. She sucked in a raw breath, only to have it get caught in her lungs when Leanne interrupted from behind.

"All right, you two, none of that."

Savannah spun around, flustered to the point of a nervous giggle when she discovered her mother with Leanne. For everyone's sake, she scrounged up what she hoped was a pleasant smile. Thankfully, her face didn't betray her and she went through the process of introducing Celia Davis to Jake. Once again, Jacob was his suavely polite self.

"Now that that's over," Leanne declared, slipping her arm through Jake's. "I'm going to steal this man away. There are a whole slew of people I want him to meet."

"I was going to do that," Savannah protested. It wasn't that she didn't trust her sister, it was that she . . . *really* didn't trust her sister. There was no telling what antics Leanne would pull.

"Don't worry, Banana." Leanne gave Jake her most harmlessly flirtatious grin. "Jake's a big boy, he can take care of himself."

"It's not Jake I'm worried about."

Jake allayed her fears. "I'll be fine, Savannah. This will give you and your mom some time to talk."

She eyed him skeptically. "All right, but you proceed at your own risk."

Jake's grin assumed a clearly devilish tilt. "Don't I always?"

Savannah had no answer for that. The man had flown in combat. She supposed he could survive some time in Leanne's presence.

"He'll be fine," her mother chuckled when they were alone and seated in a deserted corner of the room. Permanent laugh-lines were etched in her narrow face, the brown of her eyes shone brightly.

"I know." For no other reason than it was natural for her to do so, Savannah placed a kiss on her mother's graying temple. "How are you, Mom?"

Celia Davis twisted her slender torso from side to side. "My back is a little stiff today, but other than that, I'm . . . what's the right word? . . . peachy-keen."

"Have you been overdoing it?"

"Not at all. What about you? Have you been taking care of yourself?"

"Absolutely."

"Are you taking your vitamins?"

At the routine, well-intentioned-albiet-annoying inquiry, Savannah made a face at her mother. "Yes, I'm taking my vitamins."

Celia ignored her daughter's grimace. "I want you to be healthy."

"I am healthy. And happy."

"I wonder why?" her mother entreated in a singsong voice, rolling her eyes in a show of overstated innocence.

Savannah knew why, too. Her gaze softening, she asked, "Is it that obvious?"

"That you think he's wonderful?"

Savannah nodded.

Celia took hold of her daughter's hand. "It's been a long time since I've seen you looking so relaxed."

Relaxed was just a small portion of what Savannah had been feeling lately. "He's pretty special."

"He must be, in order for you to bring him home."

"What do you think of him?"

Celia's gaze was direct, unwavering. "I like him. I told you from the beginning that I had a good feeling about this man."

Savannah stroked the hand that held hers. Cautiously, reluctant to overstate feelings with which she had yet to come to grips, she said, "I've . . . uh, I've never felt this way about anyone."

"Not even Eric?"

"You know how it was between me and Eric. What I have with Jake is nothing like that at all."

"He seems to know what he wants out of life."

"You could tell that from a single meeting with him?"

"It's obvious just by looking at him."

"Yes, well, you're right. The man is determined. Intelligent. Opinionated"

"Uh, oh."

Savannah laughed and conceded wryly, "We do have our moments. Makes life interesting." Again, the brown of her eyes reflected the tenderness of her thoughts. "He possesses a depth of character that has true value. There's not a shallow bone in his body. He can be very caring and protective."

"And he's a good lover?"

Savannah squeezed her eyes shut for a second. "Mom, you're as bad as Gran'ma."

"I'm your mother. I worry about you."

"You don't have any reason to."

"You can't blame me, Anna. I've watched you hibernate these last few years. And now you're . . . what's the right word? . . . *involved* with a man."

"I didn't hibernate."

"Not with us, not with the family, but you've kept your heart closed off to others. I worry that it might be fragile right now."

"My heart's tougher than you think. *I'm* tougher than you think."

Celia's eyes, so like her daughter's, shone with all the unrelenting love Savannah had known all her life. "Oh, I know you're tough, on the outside. But in here . . ." Celia patted the spot over her heart. "In here, you're tremendously sensitive. I wouldn't want you to get your heart broken."

"I don't want that either. I'm being very cautious, trying to take my time with all the emotions involved. Jake's personality doesn't always allow for that, but he would never do anything to hurt me. He feels strongly about the important things in life, and when he commits to something, he commits one hundred percent."

"Has he committed himself to you?"

Leave it to her mother to get right to the heart of the matter. Savannah didn't mind. If she hadn't wanted to have this discussion, she wouldn't have. That said a great deal about how secure she was becoming in her feelings for Jake.

"He's committed to making the relationship work."

"That's not what I mean."

"Are you asking me if he loves me?"

Celia's eyebrows rose in a silent *yes*.

Savannah tucked a strand of hair behind her ear as she thought about the question. "I think he might . . . he hasn't said as much. Things haven't progressed that far between us."

"I understand."

And Savannah knew that her mother did. Mom would know that the full extent of her daughter's feelings were intense and private, meant to be shared in their entirety only when the time was right. For Savannah the time wasn't right.

A burst of laughter drew her gaze into the den, and a smile curled her lips. Jake stood among her cousins and aunts and uncles. In his arms, he held Christy, her pudgy little arms wrapped around his neck.

"I think your father would have liked him," her mother said.

Happiness welled within Savannah. "Yeah, I think Daddy would have liked Jake as much as I do."

"I'm going to have to diet for the next two weeks," Savannah groaned as she watched Jake unlock her apartment door.

"That was the best Thanksgiving dinner I have ever had." Jake made his declaration around a sated sigh. "And I have never seen so much food at one meal."

"It's amazing, isn't it?" Savannah switched on the light. "Hello, apartment. I'm home." Leaving Jake to lock up for the night, she crossed to the sofa and sank into its welcoming cushions. "This is it. This is as far as I can go without the help of a crane or a tow truck."

"That stuffed?"

"To the gills." She leaned her head back and shut her eyes, listening to the pleasing sounds of Jake removing his jacket and sitting beside her. Eyes still closed, she reached out and blindly sought his hand. His warm, hard fingers encompassed hers at once. "I do this every year, you know."

"What's that?" Jake slipped off his shoes and stretched his long legs out before him on the low, Oriental table.

"Promise myself I'm not going to overeat and then go right ahead and cheerfully break that promise."

"How can you help it? Your aunts could teach the best chefs of the world something about good food."

Savannah peeked open one eye. "Did you have a good time?"

"The best. You have a great family."

"They like you, too."

"I would say my being with you had something to do with it."

Savannah denied that with an adamant shake of her head. "Absolutely not. You gained entrance into the fold because of me. You gained their acceptance on your own. Believe me, if they didn't like you, you'd know."

"Oh, yeah?"

"Yeah. Besides, you remind Aunt Nell of a cross between Harrison Ford and Timothy Dalton."

"Get out."

"I'm serious. *And* she thinks you're good for me."

Shifting his shoulders into a more comfortable position, he peered at her smiling lips. "She said that?"

"Yup, and so did just about everybody else."

Jake had known that Savannah's family was going to check him out. He wouldn't have expected anything else. "Did it make you uncomfortable to have people telling you that they approve of me?"

Savannah chuckled and laid her head on his shoulder. "Nope. I'm used to their emotional hovering. In any event, it wouldn't have made any difference to me what they thought of you."

"No?"

"I want them to like you, because you're a person worth liking. And it makes things easier in the kind of gathering we had today, but their opinions would never sway me in how I feel about you."

"What way is that?"

The conversation had been easy, comfortable, a pleasant recounting of the day. Now, suddenly, with his one question, comfort and ease had been stripped away by an intense seriousness.

Savannah lifted her head and peered into the blue of his eyes. He stared right back at her, visually compelling her to face her own feelings.

She exhaled sharply and searched the ceiling. "God, this is hard."

"Why?" Jake studied her as intently as she studied the air above. She was nervous; at a rare loss for words.

She returned her gaze to his and lifted her brows in a shrug. "For years I assumed, believed, I'd be me, alone by myself. Then you barrelled into my life and nothing's been the same. I feel as if I've been swept up into the eye of your storm."

He gave her a gentle smile. "Is that so bad?"

"No, but it's going to take some getting used to. Having you in my life is rather extraordinary."

Jake shifted about, so that he faced her directly, one hand splayed on the back of the sofa, the other on the arm. Savannah was encompassed within. "Extraordinary, huh?" One side of his mouth quirked with a contented grin.

"Very." His contentment reached out to her. She smiled back. He had said that she was dead center in his life. When they made love, he gave himself to her unconditionally and demanded the same in return from her. In a hundred little ways each day, he made it obvious that he genuinely cared about her.

Curving her hand behind his head, she stroked her fingers downward along his jaw line. "In fact, Q Man, you're the best thing to ever happen to me."

Jake's smile faded, the glint of humor in his eyes gave way to something deeper. "The best thing . . ."

She angled her mouth toward his. "The absolute, very best."

Fifteen

"War seems to be inevitable."

"Tell me that isn't so."

"If the Yankee politicians cannot bring themselves to see reason, it does not look hopeful for the preservation of the union."

"That doesn't mean this country will come to blows with itself, Nathan. Surely it won't come to that?"

Savannah watched and listened as the scene in the master bedroom played out. With her legs crossed, she sat on the floor beside the fireplace, her heart going out to Nathan and Emily Jane.

The two were distraught over the possibility of what Savannah knew to be the coming Civil War. Sadly, their lives were about to be changed forever, and they didn't even know how greatly.

Nathan gathered his wife into his arms. "There is already talk of secession. That won't be accomplished without bloodshed."

"Can't this be worked out in Washington?" Emily Jane implored.

"For every one of the Yankee hotheads, the South has one of its own. Nothing can be resolved peaceably with tempers flaring. Eventually, in time, I fear the worst."

Emily tipped her head back. "I hope you are wrong, husband."

"No more so than I." Nathan rubbed his wife's shoulder

before he dropped his hand to the roundness of her belly beneath her skirts. "I would like to see my sons and daughters born into a time and place of accord."

Covering his hand with her own, Emily Jane murmured, "This one has begun to kick."

A proud smile replaced some of the grim creases on Nathan's face. "So, he's a little codger, is he?"

"He is nothing of the sort." Emily lifted her nose in a prim rebuke, but her eyes gleamed with unmistakable love and maternal pride. "He's a sweet little darling, knocking at the door to remind me he's there."

Nathan's hand lingered at his wife's waist, his expression becoming one of poignant tenderness. "I like this." He slowly smoothed his palm in a circular motion. "I like knowing that I am responsible for the changes in your body, that it is my seed that makes you swell here." His hand rose to capture the fullness of one of her breasts. "And here."

Savannah bit her lower lip. This was only the second time she had seen Nathan and Emily Jane together, but it was obvious that they loved each other deeply. They were friends as well as husband and wife. Such a relationship was a rare gift regardless of the century.

Sitting perfectly still, she watched the couple embrace, feeling once again that she was intruding on an emotional intimacy never intended for public viewing. And yet, physically she could not drag her eyes away.

Startled by her reaction, she blinked repeatedly and discovered that the space surrounding the pair glistened and shimmered with a pale light. Like a gossamer veil, it quivered around them, expanding in all directions.

Savannah leaned back, uncertain with this new twist in the fabric of things. In seconds the aura surrounded her. Well-being flooded her mind and her body. She was held captive, fascinated and enchanted.

"You are a fetching little thing, Emily," Nathan whispered, his words emerging as a caress. The air took on a warmth that stroked over Savannah's skin. "If I had the time I would go hunting tender game. As it is, I have to see that the repairs to the dock are progressing."

"As it is, husband, you have hunted this particular game before."

"I admit I have a fondness for pointing my firearm in your direction." He kissed her with tender passion before he stepped back. Grinning wryly, he admitted, "If I continue with much more of this, my firearm will be loaded and primed and now is not—"

The room before Savannah's eyes changed without warning. Nathan and Emily Jane vanished in a fraction of a second. The glistening warmth that had enveloped her was ripped away. What had been the nineteenth century was now the cold reality of the present.

It happened so suddenly, Savannah could barely grasp the transformation. And then realization set in and the too-rapid shift jerked brutally at her senses.

Her balance swung crazily, her body flushed from hot to cold and back again. She pressed one hand to her head and the other to her stomach, sucking in short breaths. Distantly, she thought that it was a good thing she was sitting because had she been standing, she would have dropped to her knees.

What happened? This abrupt disconnection from the past wasn't the norm. Things usually faded slowly, gradually. Why the sudden break this time?

Voices from below penetrated her confusion and discomfort. Instinctively, her head swerved toward the doorway. Two men. Their voices came to her in muffled tones. A little crazily, she wondered what century the men belonged to.

She came to her feet, swallowing the nausea that clogged her throat. Several deep breaths restored her equilibrium and sheer willpower calmed her nerves. By the time she made it to the top of the stairway, her body was functioning as it should with the exception of a wicked headache. It pounded away in silent testimony to the upset to her system.

"Hello?" she called down.

"Miss Davis?" someone called back.

"Up here."

A tall, slender man came to stand at the foot of the stairs. It took no time at all for Savannah to see the resemblance between him and Jacob. The angle of his jaw, the black hair and the same blue eyes marked the two as brothers.

"Miss Davis? I'm Doug Quaide."

"I figured that out." Smiling, despite the throbbing in her head, she trailed an inquisitive stare along the lines of his neat gray suit. "You and Jacob favor each other."

"So I've been told." He returned her searching stare. "I hope I didn't scare you. I called out a few times."

"Oh, I'm sorry. I didn't hear you." Of course she hadn't. She had been spellbound by Nathan and Emily Jane. "I think these walls tend to ab . . . absorb sound."

"Did I interrupt your work?"

"No, I, uh, was finished up." She had been making real progress on the ballroom when Nathan had appeared. That had been the end of work for the day.

"How are things going?" Doug asked.

"Good." She gathered her attention. "The house is a marvel."

His mouth thinned in what looked like anger. His voice, however, reflected a quiet solemnity. "It is definitely one of a kind."

Savannah's tone became as hushed as Doug's, tamed by the regret he couldn't hide. "I've never encountered anything like it. I'd like to thank you for allowing me to work here. As I promised Jake, you won't regret your decision."

"I never thought I would." Sadness invaded his blue gaze. Savannah recognized it for what it was, but Doug didn't give her the opportunity to comment. He tipped his head back toward the front doorway. "If you hear voices for the next half-hour or so, don't get alarmed. The house is being appraised again today." He shoved his hands into his pants pockets. "At the buyer's request."

Savannah didn't imagine the sting underscoring the statement. And she didn't need a crystal ball to understand its causes. "I was sorry to hear about the sale of the land."

"Yes." Doug scanned the decaying foyer. "Well." He raised a squinting gaze to the remains of the ceiling. "It's done."

She felt his discomfort keenly. Coming down several steps, she said, "I'm sorry. I didn't mean to upset you. This has to be very difficult for you."

He met her gaze as squarely as Jake ever had. "It is." The parody of the smile he gave her spoke more clearly than words just how difficult this was for Doug. He turned with that smile and headed for the doorway.

"Mr. Quaide?" Savannah descended several more steps, unwilling . . . no unable to let him just walk away. Something inside her compelled her to go after him. "Doug?"

Hands still buried in his pockets, he turned back. "Yes?"

There was only one reason she had stopped him, only one question that burned in her mind. "Who were Nathan and Emily Jane?" She felt as if her life depended on knowing the answer. Compressing her lips, she waited for his reply.

"Nathan and Emily Jane?" With a smile of genuine pleasure, Doug shook his head. "Where did you hear about them?"

"Around."

Doug scoffed out a laugh. "Good old Nathan Quaide. He was one of my ancestors. He owned the plantation around the time of the Civil War." Doug's grin slanted to one side. "The plantation reached its full glory under Nathan. Not before or since has it been as magnificent. My grandmother used to say that was because Nathan loved his wife the way he did; the land had obviously reaped the benefits."

Savannah's heart swelled, and silently she agreed with Doug's grandmother. Nathan had loved Emily with a force that had transcended time. Emily's love for her husband had been no less. Savannah firmly believed that the combined strength of that love had made Oakwood Plantation a shining jewel along the York River. It had also bridged the dimensions of time and space to contact her.

And she had been contacted. Watching Doug leave, she was convinced of that as never before. This entire affair with Nathan and Emily wasn't a metaphysical fluke. She was being allowed to see their spirits for a reason. Whatever that was. She wasn't any closer to figuring that out now than she had been weeks ago.

In time, she told herself. In time she'd have her answers. That was a major consolation, but unfortunately it didn't do anything to dim her headache. By the time she let herself into Jake's house and found a bottle of aspirin, she was fervently hoping that Nathan and Emily would speed things up a bit. On good days it was tough enough to sustain the discomfort that accompanied each encounter. On a day such as this, where cramps were beginning to twist themselves through her lower abdomen, she didn't have any energy to spare on a supernaturally-induced malaise.

The sofa in Jake's den beckoned. She curled into its cushions and gave herself up to the sheer comfort of lying there in the peaceful hush of the house. Surprisingly, Ares joined her, plopping himself at the floor beside her. A little wryly, she glanced down at the dog. Apparently, he had decided to accept her. She could live with that.

In the companionable silence, she turned her thoughts back to the old bedroom. A pattern had begun to emerge. Her encounters were becoming increasingly more intense. The first glimpse she had had of Emily's time had been less than a few seconds; a quick view of curtains and glass in the window. The following time, transparent furniture had appeared. The time after that, Emily had shown up, then Nathan. Now their beings had begun to radiate a strangely euphoric energy.

The shimmering aura. At first, she had experienced a momentary fright. Once it had enveloped her, however, she had felt joy and contentment. Emily Jane's happiness had been hers.

She fell asleep with the residual bliss, and woke up to find it was still with her when Jake sat beside her. Drowsily, she thrust ghosts aside and smiled up at him.

If she lived forever, she would never get tired of looking at Jacob Quaide. Even minus his suit jacket, he appeared every inch the impressive businessman. His white dress shirt fit his shoulders like a caress, while the dark gray slacks emphasized the corded muscles of his legs.

"Hi," she murmured a little distractedly. In her mind, she couldn't decide whether she liked him better as he was now or as the rugged-cowboy-type. In his incredibly faded jeans, chambray shirt and scuffed boots he was sinfully delicious.

Either way, it came down to the basic fact that it was the soul of the man beneath the clothes that made her heart beat faster. It was rather nice that the soul and personality were so perfectly wrapped.

"You all right?" he asked. The length of his hard thigh pressing into her hip, he stretched an arm out along the back of the couch. "I've been making enough noise to wake the dead and you've been out of it."

She started at the old saying. "I had a headache and cramps. I was feeling pretty zonked."

His eyes widened with comprehension only to narrow with concern. "Can I get you anything?"

"No." She shook her head feeling like a dishonest crumb for deceiving him. He attributed her headache to the same cause as her cramps. "I took some aspirin earlier. I'm feeling better now."

"You sure?" He placed his hand low on her belly and rubbed lightly.

Seeing, feeling his hand in that exact spot made the muscles around her heart constrict. Nathan had placed his hand to Emily in the same manner. "I'm sure." Completely flustered, she pushed herself into a sitting position and changed the subject. "What time is it?"

"Going on four."

She slid her hand up his chest and toyed with the blue and gray stripes of his tie. "You're home early. I thought you were going to be late tonight."

"That was the plan."

There was a brusque undercurrent in the tone of his voice that pricked Savannah's attention. She studied the creases in his forehead, the sharpening of his gaze.

"Is something wrong?"

Jake scoffed and shot a glance out the corners of his eyes. "More of the same."

"The plantation?"

"Yeah." Shifting, he braced his elbows on his knees and let his hands hang loosely in between. "Doug called today."

His anguish was like a painful vibration that pulsed along her nerves. "I met him earlier."

He turned his head just enough to see her. "At the mansion?"

With a nod, she commented softly, "He introduced himself."

"Did he happen to tell you why he was there?"

"He said something about the buyer wanting to have the house reappraised." She waited for him to explain. When he didn't, she prompted, "What's going on?"

There, Jake thought, was the mother question of all times. For all of the complex emotions and finances involved, it boiled down to one extremely uncomplicated fact.

Steepling his hands, he raised them to his mouth. From

behind his fingers he said, "The buyer is thinking of tearing down the old house."

The statement slammed into Savannah. Her breath escaped her in a single whoosh. "What?" She searched Jake's face, hoping she hadn't heard right. "Why?"

"Why not?" he sneered back. "In another few weeks, the land won't be ours. The owner can do anything he damn well pleases."

"I know," she wailed softly. She knew that probably better than anyone else. Every time she set foot within those three-hundred-year-old walls, the forces that be reminded her that ownership of the building was a relative matter. "Why can't the new owner leave the house standing?"

"In its present condition, it's worthless. It's occupying a prime piece of real estate, and it's an insurance nightmare."

Savannah didn't give a damn about insurance. What was going to happen to Emily Jane and Nathan? She gazed at Jacob for reassurance.

He had none to give. He knew he couldn't prevent the destruction of the old house any more than he could buy Doug out.

With a swift move, he shoved to his feet and jammed his fists on to his hips. Under his breath, he issued a string of curses that should have blistered the paint on the ceiling. Little satisfaction was his, but the gesture took the cap off the boiling pot of his frustration.

"I'm going to go up and shower," he commented, needing some time and space for himself. He had accepted the fact that the land would be gone, but he had assumed the old house would continue to stand. *Because it always had.* Its destruction was the embodiment of the loss of the land.

"Is there anything I can do to help?" Savannah asked quietly, coming to her feet.

He didn't bother to lift his gaze from the carpet. "No."

"Jake?"

At the touch of her hand on his arm, he inhaled and

finally peered her way. "I don't need an encounter group, Savannah. I've tapped into my emotions, believe me."

"That's what I'm worried about. You're a walking raw nerve encased in a shell of male pride."

One of his black brows arched in silent challenge. "We've been through this before. I'm not going to cry and carry on."

"It wouldn't hurt."

"I'm not the sack-cloth type."

She looped her arms around his neck, the mahogany of her eyes filled with fierce concern. "You're definitely the strong silent type. You're also one of the most sensitive people I've ever met. It hurts me to know that you're hurting."

Her comment locked onto the target of his heart and hit dead center. He was hurting more than he had hurt about anything in his life, including the break up of his marriage to Catherine. Sure, he could stoically avoid thinking about the land, he could bottle up the red hot rage that threatened at times, but that didn't lessen the regret. Nothing compensated for the sense of loss.

"I'll be all right," he professed, drawing her close.

Savannah knew he was too strong to let this ruin his life. He would come to grips with this in time.

Time. For Jacob, it stretched out limitlessly. For her . . . and Nathan and Emily? Time had just run out.

Sixteen

"It's called retrocognition," Leanne said, her voice sounding a bit faded over the telephone wires.

"Retro-what?" Savannah asked. Adjusting the collar of her hunter-green wool jacket, she clamped her receiver between her shoulder and ear. She had been on her way out of the cottage when Leanne had called.

Leanne repeated her information. "Re-tro-cog-ni-tion. That's what's been going on in the old house."

"How do you know?"

"I went to the library and researched it, which is what you should have done weeks ago."

Savannah had to agree with that. Her only excuse was that she had been so consumed by the events—and by Jake—that she hadn't taken the time for snooping through books. "So what is this retrocognition?"

Leanne's smile could be heard all the way from Richmond. "I'm glad you asked. It's a rare kind of haunting where a person experiences events and environments of the past. You're not going back in time or anything. It's more like the energy is still hanging around and you're lucky enough to be a part of it."

Savannah didn't know if she would classify herself as lucky. Winning a cruise to Bermuda was lucky. Experiencing a "rare kind of haunting" leaned closer to nerve-racking.

"According to what I learned," Leanne went on, "there have been reported cases where people have gone through exactly what you're going through. It seems to occur most frequently in or around old buildings."

"Oakwood would qualify for that. But what about these people? Were they telepathic or psychic?"

"Nope. Everyone that I read about was your average 'Joe Shmoe'. But I *did* come across an interesting fact."

"What's that?"

"Several people claimed they talked to the ghosts, had outright conversations."

Savannah's hands stilled in the process of fastening the buttons on her jacket. "The spirits communicated?"

"That hasn't happened to you, has it?"

"No, thank God. I'm not sure I could handle that."

"That's what you said when you saw nothing but a room full of ghost furniture. Now you're up to two breathing, speaking ghosts, just like a pro. Speaking of which, I think you should find a paranormal psychologist."

"Why?"

"To help you, that's why. Jeez, Banana, how much longer can you deal with this on your own?"

"It's a pointless question," Savannah sighed, equal amounts of sadness and bitterness creeping into her voice. "First of all, I'm nearly finished with my work there. And secondly, the old house is going to be torn down."

"Oh, my God, when?" Leanne demanded to know.

"I'm not sure. The new owner is planning to build his new house pretty close to the site of the old mansion, so I'd say he isn't going to wait very long."

"What are you going to do?"

"Stick it out for as long as I can, learn as much as I can."

"And then what?"

Savannah shook her head in confusion. "What do you mean?"

"Are you ever going to tell Jake?"

"What would be the point? He can't accept the whole

idea of ghosts. And the house will be gone. I can only assume Nathan and Emily Jane will . . . will go back to where ever they came from."

"Will they be able to do that?"

"You're asking me?" Savannah shot back impatiently. The pressure of time as it related to the old house was worse than any publishing deadline she had ever had. "You're the one who's done the research."

"Not on the afterlife of the afterlife of a ghost! I mean, ghosts are already dead, they're already doing their own thing. Can they be evicted from one place to another?"

"I don't know."

"You need to find a professional."

"I don't have the time."

"Then I'll find one for you."

"Where? It's not like finding a dentist."

Leanne dropped her frenzy and announced with supreme dignity, "I'll start where I always start, in the Yellow Pages."

That touch of cool haughtiness diffused the rapid ascent of Savannah's temper. She kneaded her forehead and reached deep for her reserve of patience. "All right, Lee, do what you want. See if you can find someone reputable."

"Of course. In the meantime, what are you going to do?"

Savannah rolled her eyes and considered her sanity. "I'm going to go see if I can talk to a couple of ghosts."

Who in the hell is she talking to? Jacob listened to Savannah's voice echo faintly off the moldy, stained walls. In the chilled musty air, the sweet tones seemed out of place.

He started up the decomposing stairwell, more aware than he cared to be that he wouldn't have this option for too much longer. His fingers trailed up the rotted banister, stroking the wood as if the tactile link would preserve his memories. Those were all that would remain of a family's legacy. Those and Savannah's photos.

Her voice came to him again. His black brows flicked upward. So, she talked to herself while she worked. It wasn't a habit he would have associated with her. He had her pegged—finally—as the intense type, prone to silences *before* she exploded with all that intensity.

He had to grin when he thought of how passionately alive she was. She was a strong-willed woman with strong ideas, and yet capable of an honest compassion that was intrinsic to her nature. That he was the recipient of such generosity of nature stirred him down to his most gut level.

No one had ever cared about him in quite the way that Savannah did. His parents had loved him, of that he had no doubt, but it had been an affection based on familial bond, not necessarily one inspired by absorbing emotion. And Catherine . . . hell, she hadn't cared about anyone other than herself. As for his friends and acquaintances, they were just what the terms implied, nothing more, nothing less.

With Savannah however, his emotional being was as important to her as his physical. The latter was heaven on earth, but the former was hard to take at times. He wasn't used to having his feelings pushed and prodded to the extent that she shoved them, especially in regard to the sale of the land.

Time and time again she had made his anger hers and tamed it, held his grief within her heart and calmed it, taken his overwhelming frustration and tempered it. She'd done it all with a loving spirit and unwavering support.

Both were as rare as Savannah was herself. She was as much woman as any man could handle, all that he envisioned himself handling for the rest of his life.

And *she* thought he was the best thing to have ever happened to her.

Well, he had a news-flash for her. She was everything he had ever wanted in a woman.

He made his way down the hall to the master bedroom,

infused with the kind of energy that made him want to snatch her up, fling her over his shoulder and carry her off. It wasn't a bad idea.

"Savannah?" he called out, entering the bedroom. "Where are you, woman?" He found her even as he spoke, standing wedged into the far corner, eyes wide and unfocused, her skin a ghastly white.

He was across the room instantly, grabbing her up by the arms. "Savannah, what is it?" He stared into her unseeing eyes, his heart pumping painfully. She was completely out of it. Her pupils were dilated, her breathing shallow, her skin icy.

"Shit." He gave her a shake, watching for signs of recovery. Her eyelids flickered. "Come on, babe," he coaxed, "that's it. Come back to me."

She blinked, swallowed, blinked again. A frown stretched slowly across her forehead as her gaze gradually cleared. With a start, she sucked in a breath and finally focused on him.

"Jake?" Her voice was a raspy whisper.

Black brows pulled into a severe scowl, he continued to study her eyes. "What happened? Are you all right?"

Savannah truly had to think about that. She had been standing there watching Emily Jane change from her workdress to a dinner gown. Nathan had been giving his wife his usual wolfish leers when . . .

She gasped and gazed straight back at Jake. "Oh, God."

"What is it?"

Shock ricocheted around inside her as she realized precisely what had occurred. Jake had walked into the scene with Emily and Nathan. At first, he had been little more than a shadowy movement. Then he had materialized right in front of her. For a brief instant, she had seen all three together. He was still there . . . and Emily and Nathan were gone.

"Did you see them?" she blurted out, her fingers digging convulsively at his forearms.

"Who?"

"Emily and Nathan." She choked and stuttered, unable to stem the crazy sensation that they had all just stepped over some invisible line. Suddenly, it didn't matter any longer that Jake believed the spirit world was a farce. He had just become part of the whole phantasmal realm. "Did . . . did you see them? They were right here, you walked right past them."

"Take it easy, babe."

"No . . . no . . ." She ground her teeth together, shaking her head in denial and excitement and confusion. "You don't understand."

"That's because you're not making any sense."

"But I am," she cried.

"Savannah, there's no one here but us."

"Emily and Nathan were in this room." She gestured wildly toward the fireplace. "She was there, and Nathan was lounging on the bed . . . you walked right between them."

Jake tried his best to weave his way through the maze of her assertions, but two names blocked his progress. "Nathan Quaide? Emily Jane, his wife?"

Savannah nodded emphatically. "Yes. I can't believe you didn't see them."

He bent low again and squinted into her eyes. "There was no one here but us."

"Oh, Jake, there was." But she couldn't convince him. He hadn't seen them.

Swallowing hard, she pressed the heels of her hands into her temples. This was worse than a nightmare. Ghosts appearing, Jake emerging into the same plane. Neither had been aware of the other's presence. And she was caught in the middle like it was some kind of paranormal joke, only no one was laughing, least of all Jake. He glared at her as if it were time to measure her for a straight jacket.

"Come on." He wrapped steely fingers around her upper arm, giving her no room for argument.

She nodded, not trusting her brain to convey the right signals to her throat and mouth. Adrenaline was having a field day with her body. All she could do was traipse silently along beside Jake, instinctively aware that it was finally time for the whole truth. Jake was going to demand it.

She stumbled at the thought.

"Shit," he muttered darkly, steadying her with his hands as well as his body. Despite the harshness of his tone, he handled her with extraordinary care. "Can you walk?"

"Yes." She kept her gaze fastened to a spot in the center of his wide chest. To raise her eyes from the heavy black knit of his sweater would have risked too much. Waves of anger emanated from Jake in hot pulses that she was too vulnerable to handle right then.

The walk back to his house was completed in a silence she used to steady her nerves. Jake retained his hold on her wrist for the entire distance; not, Savannah knew, because he was afraid she would run off or refuse to accompany him. Jake wasn't afraid of anything, least of all besting her physically. No, she was convinced he kept her manually chained to his side as a means of coping with his rage. A rage, she decided as they entered his study, to which he wasn't entitled.

Strength was returning quickly to her body and her mind, bringing with it a resurgence of her normal defenses. Why, she asked herself, was he angry with her? She could understand and accept—had even anticipated—him being critical and confused, but she didn't see any cause for his ire.

Sinking down into one of the chairs opposite the sofa, she rubbed at her wrist, all the while keeping a steady eye on Jake. He moved away to the dry sink and poured her a small shot of bourbon.

"Drink," he ordered, his tone clipped, anger contained momentarily.

One of her curved brows arched delicately at the command. She eyed the glass, eyed Jake just as pointedly and cautioned herself to choose her battles with care. She accepted the glass and took a small swallow of the smokey liquor. That was as much of a concession as she could muster.

Setting the glass aside, she gazed steadily up into his face as he towered over her, his stance a menacing display of raw, male power. "Why are you angry?"

"Why?" His exhale sounded more like a hiss. "You scared the shit out of me back there."

"I'm sorry."

"You had better be. I want to know what the hell is going on."

"How much of the truth do you want to hear?"

His features contorted with a snarl.

She nibbled on the inside of her cheek, glancing away briefly. "I tried to tell you before."

"Tell me what?"

Calmly, evenly, knowing all along that it would come to this, she said, "The spirits of Nathan and Emily Quaide are in the old house."

For a full three seconds, he stared down at her, disbelief and amazement flashing freely with his anger. Then he whirled away, shoving a hand back through his hair. "Jesus."

"I'm not lying."

"I don't believe this," he muttered.

"I'm telling you the truth. I know it's hard to believe; I had a hard time with it at first, too."

Her words jerked him around again. His jaw flexed and clenched. "A hard time with what? Imagining yourself surrounded by my dead ancestors?"

"Exactly."

He threw his hands up in a disgusted gesture. "Give me a break."

"You give me one," she shot right back. "Don't you think I've struggled with this? My life hasn't been normal since I first set foot inside that old building. How do you think I felt the first time I saw furniture and people appearing out of nowhere?"

"Will you *listen* to yourself?"

"I don't have to. I've talked myself silly over this."

"You've got that part straight."

She came to her feet, secure in what she knew to be real. "I'm not crazy, Jake. I've had time to sort through all of it."

"Just how much time are we talking about? When did all of these supposed 'visits' from the other side begin?"

"I told you, the first time I walked into the house. Things, people, didn't start appearing until about a week later, but the conditions were there from the start. That's why my watch stopped. That's why I passed out. It's been the same ever since."

"You've passed out again?" He bit the words out harshly.

"I came close once or twice. It's never been as bad as that first time. In fact, the physical discomfort gets easier to bear with every encounter."

" 'Encounter'?" he repeated slowly, softly, the low invective sounding dangerous. "Is that what you call these little visits from Casper?"

"There's no need for you to get snide. After all, you were the one who said it was perfectly all right for us to disagree about this. We're disagreeing now. I'd wish you'd accept that."

"There's a whole hell of a lot of difference between accepting a theory and blindly swallowing this crap you're shoving on me."

"It's not crap. The spirits are real."

"Quick, let me call Ghost Busters."

His contempt was all she had thought it would be. It pricked her temper big time, but she clung to her composure, wanting him to accept, and if not, to at least give her the benefit of the doubt and try to understand.

"You wanted an explanation, I gave it to you."

"I wanted a rational cause."

"And I told you what's going on. You don't have to believe, but leave me the right to do so."

"Believe in what?" He jabbed a finger at her. "A bunch of nonsense?"

"Actually what's been happening is called retrocognition. It's a kind of haunting."

Hooking his thumbs into the belt loops of his jeans, he sneered, "What's the matter, Savannah, don't you have any living friends to play with? You have to hang loose with a bunch of ghosts?"

Her temper slipped several notches. "This is exactly why I didn't tell you what was happening. You refuse to acknowledge that something other than the accepted logic is possible."

"The key word here is logic."

"That's what I'm trying to tell you, Jake. To hell with logic. I had to throw it away the first time I came face to face with Emily Jane."

"I bet that was a real Kodak moment."

"Damn right it was. I had already tried to expose half a roll of film, and do you know what I found? Nothing. Not a damn thing. Just black empty film where there should have been light and form. I was so frightened, I didn't stop shaking until the next morning."

"So you don't have any proof of all this?"

"I don't need any proof because I've lived through it. I know it's real. Aside from that, I'm not trying to convince anyone, least of all you. In fact, this doesn't even concern you."

"The hell it doesn't," he yelled, the veins and tendons in his neck straining. "For weeks I've assumed you were in there working. Now I find out you've supposedly been communicating with the dead."

There was only so much Savannah was willing to tolerate. He was being unreasonable, unwilling to meet her at all on this. Gritting her teeth, she ordered, "Don't even think about accusing me of lying."

"I don't have to. You've practically admitted it yourself. You said your camera was useless, your film black."

"Only when things change, when the spirits are present. The rest of the time my cameras aren't affected."

Doing nothing to hide the fact that he didn't believe a word she said, he gave a grating laugh and swung away for the dry sink and the bottle of bourbon. She watched as he poured himself a stiff drink, and then another.

"What a pisser this is," he muttered down at his half-empty glass.

"It doesn't have to be."

He swung back in full fury, his gaze impaling her to the floor. "The hell it doesn't." Cold, violent accusation contorted his features. "What do you take me for, an idiot?"

Savannah stepped back, an instinctive move to protect herself from his buffeting anger. She'd never seen him in such a rage. She'd never seen his eyes so coldly seething. Swallowing, she asked, "What are you talking about?"

"For weeks, you've been trespassing on ground I cherish for God only knows what kind of warped, sordid motives. You played me like a fool, little girl, and I fell for it."

"I didn't play at anything."

He went on as if she hadn't said a word, eyes glaring, mouth thinned. "What I can't figure out is why. What did you think you could gain with this tripe about ghosts? Money? From whom, for what? Publicity? It that was this is all about?"

She rejected his brutal words with tiny negative shakes of her head. "You're so wrong."

"Tell me, did you concoct this scheme before or after the first time you went to bed with me?"

Desperately, Savannah tried to understand his meaning. "What scheme—"

"Or was getting laid just a little icing on the cake? I had already agreed to help you so you decided to get a little screwing in on the side. Is that how it went?"

His accusations stabbed at her heart. Disbelief rose up inside of her as hotly, as intensely as anger. "How dare you!" she cried. "How dare you call me a liar! How dare you accuse me of using you!"

He raised his glass in a jeering toast. "What's the matter, Savannah, does the truth hurt?"

"You wouldn't know the truth if it came up and bit you on the ass." Hands clenched at her sides, her entire body shook with rage and a searing pain of the heart. The last few weeks flashed through her consciousness, betraying her for a naive, trusting fool.

How could she have been so wrong about him? About them? How could he turn on her like this? The trust she thought they shared was a delusion. That hurt worse than anything she had ever experienced.

"You want the truth, Q Man?" she whispered, hanging onto her control by a shred. "You got it. You haven't gotten over your paranoia about people exploiting the plantation. Your whole outlook is still warped to the point that you think I'd make up stories about spirits and hauntings. You're still so damned suspicious of anyone who isn't a Quaide that you're willing to think the worst about me, that I'd try to use you and the plantation for my own purposes."

She flung out a hand in a gesture as tempestuous as the seething heat in her eyes. "How could you believe I would do something like that?"

"Give me one goddamned reason why I shouldn't," he fumed back at her.

"Because I thought we trusted each other. I thought we had come to mean something to each other. Oh, you talked a good game about the land being only a part of your life; that the lessons learned at your father's knees hadn't distorted your views. But the second you assume the land is being threatened, you kiss all of those grand sounding declarations goodbye. Where's the trust in that, Jake? Where's all the balance between your history and your future you claimed to have?"

Horribly, the emotional strength needed to maintain her anger evaporated, leaving her feeling numb and drained and hollowed from inside out.

The shattering of her soul dulling her eyes, her voice choked to nearly nothing, she said, "If you trusted me, you wouldn't jump to conclusions. At the very least, you'd have listened to me without being judgmental."

He didn't say anything to that. There truly wasn't any need. His expression was eloquent enough.

There would be no reasoning with him, about either a place for her in his life or about Emily and Nathan. His devotion to the past had warped his commitment to the present.

Wrapping her arms around her middle to stem the awful nausea that seized her, she made her way to the doorway. There she turned and looked at him one last time. "Apparently I was wrong to think that I could ever be as important to you as this land."

She turned, blinked back the tears before they could fall and hurried from the house, feeling as if she had somehow betrayed Nathan and Emily Jane.

Worse, she felt as if she had betrayed herself.

Seventeen

"You can go in, Mr. Quaide. Your brother is expecting you."

Jacob acknowledged his brother's secretary with a cool smile that reflected his bend of mind. At the moment, he would just as soon have been anywhere other than at Doug's office. Nonetheless, he made his way to the wide walnut stained door just beyond the secretary's desk and stepped into his brother's inner sanctum.

Doug looked up from the stack of papers before him, a half-grin creasing his face. "I was wondering when you were going to get here. Get hung up in traffic?"

Jake didn't feel like explaining why he was almost forty minutes late, any more than he felt like being there in the first place. "I only wish."

"Uh, oh." Doug leaned back in his chair and hooked his hands behind his head. "Trouble in the 'information collection' world?"

There was trouble, Jake knew, but it was with his personal life, not his professional. Four days had passed since he'd had it out with Savannah. Four screwed up, frustrating, maddening days in which he had recounted every minute of the scene in his study, from the moment he'd asked her to explain, to the second she'd walked out of his house. He hadn't seen her since.

"No, everything is fine," he insisted. "I had a meeting

with the higher echelon of the Port Authority. One of the members is a windbag."

Doug grimaced. "I know the type. But I'm glad you could make it. When you called and said you'd be in town, I cleared my schedule for a few hours." He checked his watch. "I've still got close to an hour if you're game for lunch."

"Sure." Why not? Eating was one of those things he could do on automatic pilot. It didn't require a great deal of brain power. And Doug's company would keep him from slipping into the more obsidian regions of his mind. For the short while it would take them to walk the two blocks to Norfolk's Waterside, to settle into one of the complex's quaint restaurants with a view of the Elizabeth River and order lunch, Jake could be relatively assured that he wouldn't have to think about Savannah.

"Got an interesting call a few days ago," Doug said as soon as their waitress took their order.

Jake heard the overstated nonchalance in the statement and cocked his head to one side. "From whom?"

"Savannah Davis."

Everything in Jake slammed to an instant halt, then resumed working again far too quickly. "What did she want?" Despite his best efforts, he couldn't keep the scorn from his voice.

Doug tugged at one of his ear lobes. "Damnedest thing. She wanted to let me know that her work is going well, but that she wouldn't be needing access to your drive any longer. She's going to hike in, it seems."

Jake took a moment to digest that. When she had walked out, he'd assumed by her absence that she hadn't returned to the old house as well. It galled him to realize that he had been wrong on this count, too, just as he'd been wrong about so many other things about her.

"Why the hell did she bother to call you?"

"She thought it would be best. She had already notified

the sheriff's department to let them know she would be parking her car on that deserted stretch of Phibbs Lane, that borders the property. She wanted me to know in case I or someone else spotted her car parked there and thought it strange." He leaned forward and added a little too innocently, "I'm surprised she didn't tell you."

Jake seared the artlessly taunting gaze with one of feral intensity, studiously blocking out an all too clear mental image of Savannah, alone; miles from the nearest phone. "Why should she have told me?"

"Hell, Jake. You spent Thanksgiving with her. I'd have thought that put the two of you well past the speaking stage."

"That's what you get for thinking."

To Jake's disgust, Doug levered back from the table and teased, "Lover's quarrel?"

Jake bit back a curse. He wasn't going to sit there and flesh out the details, gory or otherwise, for his brother. "Back off, Doug."

The warning struck Doug with obvious impact. He sobered instantly, lifting both hands in a sign of surrender. "Whew, didn't mean to step into it, man. I didn't know things between the two of you had gotten that intense."

"Extreme is more apt."

"Damn. Need to talk?"

What could he say? The woman who knew how important my heritage is to me, the woman who convinced me her motives were decent and reputable, the woman I thought was special has been jerking me around?

He skirted the truth. "We had a thing going."

"Had? As in the past tense?"

"Yeah."

That one, chewed off word gave Doug pause. "I'm sorry, Jake. If I had known it was that bad, I wouldn't have mentioned any of this. I got the impression that the situation between the two of you was *certa res.*"

"Nothing in this life is a sure thing." Least of all his relationship with Savannah.

He had spent more than enough time in the last few days ripping the guts out of that issue. He didn't want to get into it again, and yet, that was what he found himself doing when Doug made a trip to the men's room.

Damn her. Did she take him for an idiot? This whole business about ghosts and spirits was asinine, especially so for a woman as smart and clever as Savannah. What he couldn't figure out was why she thought she could pull this over on him. She had to have known that he wouldn't bite, and yet she had stood right there and brazened it out, chin up, gaze direct.

His brow furrowed. She hadn't been the intrepid Savannah Davis when he had found her in the old bedroom. For the umpteenth time, he had to consider her physical condition at that time. She hadn't been faking anything then or when she had fainted into his arms weeks earlier. Both made him wonder if she was ill.

In rapid succession, he mentally ticked off every symptom she had experienced over the course of the last month and a half. Maybe Savannah had been having seizures without knowing it, and this bit about Oakwood being haunted was a resulting hallucination. It wasn't unusual to emerge from unconsciousness disoriented.

As explanations went, it was plausible, but he didn't believe it. Experience had taught him that people would go to great lengths to get whatever they could out of Oakwood. Usually, he was good at spotting a potential user a mile off. With Savannah, he had let his guard down and she had slipped right past his defenses. Worse, he had allowed himself to get emotionally involved with her.

The sense of betrayal was twofold and abhorrent.

"She must have really pissed you off," Doug observed as he took his seat.

"She's something else."

"She would have to be, in order to get this kind of rise out of you." Placing his napkin over his lap, Doug requested, "Do me a favor, will you? Quit thinking about her. I'm the one who has to look across the table at you. Either that or tell me the whole story, so I at least know why you look like you're ready to fly into a war zone."

Jake liked the suggestion of forgetting Savannah. He set his mind to that. "How are the kids?"

Doug gave him a dubious looking frown, then amiably followed his brother's lead to change the subject. "Growing. They're getting to the ages where Iris has become their chauffeur. Soccer games, piano lessons, Brownies. It's a real madhouse some days." He paused when the waitress arrived with their salads. With her departure, Jake resumed the conversation.

"How are things otherwise?"

Doug needed no interpretation of the query. "Better than I expected. Our budget is going to be tight for a while, we won't be vacationing in . . . actually, vacations are out. But we didn't lose the house, and my practice is solvent. We have an income, a better-than-nice place to live, and our health. That's all I can ask for."

Jake studied his brother's expression and saw acquiescence as well as acceptance. "I'm glad it worked out for you."

Doug's gaze quickly lifted from his plate. Around his mouth, lines of embarrassment formed. "I was worried you wouldn't feel that way."

"Why?"

"You weren't expecting me to screw up things as badly as I did."

"It wasn't intentional."

"But it was avoidable. That's made it tough because I know how much the plantation has always meant to you."

"And you."

Doug denied that with a slow shake of his head. "Not in the same way, Jake. For you it was a sacred quest to carry on tradition. For me it was a responsibility complete with burdens."

Jake lowered his fork, surprised and a bit disbelieving. "When did you start feeling this way?"

"Consciously?" Doug shrugged with his brows. "For the past ten years or so, but I think it's gone back to my days in law school."

"You never said anything," Jacob reasoned, unsettled by Doug's revelation.

"How could I? Oakwood's our birthright and no one ever let us forget it. If Grandfather wasn't there recalling the glory days, then it was Father going on about how he expected us to preserve the land for the future. We sucked it all up."

"You didn't seem to mind."

"I didn't." Doug leaned back, his sight patently turning inward. "Hell, we were the Quaides of Oakwood, Southern gentility at its best. Believe me, that got me into more than one back seat of a car with my date when I was in high school." His vision cleared to return to Jake. "But even then, you felt a whole hell of a lot stronger about the place than I did. I used to get blown away at how you would hang onto Grandfather's every word."

Jake could remember doing just that. Humid, hazy days seated in the shade of a towering elm; their grandfather had recounted tales that had obviously been embroidered with a grandeur and splendor that simply didn't exist any longer. To an impressionable child, those stories had been bigger than life.

"I'll tell you something." Doug laid his fork aside and braced his forearms on the table. "Now that it's almost over, I can honestly say it's a relief."

Something inside Jake stilled. The impulse to refute surged hotly. "You're glad you sold the land?"

"For obvious reasons aside, yes. I didn't realize until just recently how much emotional baggage the plantation has been all these years."

"Baggage?" Jake repeated, his black brows angling severely.

"And then some." Lacing his fingers together, Doug studied his palms. When he spoke again, his voice was low, steadfast and tinged with a certain sadness. "For years I've laid a guilt trip on myself because I didn't feel the bond the way you did, the way Mother and Father expected. All this time, I've assumed that my personality was fundamentally lacking. After all, every other Quaide that lived had supposedly been devoted to the land. What was lacking in me that I couldn't feel the same way?"

His mouth curled with a smile of obvious resignation. "It wasn't until last week that I finally, *finally* realized that there isn't a damn thing wrong with me. I love my wife and my family. I'm committed to my practice. I'm a loyal American. It's *all right* for me to be devoted to someone and something other than the Quaide legacy."

In the silence that followed, Jake mentally combatted the sensation that he had just stepped into a Salvador Dali painting. To say that Doug had surprised him would have been an understatement of grand and surrealistic proportions.

Jake worked his jaw in prolonged silence. He didn't like being taken by surprise. "I don't know what to say," he professed, his unease adding a congested quality to his voice. "I took it for granted that . . ." Hell, he had assumed that he and Doug shared the same attitudes. It was like a kick in the pants to unexpectedly realize that for years he had been wrong in a basic belief.

"Are you angry with me?" Doug asked.

Jake studied his brother as he waited for his emotions to sort themselves out. Neither anger nor resentment were present in the unsettling mixture of things he was feeling.

"No, I'm not angry. Amazed . . . but not angry."

"Yeah, I can see why you'd be surprised. I'm still rather stunned myself."

"What made you come to this realization?"

"Not what, who." Doug offered up a droll grin. "Having to tell you about selling the land was one of the hardest tasks I'd ever faced. For weeks I stewed and chafed until somewhere along the line, it hit me that I wasn't stressing about the land so much as I was about how you were going to react; how this was going to impact you. When I accepted that, I accepted the truth." Leaning back in his chair, he shoved his hands deep into his pants pockets and added, "And some of it isn't pretty."

Jake didn't like the sound of that and it showed.

"Don't you see, man?" Doug scoffed, any trace of humor wiped clean away. "Mother and Father had no right to lay this crap on us. We were kids, for Christ's sake. This is the twentieth century. We had other options, other opportunities and yet they perpetuated that so-called time-honored practice of indoctrinating the next generation in responsibility and dedication to a piece of real estate."

"You can't blame them for that, Doug."

"Like hell I can't."

"They were products of their times." In his mind, Jake heard the same grating words echo from nearly the exact discussion he'd had with Savannah. "The responsibility inherent to Oakwood was part of Father's life."

"That didn't mean I wanted it to be part of mine." Doug lifted a placating hand. "Okay, I can swallow the facts, I understand how things were, but we were never given the choice. No one ever asked either of us what we thought or how we felt. It was presumed, understood and expected that we would carry on like every other little Quaide that came before us."

"There's something to be said for that kind of tradition," Jake countered.

"I'm not saying there isn't. If it works for you, and it obviously does, then more power to you, Jake. I mean it, I'll be the first to pat you on the back and genuinely sing your praises." Sighing heavily, Doug tossed his napkin onto the table. "But it doesn't work for me. It never has, it never will. I only wish I had realized this sooner. I could have spared myself a whole hell of a lot of mental anguish."

In a gesture identical to Doug's, Jake threw his own napkin onto the table. But where Doug's move had been rife with finality, Jake's was teemed with pent up frustration.

For some damned reason, Jake felt singled out. Alone. "Shit." As far as Jake was concerned, that summed it all up.

"I suppose you think I'm a disloyal bastard of a son," Doug asserted.

Jake flicked a sharp indigo gaze across the table. It would have been easy to have agreed with Doug. In all honesty and fairness, he couldn't. "You're entitled to feel any way you want."

Another prolonged silence stretched between them. Finally, Doug mused aloud, "Didn't mean to ruin the meal, man. I was going to tell you eventually. Now seemed to be as good a time as any."

If there was one thing Jake admired above all else it was honesty. He wouldn't fault Doug for being honest, even if it had been hard to take. "You couldn't go on living a lie."

A full smile stretched over Doug's features. "If only Mother and Father had been as open-minded. But then, that's you, Jake, tolerant and impartial. You may not always agree with someone, but you've always been honest enough to give him the fair shake."

The words skittered along Jake's nerves, jerking to mind Savannah's face just before she had left him standing in his study. Her expression had been wounded, devastated, brave. Then she had corralled it all behind a blank facade and walked away; leaving him alone with his supposed impartiality and tolerance.

Right now, both felt hollow.

Eighteen

I'll be damned if I'll cry another tear.

Savannah made her silent declaration as she emerged
from her darkroom. Contact sheets in one hand, her habitual
cup of tea in the other, she determinedly resolved that her
heart was going to have to toughen up. Nothing would be
gained by crying, or ranting at the walls or tossing sleep-
lessly through the night.

She had made a big mistake with Jacob. Now, she had
to pay the price. If her heart suffered along the way, then
that was the way it had to be.

Her heart; poor, pathetic little thing. After all these years
of being wrapped away, it didn't have any real armor. It
was as fragile and as vulnerable as it had ever been. More
so because this time she had let herself love. Dear God,
how she loved him. Deeply, ardently, so completely that she
ached inside. Her heart had never stood a chance.

Folding herself sideways into the chair in the corner of
the living room, she gazed through the window, studying
the street below instead of the sheets of miniature photos
in her lap. An unusually early snow had powdered the
ground with a layer of white. The temperatures were chilled
enough to insure the snow lingered.

Savannah felt some of that chill inside her. She wrapped
her arms around her torso and rested her cheek against the
back of the chair. Despite her avowals to the contrary, tears
rose up and glistened her eyes.

God, what a fool she had been. Forsaking her normal caution, she had left herself open to being hurt. And she couldn't find any solace in knowing that she hadn't told Jake that she loved him. She had bared herself to him in so many other ways that she already felt stripped down to her soul.

In the region of her heart, she shriveled a little more. For that, she had no defense. She tried to reason that time would help—good old time, the great healer—but that rationale stung. She didn't want to wait to feel whole again and if she thought talking to Jake would help, she would have been at his front door days ago.

Therein lay the source of yet another hurt. Not only had he thought the worst of her, but there was also no approaching him. When it came to Oakwood, he was unrealistic. Forget the possibility that spirits might exist, Jake had automatically assumed she was scheming and conniving. Where were his declarations of commitment now?

You've got me in your life and whether you like it or not, you're dead center in mine.

If this is how he treated the woman who was "dead center" in his life, than Heaven help any woman who was unfortunate enough to exist in its periphery.

She jumped at the sound of the downstairs buzzer. For an instant, she froze inside, thinking that it might be Jake. Crossing to the door, she thrust the part-fear, part-hope aside.

"Who is it?" she asked into the speaker by the front door.

"Who were you expecting?" Leanne returned.

Savannah winced. She had forgotten that they were supposed to look for a birthday present for their mother today. They had discussed it on Thanksgiving and settled on this particular Thursday.

Even as Savannah buzzed her sister up, she glanced down at herself. Her jeans and sweatshirt were presentable, but her hair was clipped to the top of her head, and her face lacked all and any makeup. She wasn't nearly ready to hunt for a birthday present. More to the point, her heart wasn't in it.

"I thought you'd be ready," Leanne accused lightly the second she walked in.

"I'm sorry, Lee, I completely forgot about today. I got busy in the darkroom and, well, you know how I get."

"Don't worry about it. Brush on a little blush and you'll look fine." Leanne scrunched up her nose. "On second thought, you might want to do something about the smudges under your eyes. The tired look is definitely not in this season."

Savannah headed for the living room, throwing Leanne a pointed stare over her shoulder. "Is this your way of telling me that I look like hell?"

"Of course not. Worn out is a better word." Leanne tossed her purse and jacket onto the sofa before planting her hands on her hips and giving Savannah a blatant, scrutinizing once-over. "Have you been feeling sick?"

"No." Savannah moved away to gather her contact sheets from the chair in the corner.

"Things at the old house are getting to you, aren't they?"

"No."

"Are you sure?"

The insistent prying depleted the meager reserve of Savannah's poise. "Don't you think I'd know?" she snapped.

Leanne blinked, her amazement as apparent as her concern. "What's the matter with you?"

Savannah scrubbed at her forehead. "Nothing."

"Don't give me that."

"Don't nag."

"I'm not nagging. I asked a simple question, I think I deserve a simple answer."

Savannah dropped her hand to her side, resigned to her

fate. Leanne would badger until she got what she wanted, in this case, the truth.

Heaving a sigh, Savannah lowered herself onto the sofa, uncertain if she was ready to discuss this. Up until now, she had kept her silence hugged close as if it were a barrier.

"Jake and I have had a . . . parting of the ways."

"Ooohhh, nnnooo," Leanne wailed instantly, joining Savannah on the couch. "Why? What happened?"

"Take an educated guess."

"The ghosts?"

"Exactly."

"I thought you weren't going to tell him."

"I wasn't going to, but he found me in the middle of watching Emily and Nathan. He wanted to know why I was 'checked out' so I told him."

"Uh, oh. Did he believe you?"

"What do you think?"

"I think he was pretty skeptical."

Savannah rubbed at the nape of her neck. "You're being too kind. He was furious."

"Why would he be angry with you?" Leanne asked indignantly.

Try as she may, Savannah couldn't keep the tears at bay. Her fingers slid from her neck to her lips. "Because," she whispered, "he thought I was making the whole thing up. You wouldn't believe the things he accused me of."

"Like what?"

"Sleeping with him for no good reason, using sex so I could sway his thinking . . . I don't know. He thinks I was planning to use my claims of ghosts for my own benefit."

"How could that benefit you?"

"I'm not sure. A publicity stunt, maybe, interesting cover copy. Who knows!" She could see Leanne's insulted wonder. "Amazing, isn't it?"

Leanne shook her head from side to side. "I cannot believe this. Why on earth would he think such a thing?"

"I've told you how he is when it comes to that place. He's extremely defensive."

"Yeah, but this is ridiculous. You aren't just anybody. You're supposedly special. He should have known you wouldn't do anything so selfish. Didn't he trust you at all?"

"Apparently not."

"What did you do?"

"What could I do? I walked out."

"Did you try to reason with him?"

"I tried to explain about Nathan and Emily, but he was so convinced of the impossibility of a haunting that he wouldn't listen to anything else I had to say.

All the hurt she had been trying so hard to control surged up inside. She came to her feet and crossed to stand at the window in the corner. "I knew he would never accept the idea about there being spirits." Her voice emerged as a tragic murmur. "But I never thought he'd turn on me. I never thought it would destroy what we had." She lowered her head. "Stupid, stupid me."

"Oh, Banana," Leanne consoled, slipping her arm around her shoulder. "You can't blame yourself."

"Yes, I can. I should have never gotten involved with the man."

"It hasn't been all bad. Ya'll were doing fine until this mess happened."

"If we had been doing fine, Lee, I wouldn't be here crying on your shoulder. Jake would have trusted me, even if he didn't believe in Nathan and Emily."

"Is there anything you can do?"

"Like what?"

"I don't know, talk to him."

Savannah's head jerked around, her gaze lighting with a spark of ire. "Why should I? The man accused me of scheming behind his back, of knowingly exploiting the thing he loves best in life. Would *you* waste your breath on someone who preached trust out of one side of his mouth and condemned you for deception out of the other?"

Leanne gave another of her purging sighs. "No, I wouldn't, but this is the pits. I thought ya'll were so perfect for each other."

"You wanted us to be perfect for each other." More importantly, Savannah had wanted that, too. Worse, she had begun to believe it. In the dark hours of the night, Jake's arms holding her to his body, his heat warming her mind and senses, she had never felt more perfect about anything in her whole life.

"I'm so sorry about this, Savannah."

She shrugged with one shoulder. "Thanks."

"You can't go into a nosedive about this."

"I don't intend to. At least I have my work."

"How's that going?"

Savannah actually managed a smile. With it came a small dose of enthusiasm. She gathered up her contact sheets and flipped though them. "I've done some of my best work at Oakwood. The pictures I choose from that group will epitomize everything I was looking for when I began this book." Carefully, she placed the pages on the coffee table, her gaze filling with a wistfulness. "I'll be sorry to leave it behind."

"And Nathan and Emily Jane?"

"I'll be sorry to leave them, too."

"I'm still looking for a paranormal psychologist who'd be willing to advise or maybe even help out."

"Don't look too hard, Lee. It isn't necessary."

"A matter of opinion, I'd say. You need help."

"No, I don't."

Clamping her hands behind her back, Leanne made a great show of pretended nonchalance. "I wouldn't mind going along for moral support, you know, making observations when you have one of those encounters."

Savannah knelt to fold up the newspaper she'd left on

the floor that morning. "You can wish all you like, but it won't happen."

"Why not, Banana? I promise to stay out of your way."

"I'm sure you would, but that isn't why you can't come with me. I think people interfere with whatever forces are needed for Emily and Nathan to appear."

"How do you know?"

"Because Jake's brother came into the house last week and the force shut down at once."

"So?"

"So the encounters don't end that way. They usually fade away gradually."

Leanne accepted that at first, but the more she obviously thought about it, the deeper her frown became. "Wait a minute. You said Jake found you while you were in the middle of an encounter. Did the force turn off then?"

Savannah rose with the paper, and with the conflict of unanswered questions tugging at her serenity. "No, it didn't. But I've felt from the start that he's very much involved with this haunting."

"You mean the ghosts are trying to tell him something?"

"Possibly. There's no reason for them to contact me."

Leanne lowered herself to the sofa, exhaling through pursed lips. "Wow. Maybe there's a treasure hidden somewhere in those old walls."

"You've been watching too much late-night TV, Leanne."

"No, I haven't. And how do you know I'm not right? Maybe Nathan and Emily have come back just in the nick of time to save the plantation." Leanne warmed to her subject with gleeful enthusiasm. "They show you where the fortune is hidden, you give it to Jake so he can give it to his brother. The plantation is saved."

Savannah gave the suggestion a brief consideration, but her instincts told her Leanne wasn't right. Whatever the spirits were trying to accomplish was for a different purpose.

Her feelings on that hadn't changed. She was convinced that Jake was the sole purpose for Emily and Nathan's return. Unfortunately, there would be no convincing him of that.

The heartache was imprisoned somewhere in the nether regions of her psyche, tamed to a whisper of grief and a hint of chagrin. All the walls that had ever guarded her heart were back in place, fortified this time by the edicts of her mind. She would not give in to sorrow, she would not let this break with Jacob interfere with her work, she would not let him destroy her happiness.

That was what she told herself. It was what she believed until . . . she saw him standing at the front entry to the old house. Then, in less than two heart beats, the tenets of her private counsel crumbled around her feet, joining the decaying remnants of the structure before her.

She came to an instant halt just within the clearing that surrounded the house. In the frigid morning air, her breath emerged as white, raggedly spaced puffs. Through the mist, her gaze connected with Jake's and she felt the jolt of suppressed emotion spear its way though her.

He stood tall and unmoving, the navy collar of his heavy jacket raised up to frame the hard edge of his jaw. The black of his hair picked up the cobalt highlights, glints that were reflected again in the deep blue of his eyes. She'd never be able to view that shade of blue again without thinking of Jacob.

Her conscience mocked her. The bracing words she had heaped upon herself for days were nothing more than feeble props, rendered useless by a single glance into that handsome, austere face. Disillusionment and regret swelled up and she knew she had been ridiculously naive to have thought she could remain unaffected.

Naive; yes. A fool; absolutely. But she was also proud and angry and hurt. And she had a job to finish.

Slipping her thumbs under the straps of her backpack, she closed the distance between herself and Jake, knowing full well that he watched her every move.

Good, let him look. If he expects to see me grovel at his feet, he can go take a flying leap.

She didn't come to a stop until she was halfway up the brick steps. There, she placed one foot on the next row of bricks and raised her eyes to Jake's. The hard orbs lacked all the compassion and humor and concern that had once touched her so deeply. Instead, as his gaze visually traced her features, she saw censure and a well guarded anger.

"What happened to your cheek?" he asked.

His voice stroked over her flesh like a vibrant caress. A little frantically, she asked herself if it had truly been only a week since she had last heard those deep and gravelly tones.

In answer to his question, she dabbed gloved fingertips to her right cheek and noted the resulting stain of blood on the beige wool. "I had a run-in with a tree limb, as to right of way; I lost."

He nodded. She remained silent, her nerves stretching as the awareness between them increased to an uncomfortable degree.

"Excuse me," she said at last, moving up the last few steps. "I'd like to get started." How wretchedly polite she sounded; cool, professional, her inner trembling nowhere in evidence. All the while, part of her wanted to give in to the turmoil he inspired by just standing there.

"You could have parked in my drive," he told her, planting himself directly in front of her. "There's no need for you to walk all the way from the county road."

"I don't mind the walk." As casually as possible, she stepped to her left with the intention of going around him.

He shifted to meet her move. "Don't be stubborn, Savannah."

Hearing that particular criticism from him, of all people, sent her blood pressure rocketing. "What do you want from me?" she railed, serenity instantly a thing of the past. The hurt and anger she'd been shoring up for too long burst forth in a scorching torrent.

"You've, in essence, called me a liar and a cheat. You refused to listen to what I had to say and now you show up here and pretend to be concerned?" Her chin angled to one side as her eyes took on the fierce light of her indignation. " 'What happened to your cheek, Savannah? You could have parked in my drive, Savannah.' For whose benefit is that? Mine?" She scoffed, sidled around him and stepped up onto the landing. "Thanks, but I can do without your brand of concern."

She managed two paces into the foyer before he caught her up by one arm and swung her around to face him.

"Save your wounded pride," he ordered, towering over her in a black rage. His eyes were narrowed to icy-blue slits, his jaw hard and unyielding. Every line of his body broadcasted an aggressive anger that should have stopped Savannah in her tracks.

It didn't. "Let go of me," she bit out, her voice as low and controlled as his.

His fingers only tightened through the thickness of the heavy green wool of her sleeve. "This isn't settled."

She threw her head back, facing him head on. "Just because you say so?" With surprising strength, she wrenched her arm free. "A week ago, you were done talking, so we didn't talk. Now you want to talk and I'm supposed to fall right in line like some good little soldier? Think again."

She paused for breath, at the same time striving for control of her temper and the pain squeezing her heart. "I have a say in this, too, or doesn't that count? Did it ever? Or was I just a temporary convenience for you? The photographer is handy, so to use your words, why not get a little screwing in on the side. Or was that the price I had to pay to get your help?"

"Shut up, Savannah."

"You got your jollies, all right, but the minute I didn't conform to what you expected of me, I was no better than pond scum."

His hands captured her again, holding her immobile for the full blast of his fury. *"I said to shut the hell up!"*

"Why should I?" she railed, losing her battle for inner control. "Can't you see it doesn't work that way? Relationships are supposed to be built on *mutual* sharing, *mutual* respect. And trust. Both parties are supposed to *trust* each other, have some faith and understanding. One party isn't supposed to suspect the other, or order her around, or make decisions that affect them both."

Overwhelmed by frustrated rage, she clenched her fists and raised them into the tight space between their bodies. In comparison to his inexorable strength, her gesture was impotent and sobering.

Like the air being released from the neck of a balloon, her anger dissipated rapidly, leaving her feeling deflated, empty, save for the wounds he'd inflicted.

Dropping her hands, she looked away, in the aftermath of her rage, suddenly too tired to go on. "What do you want, Jake? Why did you come here today?" Hating herself for her weakness, tears gathered as she peered back at him. "If it was to make me miserable, you succeeded."

She didn't know what prompted him to release her. It didn't really matter. In the end, she stepped back and gave him a last look, noting through her misery that his eyes contained a bleakness to match her own.

As she headed for the west wing, she told herself she did not care.

Nineteen

What do you want, Jake? Why did you come here today?

The remembered queries clicked off in Jake's mind, keeping perfect timing with the cadence of his stride.

As he rounded a small cropping of rocks at the far end of his property, he jeered at himself for letting his concentration slip. He had purposely sought the physical outlet of running to keep his mind off Savannah. Instead, her voice hounded his every step.

Damn her, he silently cursed. And yet, the charge didn't sit well. And that in itself didn't sit well.

"Goddamnit."

Loping beside him in an easy stride, Ares cocked his head toward the sound of his master's voice. Jake ignored the canine look of inquiry. He wasn't so astute at avoiding his own inner search.

Why did you come here today?

Once again, the question brought with it the sound of Savannah's voice, low, defeated. And the brown of her eyes glassed with tears. His chest clenched uncomfortably at the memory of both. She had looked tired then, more so than when she had first stepped out of the tangled forest; skin pale, dents of weariness under her eyes.

And, too, there had been the ugly scratch across her cheek. Every time he thought about it, he was filled with a mixture of irritation and worry. It pissed him off royally that she chose not to spare herself the grind of walking in from the county road. It bothered him even more that he cared.

"All right, so I damn well care," he admitted aloud. He was feeling a great many things about her, but nowhere in the melange of emotions was there the desire to see her physically hurt. His protective instincts aside, he couldn't dismiss the last several weeks. He couldn't turn off emotionally simply because it would have been easier to do so.

He fought the urge to draw in a deep breath of relief. The pace he kept precluded that, but he did feel better for having made his confessions.

So *why* had he gone to the old house yesterday?

To see her, that much was obvious. What wasn't so obvious was what had prompted him to *want* to see her.

"You can't let it rest, can you?" he asked himself. "You just have to keep picking away at it."

Yeah, well, he wasn't playing any great mental games with himself. He was well aware that his conversation with Doug had provoked him to do a shit load of thinking, not only about the plantation, but about his life as well.

His contemplations had resulted in several conclusions, some rather obvious and others more startling. The most easily accepted truth was that Doug was entitled to feel any way he damn well pleased. The second was that even though he didn't resent Doug for harboring his beliefs, he was saddened. And the third was that he could accept and even appreciate Doug's strength in having reached his decisions.

As to the conclusions that were more unusual, even now they sat uncomfortably in the middle of his chest. He ran for thirty yards before he came close to making his confessions.

"God . . . Almighty." He ground the words out between a carefully controlled pattern of breathing. "Say it . . . you ass, admit that when it comes to Oakwood . . . you're unreasonable."

Doug's views of their childhood and Oakwood had made

him realize that. He had been single-minded all his life, but he had never perceived it that way until now.

Scanning the fields and trees in every direction, he felt the familiar tug of the bond he shared with the land, with his past. However, for the first time, the feeling was curiously empty. The satisfaction he had once derived wasn't as rich or abundant. It was as if he had his land, but little else.

As admissions went, he could have done without that one. But he had to be honest with himself.

He scoffed at the thought and growled low in his throat. Self-examination was tough on the ego. Still, he forced himself on, forced himself to take a hard look at his actions, his convictions.

"I'm not as honest and fair . . . as Doug thinks I am. As I've . . . believed myself . . . to be."

And *that,* he realized, was why he had gone to see Savannah yesterday. Because now, one day too late, he could openly acknowledge that he hadn't been fair to her. He didn't know jack-shit about this business with ghosts, but he shouldn't have accused her of taking advantage of him and the plantation.

He had overreacted out of a habit that had blinded him to the truth. Savannah didn't have it in her to take advantage of him or anyone.

With no advance thought, he came to a jarring halt, and planted his hands on his knees. Bent low, he inhaled cleansing gulps of air.

"This sucks." He mentally kicked himself for yesterday's fiasco. Savannah was convinced that she had been nothing more than a piece of ass to him.

What do you want, Jake? Why did you come here today? If it was to make me miserable, you succeeded.

He didn't want her miserable, or hurt or alone.

What do you want, Jake?

He may not have known yesterday, but he sure as hell knew now.

A sense of love and devotion encompassed Savannah in a vibrating warmth. Entranced, she smiled at Nathan and Emily, and let their shimmering emanations curl over and around and through her. She felt their gladness in her veins, their contentment in her heart.

It was a bittersweet moment, tugging at her lost hopes of what might have been. More so than ever, she envied the pair; their love and devotion to each other. She could only imagine what it would feel like to be so cherished and adored.

From within the circle of her husband's arms, Emily whispered, "You know full well, Nathan, that when you captured my heart, my body had no choice but to follow."

"Without your heart," Nathan returned, "the body was not worth capturing." He rolled his eyes, his characteristic mischief tugging at the corners of his mouth. "Although I admit I'm rather pleased that the heart's packaging is so prettily constructed. You are a delectable little thing."

Emily Jane gave him a playful cuff to the shoulder before wiggling her way to freedom. Around a feigned pout, she protested, "You speak in a manner not fit to be mentioned."

He grabbed hold of a fistful of unbleached muslin and pulled hard, catching Emily as she tumbled backward into his embrace. His voice lowered to a seductive purr. "Then I will not mention the manner of things in which I truly wish to engage."

"You take advantage of the easiness of my nature. You are a hard man, Nathan Quaide."

"Let me prove just how hard I can be."

Emily gave in to laughter, then leaned her head back against her husband's shoulder and sighed deeply. "I do love you, Nathan."

He lowered his hands to the swell of her belly rounded with their child. "As I do you, Em. You make my life worth living. Without you, all that I am, all that I own, would be worthless."

"That is not so."

"But it is. You are the heart of me. You are the soul of Oakwood. Our children and their children and theirs will have you to thank for the goodness you have given this fertile earth."

Tears trailed over Savannah's cheeks, the moisture catching on the creases of her smile. If she lived forever, she would always remember this moment. It was fine and pure and . . .

And . . . the thought escaped her, driven away by a subtle change in the air. Her brows quivered upward, then down as she tried to determine what had disturbed the moment. Eyes languid and dewy, she searched the room, looking through and beyond the bright aura.

Jake. He was there. She blinked, blinked again and turned to see if Emily and Nathan had remained. They embraced by the foot of the bed while Jake stood immobile in the doorway, staring at her.

In that split second, past, present and future felt as if they merged into one. Time and space seemed to collide. The glowing heat in the room was joined by a frigid cold and both pierced her, jerking her spine straight.

Happiness, joy, love, grief, sorrow, bitterness and ecstasy; those emotions and so many more became tangible pulses that beat against her skin in unison and in opposition. Light dimmed only to burn brightly in contradictory wavelengths. And saturating it all were the pungent scents of summer mingled with the serene odors of winter.

"Savannah."

She felt the touch of Jake's hands, long seconds before she was actually aware of him holding her. The awareness was electrifying.

"Jacob." In the edges of her consciousness, she was mindful of the animosity between them, and yet she couldn't muster the ire or the hurt. Instead, she gave into the overwhelming compulsion to lift her hand and lay her palm along the hard edge of his jaw, smiling at him, and then, through the twists and curves of cosmic swirls, at Emily.

And Emily, eyes sure and content with all the answers to the universe, looked right back at her.

"Emily?"

The spirit continued to stare serenely, steadily, knowingly until she and Nathan gradually faded away.

The room's temperature evened out, mustiness replaced sunshine and hearth smoke, light and shadows returned to their logical places. Around her, Savannah saw the emptiness of a barren room. And Jacob.

Her immediate reaction was to draw away, but by the time her sluggish mind followed her instincts, Jake's hands had her held firmly in place.

"If you don't want to witness what comes next," she told him breathlessly, "you had better leave right now."

"I've already witnessed more than I care to."

"No one's keeping you here." In fact, she sincerely wished he would take her advice. She could feel the start of the shaking that always accompanied the physical letdown. She would just as soon not have Jake witness her temporary falling apart.

A quick attempt to step away proved futile. Her only resort was to wrap her arms about herself, tuck her chin and shut her eyes.

"God Almighty." Jake felt the tremors, and scowled down at the top of Savannah's head. What in the hell was wrong with her? When he had walked in, she had been barely conscious of him. Her pupils had been huge and unfocused for the most part, clearing only when he had touched her. And now she was trembling uncontrollably.

"Savannah, can you hear me?"

"I'm . . . fine."

"The hell you are."

"It'll pass in a few minutes."

"What's going on?"

She didn't answer.

"I'm getting you out of here."

"There's no need," she insisted around a shudder. "Just give me a few seconds and I'll be okay."

"Right." And in the meantime, he was supposed to let her shake herself silly. Ignoring her ineffectual protests, he circled her with his arms, caught her up against him and absorbed her quaking with his own body. "Hang on, babe."

Even the physical discomfort couldn't dim the impact of hearing that one sweet endearment. It wrenched at her heart, making her feel things she had no business feeling. With her face pressed into the wall of his chest, it would be so easy to pretend that he loved her the way Nathan loved Emily. Unconditionally, forever, through this lifetime and into another.

But Jake didn't want her. He didn't love her.

Sobered by the truth, she pushed away slightly and tipped her head back to produce what she hoped was a credible expression of well-being. The fact that the shakes had ceased, helped.

"You can let go of me now," she prompted.

"I want to know what happened here, Savannah."

"That isn't a good topic for us." She managed to shrug out of his hold, knowing full well that he let her go. She wouldn't have gone an inch if he hadn't allowed it, and they both knew it.

Moving to the windowsill, she sat in the open space. Despite the brisk chill coming in, she preferred that spot to being in his arms. It was safer, more realistic. She needed reality just then. "Is there anything I can help you with?"

He swore distinctly, not bothering with the niceties of

manners. "Cut the polite crap, Savannah. I came to see you because there are things we need to discuss and I find you having a seizure. I want to know what's wrong with you."

"Nothing's wrong with me. And I didn't have a seizure."

"Then what would you call what just happened? You weren't fully conscious."

She had been and she hadn't been. The duality of cognizance was difficult to explain. In any event, she wasn't going to waste her time trying to make him understand.

"What did you want to talk to me about?"

"Don't change the subject."

"Don't tell me what to do," she warned softly. "We've been through that route before."

To her surprise, the lines of his face softened. He relaxed his stance, cocking his weight onto one leg. "You never could take orders worth a damn."

"You never could remember not to issue them."

"So, I won't now." He worked his jaw and arched his shoulders back, taking his time before he said, "I made a mistake."

For a few moments, Savannah actually forgot to breathe. And words were beyond her capabilities. When her lungs finally protested, she exhaled only a small portion of her dubious wonder.

In a pointedly bald declaration, Jacob Quaide, the most proud, autocratic, pigheaded man she'd ever met, had just apologized to her. Just like that. No preambles, no gentle leading up to the subject. Just a bottom-line announcement that reeked of his leftover military mentality. See that hill, take that hill. Apology required, apology given.

"I don't understand. What . . ." She shook her head, feeling as if she had missed something vital along the way. ". . . what are you apologizing for?"

"Isn't it obvious?"

A little helplessly, she scoffed. "No, it isn't."

"You're going to make this tough, aren't you?"

"You've already done that to yourself." She pushed to her feet, her incredulity giving way to annoyed disbelief. The words that had escaped her just seconds before were snared, lined up and delivered with stinging accuracy.

"You've said and implied a lot of things recently, Jake. Which of the insults should I assume you're referring to? Let's see, there was the one about my using this house for a half-baked publicity stunt. And then there was the one about my being nuts for believing that spirits exist." She sauntered toward the center of the room and swung back around with a jeering smile. "And of course, there's my personal favorite, the one about my using you, lying to you, taking advantage of you."

Jake literally chewed back the retort he wanted to hurl at her. To tell her that she could stow the sarcasm wouldn't help any. Besides, she was fully entitled to her hurt and anger and indignation.

"You're right, I shouldn't have accused you of being deceitful. I jumped to the wrong conclusions and that wasn't fair to you." He spread his hands wide, watching every subtle nuance that crossed her face. "I'm sorry."

Again, Savannah was held silent. She wouldn't have expected this of Jacob, ever. He was so entrenched in his thinking that this unexpected reversal made no sense. "Why? Why should I believe you?"

Again, his to-the-point reply came quickly. "Because I realize I haven't been entirely impartial or sensible about the plantation."

Her brows shot straight up and she didn't even try to hide her astonishment. "That's an awfully big realization."

One which, Jake admitted to himself, would take some time for him to become completely comfortable with, but he had made a start. Scratching at his left ear with his right hand, he muttered, "Yeah, well, some lessons are learned late. And at great expense." He dropped his hand to his side, his gaze intensifying with the seriousness of his thoughts. "I never meant to hurt you, Savannah."

She wanted to look away, didn't want him to see in her eyes just how deeply he had hurt her. "Could have fooled me," she quipped, trying for indifference and failing.

"I'm not out to fool either one of us. I'm *asking* you to forgive me."

He was asking for forgiveness, not demanding it, not expecting it. And he meant it. One look at his eyes and Savannah knew to her soul that he was well and truly sorry.

A fluttering little pain danced over her nerves. She hadn't let herself hope that they would reconcile. To have it occur was beyond her wildest dreams or expectations. And still, she was afraid to hope.

"What are you saying? That you want us to . . . to get back together?"

"That's what I'm saying." He winced. "Asking."

A touch desperately, she stuttered, "I don't know . . . what to say."

"Say yes, say you'll give us another try."

He made it sound so easy, but she wasn't a glutton for punishment. "What's to stop this from happening again? You say you're sorry, and I think you honestly mean it, but what happens when you forget all your good intentions?"

"You're assuming I will."

"And with good reason. You've been 'keeper of the faith' all your life. Now suddenly, you claim you've changed your attitude, but I don't think that's entirely true."

"The hell it isn't."

"Let me finish," she retorted, flinging a hand up to silence him. "I'll tell you what my shrink used to tell me, that you're in the *process* of changing your attitude. That's a long way from accepting it completely. You'll slip up, have days of reverting back to old instincts and habits . . . because you're human."

"I'm human and bound to screw up. So?"

"So I won't be your whipping post again!" She clutched a fist to her chest, her chin angled just off center to accommodate the intensity of her feelings. "I'm not going to put myself in the position of being criticized every time we have a difference of opinion, whenever we don't agree on . . . on politics or religious beliefs or *ghosts*. And I'll be damned if I'll be your scapegoat whenever you have a minor emotional meltdown over the plantation. I can't go through it again, I won't. I'd rather—" Hated tears rose up. "I'd rather live without you, Jake, than have you in my life and not be able to trust you."

With hands shoved into his jacket pockets, Jake absorbed the full force of her torment, feeling her pain as his own across the six feet separating them. Until this point, he hadn't truly comprehended the depth of the anguish he'd caused her.

He did now, and if he could somehow erase it, he would. It wasn't possible. All he could do was proceed as fairly and as honestly as he knew how, and pray that that would be enough for their future, for their happiness.

"You don't have to live without me, Savannah. And you won't have to worry about me betraying you again. I promise you that."

With all her heart, Savannah wanted to believe him. Running a finger under her eye to catch a tear intent on slipping, she asked, "How can you make that promise?"

"For one very good reason. For the best and only worthwhile reason. Because I love you."

Savannah stared without so much as blinking while her heart flipped over. "You—"

"I love you," he repeated, forcing her by sheer will alone to accept that, to accept him. He wasn't a gambling man. It wasn't in his nature to leave anything to chance and yet he was taking the biggest gamble of his life, laying his guts out on the line, waiting for her to accept or reject him. "I love you, babe. I didn't know how much until today."

The tears she had been so valiantly trying to control, spilled unheeded down Savannah's cheeks, ignored before the onslaught of hopes and dreams coming true.

He loved her. Oh, God, he loved her! By slow degrees, the notion sunk into her mind, took root and finally, hesitantly, bloomed as actuality. Then as the seconds slipped past, faith and conviction slaughtered her shock.

"You love me," she repeated, as if hearing it again would cement the fact into her brain. "You really love me."

He spread his arms, hands held out in invitation. "More than I've ever loved anything or anyone."

Her eyes rounded with the unspoken question. He read it and gave a sadly tinged smile.

"Savannah, I love you more than this land."

"Oh, Jake," she cried, the last of her defenses tumbling down. She closed the distance between them, threw her arms about his neck and hugged him as tightly as she could, wanting to hold him close forever.

"Tell me you forgive me, Savannah," he grated against her temple, his arms steely bands around her. "I need to hear that."

"I forgive you."

"Tell me you love me."

It was the sweetest order he had ever given, its audacity tempered by an underlying vulnerability. Tilting her head back, she gazed into the blue of his eyes. "I love you, Jacob. Now and forever."

Twenty

"All of me, babe, take all of me."

Savannah lifted her hips and joyously did exactly what Jake asked of her. She met the thrusting of his body with all the love bursting inside of her, soaking up every sensation and sentiment and emotion.

In her mind, the last half-hour was a blur of happiness, desperate confessions of mutual love, of a hurried rush through the woods to Jake's bed, and a frenzied stripping of clothes. Overlaying all of that was the heat and urgency and passion that engulfed them now. Mouths open and tongues entwined, hands grasping while their bodies surged together, she gave herself up to the all-consuming desire, to the bottomless well of love, to Jake.

"I love you," she gasped, feeling the tension low and inside increase with every thrust of his body.

"God, how I love you," Jake rasped out.

He pressed his face into the tumble of her hair and sucked in short, uneven breaths. To the marrow of his bones, he felt her along every pulsing inch of him and still, it wasn't enough. It would never be enough. He wanted to bury himself so deeply inside of her that they would fuse into one. And all because he loved her.

He had never loved before, not like this, not to the point where his body and his mind were overwhelmed for and by another person. He didn't know what to make of this staggering sense of needing someone the way he needed

Savannah. She was his in a way that defied reason or definition. And he belonged to her in the exact same way.

It crossed his mind to curse himself again for his idiocy of the last week, but the clenching of Savannah's delicate muscles around him robbed him of thought and breath.

"God Almighty," he groaned.

From a distance, Savannah heard his growled moan and understood precisely what he was feeling. The intensity of their lovemaking was beyond anything they had ever shared. And it was happening so quickly, the sensations building so powerfully, that she was half-afraid of the ultimate end.

"Jake . . ."

He smothered the sound of her plea with his mouth, blindly seeking his climax and hers. More than anything he wanted her to come apart in his arms while he drank her cries and felt her body squeezing his in the most intimate of all caresses.

The tempo of his driving rhythm increased, and in the next second, Savannah arched wildly, a low cry parting her lips. In the succeeding second, Jake followed her into his own blissful release. He poured himself into her waiting warmth repeatedly, for eon-long moments that didn't seem to want to end.

Through it all, Savannah held him tightly, telling him again and again that she loved him.

For long minutes after, they held each other without moving, without speaking. It wasn't until Savannah exhaled a sigh that Jake moved at all and then it was only to settle her in the crook of his arm. In the soft hush that followed, she lay with her head on his shoulder and leisurely traced a path through the nest of dark curls on his chest.

"What are you thinking?" Jake asked, the sound of his voice a deep rumble beneath her ear.

"I'm thinking that I can't believe we're here together. I never thought to have this again."

He tightened his arms around her and placed a kiss on the top of her head. "I'm sorry, Savannah."

Tipping her head back, she lay a quieting finger over his lips. "Sshh. You've said that enough. Let it go."

"It'll take a while. Every time I think about what an ass I've been, I—"

"Everyone's entitled to be an ass at some point in life," she cut in. "Your time was now. Don't beat up on yourself."

He smoothed the back of his hand over her rosy cheek. "You're something else, you know that?"

"You've mentioned it a time or two," she said around a flirting little smile.

"I've meant it."

"I should certainly hope so, because I think you're wonderful." Shifting slightly, she pressed a lingering kiss on his lips. When she settled into the crook of his arm again, she surrendered to a curiosity that couldn't be contained another second.

"Jake?"

"Mmmm?"

"What made you come to the decision about the plantation?"

He didn't answer at once. Instead, he toyed with strands of her hair, watching them slide through his fingers in a silky cascade.

Finally he said, "Losing you was a wake up call, but I didn't understand that until Doug hit me upside the head with some truths."

"What kind of truths?"

"About our childhood and our parents. He told me pretty much the same thing you did about our folks."

Without the least bit of censure she asked, "Why did you believe him and not me?"

He shook his head, and inhaled a hissing breath, wading through the convoluted reasoning involved. "I believed him *because* of you, because I didn't have you in my life any longer. To use your words, you were the best thing to ever happen to me and I let you go. No, I threw you out because I couldn't see up from down when it came to this property." He cursed fluently. "You were gone. I was left with nothing but the land, and I realized it wasn't enough. That's when I knew I was in need of major attitude readjustment."

She levered herself up so that she rested across his chest, her chin propped up on her hands. "I was serious earlier when I said that would take time."

The slant of his black brows deepened above candid blue eyes. "I'd like to disagree with you, but I can't. Oakwood is part of me. I won't be able to completely alter my thinking overnight."

"I'm not asking you to, and I'm certainly not expecting you to forsake your heritage." She rolled her eyes from side to side. "Only get a firm grip on its relative importance in your life."

Once again, he skimmed the curve of her cheek with the back of his fingers, tenderness replacing the brutal candor in his gaze. "I'll do everything I can, but be patient with me, babe. Like you said, I'm bound to screw up."

A slight grin tugged at the corners of her mouth. "Well, when you do, Q Man, I'll just have to keep you in line."

"Oh, yeah?"

"Yeah," she murmured, circling one of his nipples with a teasing finger. "I can think of some very interesting options you might want to explore whenever you need 'attitude readjustment.' "

"I like the sound of that," he muttered, his voice a lazy, sexy drawl.

"Of course, you'll need the right mind-set, and you'll have to remember one very important thing."

"Which is?"

"That I love you."

His humor gave way to deeper emotions. "You won't have to worry about that. You're in my blood, my mind. I recognized that about the same time I realized that I love you."

"When was that?"

"Weeks ago," he replied easily, instantly.

Hearing his answer, she reared up and stared at him in awe. "You never told me."

"Knowing something, admitting it and acting on it aren't all one and the same. Besides, as you've mentioned, I needed to get a few things straightened out in my head." His gaze dropped to the creamy swells of her breasts. "What about you?" he inquired distractedly. "When did you realize you loved me?"

She flopped back down onto his chest. "Oh, I think I've loved you from the moment I fell through your door and you caught me."

"You're kidding."

"Nope. But I didn't consciously acknowledge it until Thanksgiving."

"And yet *you* didn't say a word."

"I know." Her hand resumed it's gentle exploration of the muscles and planes of his chest. "I guess we were both reluctant to admit to what we were feeling."

"Which reminds me," he recalled, his voice becoming inflexible. "How *are* you feeling?" He searched her features, his gaze tender with concern and yet flinty with resolve.

She felt the pressure of his insistent, probing attention and shied away from the underlying cause. Without being aware that she did so, she also withdrew from Jake.

"Oh, no you don't," he said, cupping her shoulders in his hands to keep her from slipping away. "We may have gotten off the track earlier, but you haven't told me what happened to you back there."

Savannah suppressed a heavy sigh, more than a little reluctant to enter into this particular discussion. She couldn't explain the physical state she'd been in without bringing up

Emily and Nathan, and she would prefer not to have to do that. More than likely, Jake wouldn't make wild accusations again, but neither did she think he was going to believe her.

Giving him a doubtful look, she mused, "I don't suppose you'd be willing to forget about it."

"You suppose right."

She did sigh then, and despite his solid grasp on her, slid from his side. Sitting on the edge of the bed, she picked up his shirt and shrugged it on, fully aware that Jake followed her every move.

"I really don't want to get into this," she insisted, concentrating on fastening the row of buttons.

"We have to, Savannah." He sat up, his determination marked in the set of his shoulders, the angle of his chin. "This isn't the first time this has happened." In a fluid shift of muscle and sinew, he threw back the covers and rose to stand on the other side of the bed. "If you're sick, if there's something wrong, I want to know about it."

Damn, damn, damn! she silently swore. Why did he have to be so persistent? And why did he have to look at her with just enough concern in his eyes to remind her that he loved her?

As was his way, he would keep pressing until he had his answers, except they weren't going to be the ones he expected. She wasn't going to be able to tell him that medically something was wrong with her. She was going to have to tell him the truth. The last time she'd told him this truth, he'd thought her crazy.

Wrapping her arms about her middle, she turned to face him fully. "If you're waiting for me to tell you that I have a brain tumor that's causing seizures, or that I'm strung out on drugs, or that my nervous system is shot, you're going to be disappointed."

"That's a hell of a thing to say," he barked roughly. "Why would you think I'd want to hear any of that?"

"Because those are the more likely explanations for what you witnessed." She glanced away briefly. When she looked back, it was with a gaze that was direct and purposeful. "Because I told you once before why I go into a trance of sorts. You didn't want to hear it then. I can only assume you don't want to hear it now."

The line of his lips flattened as he stared at her in stony silence. Finally, he swung away to yank on a pair of jeans, the word 'ghost' boomeranging around in his head. Ghosts, for God's sake. The absurdity of that would have been laughable if anyone other than Savannah were making an issue of it.

How in the hell was he supposed to handle something so illogical and nonsensical? Carefully, no doubt, since this was a matter of major importance to the woman who had come to mean everything to him.

"Maybe you should explain this from the start," he suggested evenly when he had his jeans in place.

"On one condition," she countered.

"Which is?"

"That we can agree to disagree."

"I thought that was a given with us?"

"I thought so, too." With arms still tucked beneath her breasts, she shrugged slightly. "In this case, that might be stretching things a bit." Even to her own ears, that sounded like an insult. Kneading at her forehead, she added quickly, "I'm not asking you to believe, only to listen with an open mind, and if nothing else, to let me believe."

If this had been a game of chess, Jake knew he would have been in check. Unfortunately, this wasn't a game where he had only so many moves to extricate himself from a precarious position. Savannah was dead serious. He could react no differently.

"All right. Talk to me."

She nodded slowly, feeling as if she had just cleared a major hurdle. Her gestures as deliberate as her nod, she sank back to the bed. However, now that she had his complete if skeptical attention, she didn't know where to start.

"This is strange. With the exception of Leanne, I'm not used to talking about this."

"You've told your sister." It was both a statement and a query.

"Yes." She shrugged her hands in a helpless little move. "She knows all about Nathan and Emily."

"How do you know these . . . these . . ."

"Spirits," she supplied for him.

"Mmm, yeah, these 'spirits' are Nathan and Emily?"

"I didn't at first. Not until I heard them call each other by name."

His head jutted forward at that. "They talk?"

"To each other. Not to me."

"Why am I glad to hear that?" he muttered.

"Jake, you promised," she reminded him.

He held up his hands at once. "All right, all right. Go on. What do they do?"

"They carry on with their lives."

"Where, when?"

"As near as I can tell, what I've been seeing is the nineteenth century." She smiled in pleasured remembrance. "Their clothes and their speech aren't modern. And the furniture is what today we'd call antiques."

He digested all of that for a long moment. "And that's it?"

"For the most part."

"You just stand there and watch them?"

Tipping her head to one side, she grimaced. "It's a bit more complicated than that. Every time I have one of these encounters, the level of my involvement seems to increase."

"What the devil does that mean?"

She noted the aggressive posture of his stance and waved to the bed. "I wish you'd sit down. This is difficult enough without you bearing down on me." Thankfully, he did as she asked. His gaze was the same unrelenting blue, the set of his shoulders as intimidating, but at least they were at eye level with each other and that made the telling easier.

"At first, I was an observer. It was like watching a movie, I was there and yet removed, if that makes any sense. But as time passed, the atmosphere around the two began to change." Caught up in her own remembered excitement, she leaned forward, eyes alight.

"Nathan and Emily give off an aura. I don't know if that's the right term, but I can't describe it any other way. The air around them glows and shimmers and then it becomes warm. I've begun to feel that now."

"Meaning you didn't at first."

"Right. And I've also begun to feel their emotions." She paused, her heart swelling with affection for the centuries old husband and wife. "They love each other very much, Jake. It's so moving to see them together. She looks at him like he's the center of her universe. And when he kisses her, it's enough to make me breathless."

Jake ran his tongue around the inside of his cheek before he asked dryly, "Don't they mind you watching them?"

"They don't know I'm there." At a sudden, thrilling thought, she amended that instantly. "At least, they haven't known up until today."

"Why, what happened today?"

"Emily looked right at me. She and Nathan had been kissing again and—"

"They seem to do that a lot."

She gave in to a full fledged grin. "Nathan is a horny old dude, forever chasing Emily from one bed to the next. And he talks in bawdy double entendres. Anyway, today I was listening to them tell each other how much they love each other when I sensed you were in the room. When I finally did see you, I looked back to see if Emily and Nathan were still there and that's when Emily stared right back at me. That's never happened before."

"Why not?"

"I don't know. I've tried talking to them several times, but it's been useless."

"Does something happen to your eyes when all of this is going on?"

"Not that I know of, why?"

"You said you *finally* saw me. Didn't you see me when I walked in?"

"No." Pursing her lips, she struggled to find the best way to explain. "It's as though the twentieth century is gone and the air is charged with objects and people, emotion and light and scents from another time. I didn't become aware of you until you were close to me."

"What did you see then?"

A smile as glorious as love itself spread across her face. "You," she whispered gently. "As I've never seen you or anything else in my life. It was like the whole universe shifted and time and space were suspended between the two of us."

Love and tenderness radiated from Savannah with such force that Jake was shaken. Everything she had described went against some very basic tenets of his life. And yet despite his skepticism, he found himself unable to shake the impression of Savannah's conviction, nor her apparent contentment. She honestly believed what she was telling him. And now she was waiting for him to make a reply.

The trouble was, it wasn't a simple case of their agreeing to disagree. He couldn't bring himself to believe in ghosts. That would be like asking him to give credence to all the half-assed stories of pilots and planes disappearing inside the Bermuda Triangle. He knew firsthand that air space was exactly that, air space and not some friggin' extraterrestrial portal.

On the other hand, he couldn't shrug off Savannah's claims as hallucinations. She was as rational as he and ten times more sincere.

So where the hell did that leave him?

The buzzing of the phone on the nightstand wrenched him out of his brooding. He shot the instrument a malevolent glare, consigning the thing to hell for its intrusion. When he spoke into the receiver it was with a snarled "hello."

Less than five minutes later, he hung up.

"Jake, what is it?" Savannah asked when he continued to stare down at the phone.

He dropped his hands onto his waist. Without bothering to face her he said, "That was Doug."

"What's wrong?"

"They closed on the land today. The old house comes down next week."

Twenty-one

Blue shadows. Black silence. Jake felt their combined weights as he stood at the kitchen window, staring out into the ebony night. Hands braced high on either side of the panes, he squinted for a better look at the familiar landscape. All he saw were indistinct suggestions of what he knew was actually there.

Winter's coming.

He flicked his brows up at the nondescript thought, not finding it particularly relevant right then. It did suit his mood, however. Winter implied an ending, a death, a certain coldness. Wearing nothing but his jeans, he didn't feel the chill of the air on his feet any more than he did on his back.

"Jake?"

Savannah's voice floated out of the darkness from behind. He looked over his shoulder and found her standing just inside the room. Even in the murky light, she banished the gloom.

"What are you doing down here, babe?" He scanned the lines of her wrapped up in his shirt. He'd never be able to wear the thing again without thinking about how it had touched her warm, silky skin.

"I woke up and you weren't beside me." She came forward with her words, not stopping until she slipped her arms around his waist and snuggled contentedly. "Bad night?"

He curled one arm around her shoulders and hugged her close, breathing in the subtle scents of woman and flowers. "Yeah, bad night."

"Anything I can do to help?"

"Holding you, having you near helps."

"Would you like to talk about it?"

"It?"

She lifted her head from his shoulder to waggle her brows at him. "The nasty nighttime demon that woke you from a sound sleep. The emotional baggage you took to bed with you."

"Ah, that 'it'." He scoffed lightly, wondering why he had ever thought he could keep this to himself. She read him so well. "No, I'll be fine."

It was one of those pat male answers Savannah so disliked. And it was typical of Jake to think he could cope on his own.

"It's a good thing I love you," she commented, looking him straight in the eye.

"Oh, yeah? Why is that?"

"Because sometimes your masculinity can be so annoying."

"What did I do?" he asked, genuinely confused.

"You're the strongest man I know, Jacob Quaide, but that doesn't mean you can handle everything by yourself. There are times when you might need help. Mine."

He knew where she was headed and he appreciated her concern. "And you think now is one of those times."

The corner of her mouth quirked into a knowing grin. "You're standing at a kitchen window at three in the morning. I'd say now is definitely one of those times."

As much as he would have liked to deny that, he couldn't. Dropping his arm away, he stepped to the kitchen table and leaned back, hooking his thumbs into his belt loops. "What do you want to hear, that I couldn't sleep because of Doug's call this afternoon?"

"I figured that out by myself. That old house epitomizes Oakwood." Her heart went out to him. It had to be tough to know that in a few weeks there won't even be a sign that the old house had ever existed. "Perhaps if the new owner were to leave it standing, this wouldn't seem so final to you."

He scrubbed a hand at the denim covering his thigh, taking exceptional interest in the friction created against his palm. "Final sums it all up."

"Does it?"

Head still angled downward, he peered up at her, his eyes narrowing. "Just spit it out, Savannah. Say what's on your mind."

"I thought perhaps there might be other things keeping you awake."

"Such as?"

"Your parents."

The sooty hues of the room couldn't hide the flare of cobalt that lit his eyes, turning the shadowed blue orbs fiery for a second. Jaw tightening to a hard line, he glanced down at his feet, reluctant to admit that his parents had crossed his mind more than once in the last few hours.

"How did you know?"

"Educated guess," she claimed, leaning one shoulder against the same window sash Jake had just vacated. "You haven't said much about them."

"What makes you think I should?"

"It would only be natural. You've been dealing with some weighty issues lately that are directly and indirectly related to your parents."

He dropped his head back, his gaze aimed at the ceiling, an instinctive ploy to keep from examining his thoughts too closely.

"Do you resent them, Jake?"

"I might," he replied, his tone defensive. Mentally, he swore, then slowly, softly conceded to a more accurate truth.

"I'm not sure what I feel about them at the moment. All my life I've accepted my parents for what they were, but Doug brought up some irrefutable points that have me thinking."

"Does he resent them?"

"To some extent. He feels we were denied the right to make our own choices about this place."

"Is that how you feel? Do you think your parents forced—" she lifted her hands to indicate all of Oakwood "—all of this on you?"

The query struck him at gut level, prompting an immediate denial. He waited for a second, less habitual response, but it didn't come. He didn't feel imposed upon, he had never felt that way.

As far back as his memories went, there was satisfaction and affinity waiting for him. He had been the eager host for the legacy; even as a child, willingly, gladly taking pride in the land. His parents hadn't had to coerce him into feeling that way.

"No," he sighed. "For me, it was never a matter of being forced to think a certain way or to blindly accept the past."

The pleasure in knowing that was equal to the relief found in knowing he didn't resent his parents. Damn, he was glad of that. He didn't want to hate them or his memory of them.

"Doug and I are different in that way," he said, his tone full of dawning revelation. "We don't see life in the same terms, we don't react identically."

"That's how it's supposed to be, Q Man." Leaving her spot at the window, Savannah made a place for herself between his spread thighs and looped her arms around his neck. "You're brothers, not clones of each other. You feel a unique bond with Oakwood—"

"A bond that is becoming more realistic, thanks to a certain lady photographer I know."

"I'm glad to hear that." She pressed her cheek to the

hard warmth of his chest. "I love you, Jake. I want you to be happy."

"How can I not be? I have you. When will you marry me?"

She jerked back as far as his encompassing arms would allow, her heart lodged somewhere in her throat, her eyes rounded with surprise. "Marry you?"

The grin he gave her was both arrogant and skeptical. "Don't look so shocked. You had to have known—"

"I didn't know anything of the sort. Until this afternoon, I had stopped thinking of *us* as a couple all together."

"Well, this half of the couple wants to be bound to your half permanently and legally. So pick a date."

For a full count of five, Savannah could only stare up at him, happiness welling inside of her, doubling and redoubling in on itself until she was nearly giddy. "This is so like you," she protested, its effects ruined by her laugh. "You no sooner settle one problem in your mind before you move right on to the next without any downtime."

"Think of it as one of my more endearing qualities, if it makes you feel better."

"I wouldn't call it endearing. You can be extremely unsettling at times, and autocratic."

"I am not autocratic."

"Oh, my God, Jake, you define the word! Perfect example; you didn't ask to marry you, you ordered me to. That's so arrogant and imperious, not to mention unromantic that it—"

He cut off her supply of words by covering her mouth with his. His tongue swept past her lips with devastating accuracy and suddenly she couldn't think of anything else she really wanted to say. Instead, she molded herself against him, and surrendered to the hard pressure of his mouth, the demands of his body and to the love they shared.

"Savannah?" he murmured, his lips caressing hers.

"Yes. Oh, yes, I'll marry you."

* * *

She stirred from the depths of sleep, tickled awake by the muted light of dawn as it crept around the edges of the blinds in Jake's bedroom. Grumpily, she decided she didn't want to relinquish the contentment of her dreams. They had been of Jake.

His heat and strength lured her, tantalized her, called to the core of her femininity. Still half-asleep, she rolled closer and . . .

The nerves at the back of her neck tensed and her stomach rolled. Even lying down, she felt as if the bed dipped and swayed. Instantly, she snapped to full awareness, recognizing the symptoms with a sense of dismay and confusion.

Sitting up, she scanned the room, her mind and body struggling to absorb the mild discomfort while shaking off the grogginess of a too rapid awakening. A bit frantically, she told herself this couldn't be happening, not here, not in Jake's room, not in his house. The ghosts' visits had always been contained to the old house.

"Jake," she panted, breathing brokenly to counteract the loss of her equilibrium. Blindly, she reached out and connected with his shoulder. "Jake, something's happening."

That was all it took to wake him. He jackknifed to a sitting position, instantly alert, every sense sharp. "What's wrong?" he grated, catching hold of her.

"It's them, Emily or Nathan. Or both." She tensed, anticipating the wave of iciness that would wash straight through her.

"Savannah," he growled in a sound somewhere between a snarl and a scoff.

She ignored him and scrambled to her knees, listening, gazing, waiting . . .

"Oh, God." The cold caught her off guard even though she thought she had been prepared. Her entire body stiffened, her shoulders going back, her hands clutching at air. "Jake . . ."

"Jesus." Kneeling before her, he grabbed her by her shoulders, his expression fierce. "Savannah, can you hear me?"

She could. In a low, soothing, dip and fall of tones, his voice came to her. Helplessly, she gazed into his eyes, noted the stormy light of battle and tried to reassure him. "It'll pass."

And it did. The precluding cold departed as it always did, suddenly, leaving her momentarily drained. Unable to help herself, she sagged slightly, thankful to have Jake's support, but she wouldn't let herself relax completely. If the pattern followed its normal course, Emily Jane would show up at any second.

"She's coming," she warned, her heartbeat resuming a more normal cadence.

"Who?"

"Emily Jane Quaide. I don't know why. She's never done anything like this before."

Jake tamped down his more innate responses, and concentrated on Savannah's physical condition. She was trembling and her skin was icy.

He didn't wait for her approval or agreement. He simply scooped her into his arms and headed for the shower.

"Jake, put me down."

"When you're warm again, I'm going to take you to the doctor and I don't give a rat's ass how much you protest. Something's wrong and I'll be damned if I'm going to let it continue."

Savannah shook her head. "No, you don't understand. Emily's coming." Over Jake's shoulder, she searched the room again and discovered her prediction was right.

Hovering just beyond the bed, the atmosphere around her shimmering with light, Emily Jane smiled and nodded in greeting.

"She's here, Jake."

It was the utter calm and certainty in Savannah's voice that stopped him. Three paces from the bathroom, he studied her features and saw the dreamy-eyed, nearly vacant look he'd seen on her face twice before. As baffled as he was worried, he followed the line of her vision, wondering what it was she stared at so intently.

The answer was there for him to see, and his heart nearly stopped.

"God Almighty." He spoke the words without conscious thought. In truth, he was beyond thinking. His mind, that logical, rational device that had seen him through more than one hazardous ordeal, could not get past the vision of a woman standing on the other side of his bed.

Savannah's woman, Savannah's Emily Jane. She was right out of the antebellum South in her wide hooped skirt and her neatly plaited dark hair parted down the center.

"Is . . . that her?"

At first, Savannah didn't understand his question. When his words sunk in, her gaze flew to his. "Do you mean you can see her?"

"If you're referring to the lady in the pale pink dress, gesturing for us to come to her, then yeah, I see her."

Joy surged up sweetly to claim Savannah's heart. "That's Emily. Oh, Jake, I can't believe you're finally seeing her. This is wonderful."

He wanted to say, "this was crazy," but he couldn't. The ghost was all too real, in a strangely ethereal way.

A ghost. Sonofabitch, a real ghost. "What does she want?"

Savannah looked back to Emily, her pulse tripping with happiness and excitement. "I don't know. This is new to me. I told you before, with the exception of yesterday, we've never made contact. I've always been the spectator."

"I don't think watching is what she has in mind."

Savannah agreed. Her gestures graceful, Emily repeatedly beckoned to them. "What do you want, Emily?"

Emily Jane's smile broadened then she turned and lifted a hand to indicate the door.

"She wants us to leave," Jake surmised.

"Why?"

"How the hell should I know. She's your ghost."

"She isn't anyone's ghost. She belongs to herself."

Again, Emily waved them forward and finally, Savannah understood. "She wants us to follow her." She became a whirlwind of motion, squirming her way out of Jake's arms. "Put me down, Jake. We need to get dressed."

In the chaos of the moment, Jake had forgotten that he and Savannah were both naked. As he set Savannah on her feet, he threw Emily a rueful glare. "She's probably a one-hundred-and-twenty-year-old voyeur."

Savannah didn't spare him an answer. Impatience consumed her, racing along her nerves while she dressed. "We need to hurry."

"Why?" Jake asked, shrugging into a faded sweatshirt.

"I don't know. I just feel we have to."

Two days ago, two minutes ago, he would have dismissed her "feelings" for any number of reasons, but not so now. Savannah was the connoisseur in this guided tour into the metaphysical realm. He wasn't about to question anything at this point. He couldn't, not with Emily Jane smiling so serenely at him.

God bless America, a real ghost! "Does she know who we are?"

Straightening, Savannah returned her gaze to Emily. The first waves of the spirit's aura began to radiate and whirl in curling ribbons of light and heat, whispering steadily toward Savannah.

"Yes," she breathed, feeling the initial calming effects of Emily's emanations. "She knows us, and she's happy. Very,

very happy." The osmotic euphoria dazed her wits as never before. It was as if she didn't have a thought of her own.

Turning to Jake, her body felt languid, her mind gifted with a sure, inexplicable knowledge, Emily's knowledge. She questioned neither the 'hows' or the 'whys' of it. She simply accepted, because she sensed that she had to, because it was what Emily wanted and needed.

"It's important that you stay near me. Hold my hand or . . . or . . . just stay close."

"As if I would do anything else," Jake vowed, wrapping his arm protectively, possessively about her waist. He wasn't comfortable with what was happening, least of all Savannah's present state. He would let nothing harm her, especially not some specter from his past.

Savannah gave him a lazy laugh. "It's all right, Jake. Emily wants you to know that she won't hurt me. Or either of us."

He sliced a gaze back to the still smiling Emily, not liking it one damn bit that she could read his mind. "As long as she knows how I feel."

"She does." Her smile gradually faded with the onslaught of new sensations saturating her brain. Her sight grew distant. "The old house . . . she wants us to follow her to the old house."

The walk through the forest was slower than Savannah would have liked. Underscoring the peace that permeated her being was the impression of urgency, that something was waiting.

At her side, Jake cleared the path of any obstacles with one hand, his other firmly gripped about her fingers. One level of her mind acknowledged a bone deep gratitude for his constant touch, for the closer they came to the house, the more intensely she felt disassociated from reality. Her head was filled with Emily's thoughts, and yet the spirit was nowhere to be seen.

"Jake," she rasped with her last reserve of awareness.

Colors deepened, odors changed, sound dimmed. Her skin felt foreign, as if it didn't belong on her body. Her pulse fluttered erratically. "Don't let go of . . . me." It was important that she tell him that. If she knew nothing else, she knew that.

"We don't have to do this," he told her.

Her moves lethargic, she nodded. "Yes, we do." Not giving him any time to debate it further, she stepped though the row of shrubbery bordering the old house and pulled Jake in after her.

Twenty-two

It was as if for several seconds the sun shut off its brilliant radiance. Not even a scrap of light could be detected as Jake followed Savannah through the shrubs. Sounds were no more than insipid, deadened echoes that seemed to come from a long distance away. The combined sensations were disorienting.

Reason compelled him to stop and get the hell out of there. The gentle touch of Savannah's hand overrode reason, urging him past the low, clinging branches. Swearing, he emerged into the clearing and the moment he did, the sun seemed to come shining back a thousand times more brightly than it did on any hot August afternoon.

Grinding his eyes shut, he hauled Savannah against him. Every one of his protective instincts went in overdrive, primed to battle whatever danger awaited in the oppressive warmth. Sweet smiling Emily be damned. They were facing an unknown. Everything inside him impelled him to keep Savannah safe.

Both arms wrapped about her shoulders, he pressed her face to his chest. "Keep your eyes shut," he ordered. "Don't look." And yet, no sooner had the words left his mouth than the light dimmed to its normal hues. Sounds returned, bringing with them scents that were out of place; English boxwoods, newly turned earth and . . . honey?

Cautiously he opened his eyes, his field of vision going no further than the top of Savannah's head. "It's over."

Whatever the hell *it* was. They were dealing with the supernatural, there was no doubt of that. Anything could have just happened.

Against his chest, he felt Savannah's slow, deliberate nod, but she didn't stir, didn't move to put any distance between them. Cupping her face between his hands, he levered her face upward, his expression turning grim when he saw the far away, dazed look in her eyes.

"Savannah, can you hear me?"

Through centuries and over horizons, she heard his voice, reaching her not so much from without but from within. His voice was in her mind, and her body, as if it had always been there, as if there was no other place for it to be.

Subconsciously, intuitively she understood this and accepted it with a joy that was boundless. Pleasure of the soul, straight from the heart, welled up and she smiled.

"For you," she said.

"What?"

Her eyes drifted shut and yet she could still see. Images filled her mind and she saw them not only from her own perspective, but from Jake's.

It is time.

The instinctive voice trembled in her nerves and she waited, unaware and oddly enough, completely familiar with what would happened next. Energy rose from the ground beneath her, surged into walls of her body and exited through her hand held locked within Jake's.

Vibrating heat raced from Jake's fingertips, up his arm and into his body. He instantly tensed for the impact of a blow. Instead he felt a comforting warmth undulate in languid waves.

Contentment was his for no reason that he could discern. That part of his mind that should have retained his logic, that should have been shouting warnings to be on guard, suddenly didn't see the necessity for a defense. He was at peace.

He tried to fight it. Instincts and good old-fashioned common sense demanded that he not accept this like some green kid. But a confrontation would have required a certain amount of energy and he seemed to be lacking that right then. And the damnedest thing was, he didn't seem to mind.

Shit, but his head was a friggin' mess.

Savannah smiled, knowing, feeling all that Jake did. "This," she whispered, lifting her free hand, "is for you."

He followed the direction of her arm and watched in shocked silence as the view before him shimmered and trembled, colors intensifying and shadows deepening, transparent objects overlapping themselves, quickly solidifying while the air became pure and redolent of another time. Everything was the same and not. The final result was a new version of reality.

"God Almighty," he breathed, absorbing the sight with senses raw and exposed. In every direction, surrounding him as he had never seen it before, lay Oakwood.

He turned and stared in the direction from which he and Savannah had just come, where the tall hedge was no longer in evidence. The forest that should have been there wasn't. Instead, he saw strategically located crepe myrtles and hollies, magnolias and boxwoods. And acres of verdantly rolling lawns that gave way to fields ripe with crops.

Pivoting slowly, taking Savannah with him, he scanned his world. To his left were what he could only assume were out buildings. Cook house, laundry, dairy, smoke house . . . all aligned in a tidy row, all gleaming with a fresh coat of white paint.

Continuing to turn in a tight circle, he noted the vegetable garden beyond the kitchen and beside that, a small fish pond. A split rail fence coursed a path toward a grouping of cabins, again, the structures well cared for and neatly arranged.

Another eighth turn to the left and he spied a forest set against the horizon. A graveled path broke the uniformity of the stand and wound its way forward, coming to a stop only yards away . . . directly in front of the house.

"Oh, God." The house. It was whole and sound, no traces of age or fire or deterioration. Every wall was complete, every window filled with panes of glass. The shingles on the roof looked new and not one brick was missing from the chimneys.

"Come . . . inside," Savannah urged in a soft, detached voice.

It wasn't in his nature to acquiesce easily to anything, however, he willingly yielded to Savannah's instructions. The sensation of peace still saturated him. He had no fears, no worries for either himself or Savannah. Why he felt that way was another mystery, tangled up, he was sure, in the whole jumble of paranormal events.

"There will . . . be time later," Savannah sighed, "for questions . . . for understanding."

He eyed her with a crooked frown. "Are you reading my thoughts?"

She looked at him and into him, her mind already five steps ahead, picturing them together in the foyer. Holding on to Jake's hand with all her strength, she led him up the brick steps and into the house. Like a tug at her spine, she felt his brain balk for an instant, stunned by the need for reasoning, for caution. Both were quickly replaced by assent and approval. Both bathed her senses like a benediction.

Her happiness expanded and increased, especially so when she sensed Jake's amazed joy. Through his eyes, she saw the house as they had both pictured it once might have been.

The craftsmanship was a study in pride, a testament to artisans dead for centuries, and to owners who had loved and cared for their home. Floors gleamed dully with layers of wax. The walls wore papers whose floral designs evoked breezy, airy impressions. To a piece, the furniture was a blend of rich woods and elegant designs.

Each room was a treasure; the sitting room with its Cupid's bow details, the dining room with its double wide windows, the library with its floor to ceiling shelves. No matter where she looked, Savannah saw signs of understated affluence and overstated comfort. The magnificence of the house could not be ignored, but at its heart, it was a home; made that way, she knew, by Emily and Nathan.

Images of them speared into her mind. They suddenly stood at the end of the room. She felt Jake's reaction immediately. His hand tightened around hers, and he pulled them to a stop in the middle of the plantation office.

For long moments, he simply stared at the couple. Emily Jane he knew. Logically—part of him scoffed at the notion—the man at her side was Nathan. Nathan Quaide. Under his tenure as owner, the plantation had reached its zenith. The land had been its most fertile, the house its most impressive.

Jake studied his ancestor with open curiosity, and then felt a spurt of humor when he remembered that Savannah had called Nathan a "horny old dude". He'd have to agree with her assessment. Earthiness clung to Nathan like a second skin. Jake could see it as clearly as day.

"Jake," Savannah laughed languidly. "Mind your manners."

He glanced her way, blue eyes alight. "If you're going to read my mind, then you're going to have to pay the consequences."

"I . . . don't have a choice. It . . . isn't something . . . I can control."

"Are they responsible?" he asked, nodding to the spirits.

Savannah's brow furrowed ever so slightly. "Yes."

"Do you know why?"

Emily answered with a graceful wave of her arm. The gesture implored them to follow. Savannah could have predicted that their final destination would be the master bedroom on the second floor.

It was as she had come to know it, but because this was Jake's first glimpse of this most special room, she felt the delight of his discovery more keenly than she had in any other room. She savored his reactions and hugged them close to her heart. Without realizing it, she tightened her fingers around his.

Jake returned the squeeze, never once breaking his study of the chamber. Even if he had wanted to, it would have been impossible. To the marrow of his bones, he felt a connection with this particular spot, an overwhelming expectancy that touched him deep inside.

There was no further analyzing the sensation. He couldn't even begin to form questions. His head, his body, his psyche . . . hell, his entire being felt as if it were being drawn inward on itself, the focus of his world narrowing and narrowing until he was aware of one, and only one, thought; that generations of Quaides had been conceived here, born here and yes, had even died here.

This one room was the heart of Oakwood.

The realization slammed into him like an electric shock, making him stagger to one side and clench his eyes shut. His mind filled with images of people he knew were Quaides. One after another, they flashed in random order, old and young alike. And damn, he could name them all; when they lived, who was cousin or wife to whom.

Three hundred years worth of faces, most bearing a marked resemblance to each other, most having dark hair and blue eyes. Three hundred years worth of identities, personalities entwined with the land, with a commitment to a way of life, to a proud and loving family. He mentally saw them all.

Thomas and Elijah and Elizabeth from the precolonial years. Mary and Benjamin and Augustine from the late 1800s. Sally, Boaz, Isaac, and a second Isaac, John Jacob, and Harriet through the revolution. Mamie and Edward, Russel and William from the depression.

The supply of faces seemed inexhaustible. They continued to reel off in his head, peeling away layers of time, each leading him closer and closer to an end he sensed was significant and inevitable.

He drew labored breaths into vised lungs. His heart thudded painfully, his entire body broke into a sweat. His nerves quaked and his muscles strained. And still the portraits continued, on and on until, finally, unexpectedly, they stopped.

And only one face remained.

Stillness settled in and around him. All was tranquil, all was balanced in a perfect symmetry of the universe. Mentally gazing at the one lone face, Jake understood that the cosmos had come full circle.

That one face. It was well-known with its squared jaw, blue eyes and thick brows. That one lone face was his own.

It also belonged to Ethan Quaide, the first Quaide, the founder of the plantation. Jake knew it, he sensed it. They were one.

The shock of that jerked his senses, but before he could react, the face filling his mind was joined by a second. Like a reticent sun emerging from out of a shrouding mist, it gradually came into view.

Savannah. And Amanda. He knew the names to be different but the features were one, the personalities the same. Savannah, his own future wife, and Amanda, Ethan Quaide's wife, mother to all the generations of Quaides that would follow.

Full circle.

And he understood. It all made sense.

The images in his mind disappeared.

The shift came without warning, giving him no time to prepare. One second he was connected with the ages and the next, he was hovering in a void. Then the present reality rushed back, bold and powerful and electric. His body couldn't withstand the shock and he dropped to one knee, stunned, dizzy, fighting for breath.

It was several seconds before he could open his eyes. He searched for Savannah at once. She lay beside him in a crumpled heap, unconscious.

Black velvet nothingness. Pure white nonexistence. No thoughts, no senses, no feeling. Nothing.

She floated, drifted. She knew she did, but she didn't know how or where, and couldn't think to wonder why.

Come on, babe, wake up.

A ripple in her voidlike world. It dragged at her. Babe? Was there a baby? Whose?

She was thinking, questioning. She realized this as she came out of the blank nothing. What was wrong? Something was, or rather, something wasn't right.

Shit.

The urge to laugh tickled her on several different levels.

. . . 911 . . .

912? Was that the right answer? Had there been a question? With painful deliberateness, she searched in her brain but couldn't quite . . . qui . . . q . . . Q. Quaide. Jacob.

"Jake!" she cried out, jerking upright.

"Take it easy," Jake said, his arms holding her steady.

She stared at him in wonder, noting peripherally that she was in his bed. Relief and love made her go weak again and she melted against him.

"Oh, God, what happened?" she asked, her face pressed into his neck.

"It got hairy back there. You passed out."

"That's becoming a habit. Sorry."

"Yeah, well, I was about to call the paramedics." Carefully, he moved her to arm's length and checked out her eyes. "How are you feeling?"

"Awful. My head is killing me."

"Wait here."

Easing her back against the pillows, he made to rise, but

she quickly clutched at him, unaccountably insecure. Still disoriented, she wasn't sure what was wholly real and what wasn't. "Where are you going?"

"To get you some aspirin."

"What about you?" She searched his beloved features. "Are you all right?"

"I feel like a wrung out wash rag, but other than that, I'll survive." He pressed a quick kiss to her pale forehead. "Don't move."

"I wouldn't think of it."

He was gone and back in mere moments.

"Those should help," he said when she had swallowed the two white pills. "If they don't, I'm taking you to the emergency room."

Sighing, Savannah leaned heavily against the pillows at her back. She was feeling better all ready. Her mind wasn't nearly as fuzzy and her perspective of the world was back to normal.

She lifted her gaze to Jake, mesmerized by the sight of him. He sat facing her, his thigh pressed to her hip, his right hand resting comfortably, intimately along the left side of her rib cage. He looked tired. The line of his lips was a thin slash, the blue of his eyes dulled.

"Why don't you lie down with me?" She trailed her hand up the outer contour of his leg until her palm curved around his buttock.

He shook his head. "No. I'll be fine. I'm worried about you."

"Don't be. I'd know if something was wrong."

"You were out cold, babe."

"And now I'm not. People pass out all the time." She gave him a good attempt at a smile. "Really."

" 'Really', my ass. I mean it, Savannah. If you're not any better in thirty minutes, I'm taking you to the hospital."

She gave him a tired, but exasperated look. "And tell them what? That I was your link to the next dimension?"

Something hot and furious flared in his eyes and he surged to his feet. A stalking pace carried him to the far wall. All the while he scrubbed at the back of his neck, muttering a string of oaths.

Savannah felt his emotions clear across the room. "Why are you angry?"

He swung back to her and pinned her with a flashing cobalt stare. "You have to ask?"

"Anger won't solve anything. And it certainly isn't going to change what happened. Trust me, the best thing to do is to accept it. You'll drive yourself crazy if you don't."

From experience, she knew it was the only way to go. True, she had been eased into the entire affair gradually. She'd been given sneak peeks and teasing hints of the other side to get her acclimated to the full haunting. Poor Jake had been dumped in headfirst without any warning. It was little wonder he was struggling so.

She patted the bed beside her.

Jake accepted the silent invitation with ill-grace. Taking up the position he had just vacated, he chewed on his frustration with visible relish.

Savannah couldn't help but smile. "You know, your anger is misplaced."

"What the hell does that mean?" he bit out, his face a fierce mask.

She kept a tight lid on the humor bubbling inside her. "You're not angry at Emily and Nathan."

"The hell I'm not."

"You're angry because you had no control over what happened at the house." She dropped her voice two octaves. "Major Jacob 'Stud' Quaide was not in command. Someone else was in charge." Her brows rose in an expression that dared him to disagree.

He couldn't. He despised the feeling of being helpless. Everything that made him who he was abhorred not being able to control himself, and the situation.

Shit, what a friggin' situation it had been. Phantoms, and visions into the past. Savannah had been used like some paranormal puppet, a cosmic conduit between who the hell knew where and himself.

"Don't worry, Jake," Savannah whispered. "It isn't going to happen again."

His eyes sliced back to hers. "How do you know?"

She shrugged, tilting her head to one side. "I know, the same way I know that Emily and Nathan won't be back. I feel it."

That bit of news alleviated his abused sensibilities to some degree. "They're gone for good?"

"Yes." And she was going to miss them. They had become a very real part of her life. "Today they accomplished what they set out to do. They gave you their vision. They gave you their answers." She offered him a contented smile. "It was beautiful, wasn't it? The land, the house . . . ?"

They had been that. Jake couldn't deny it no matter how he might have wanted to. To his dying day, he'd never forget the abundance of the fields, the aura of richness in the air, the perfection of the house. God Almighty, he had seen Oakwood at its best. Bountiful, fertile, consummate.

It was how he had always imagined Oakwood to have been, but until today, he had assumed that was because he had a commitment to his heritage. If he believed the evidence shown to him earlier, his assumption had been only half-right.

He took hold of Savannah's hand. "You know, don't you?"

"About what?"

"All of it. You were there, in my head."

She squinted ever so slightly as she tried to define an unbelievably convoluted situation. "In a way. I was aware of myself, but I could feel and see everything that you did. Your consciousness was mine."

"Then you saw all the people."

"Yes. And just like you, I instinctively knew their names and when they lived."

"You saw Ethan and Amanda."

Even now, Savannah was shocked by what they had learned. "I'm stunned, but in a way, it makes sense."

"In what way?" Jake scoffed

Her heart tightened in her chest, all the love she felt for him shining in her eyes. "It's so obvious, Jake. Ethan and Amanda founded the plantation. They were here at its beginning. Through you and me, they're here for its end." She placed her hand over his heart. "Full circle. You felt it, you sensed it, I know you did."

Again, Jake couldn't summon any denials. He understood the concept of having come full circle, but he wasn't sure he liked the idea of reincarnation.

"This is going to take some getting used to," he muttered.

"It will. But it'll be fine."

He eyed her in mild irritation. "You don't have to sound so smug."

"I'm not smug, just very, very sure."

"That's because you've had more time to get used to the whole mess. You've been playing with these damn ghosts for months."

Love glittered in her eyes and softened the curve of her smile. "There is that, but I was thinking of something else."

"What?"

"The first moment I saw you."

One of his brows flicked upward. "What does that have to do with anything?"

"Everything," she laughed, looping her hands behind his neck. "I never told you before, but the very first instant I saw you, I felt as if I recognized you, that I knew you."

"Really?"

"Absolutely. At the time, I shrugged the feeling off. I told myself I had to be mistaken. After all, portraits are my specialty. I never forget a face, and yours . . ." she pressed her lips to his, ". . . is too dynamic to ever forget."

He settled his hands at her waist, lingering in the sensations created by the touch of her lips. "Why didn't you tell me?"

"If I remember right, I was too busy defending myself from your angry accusations."

"I was an ass."

She rolled her eyes. *"MMM,* you were. You still can be, but you're mine."

His mouth hovered over hers. "For as long as you want me."

"I don't think we have a choice in the matter. Like soul mates, we were destined to be together."

Epilogue

"What do you think?" Savannah asked, watching Jake's face for his reaction.

Jake shut the book resting in his lap and sighed. Almost reverently, he studied the book's title, *Sentinels*. It was Savannah's new book. "I think it's unbelievable."

"Really?"

"Really."

A mix of pride and contentment surged through her. Smiling, she scooted across the sofa in the den and snuggled into her husband's waiting arms.

"I'm so glad you like it. I was worried."

"Why?"

"I wanted you to be pleased with the results."

"How could I not be?" he asked, his brows climbing in amazement.

"Easily, just because you love me doesn't automatically mean you like my work."

"Babe, the photos are some of the best I've ever seen. Especially those of Oakwood." Pressing his lips to her forehead, he murmured, "Those are special."

Savannah shut her eyes and savored being held close to the man she loved with all her heart. In terms of being special, Jake epitomized the meaning of the word. He was all and everything she could have ever hoped for in a husband. Best friend, lover, confidant, father of the baby that grew inside of her.

Laying her head on his shoulder, she mused out loud, "I think you're going to make a great father."

Jake lay a protective, possessive hand on the swell of her stomach. "I'm glad you think so."

"I know so."

"You're biased."

Grinning, she tipped her head back to place a kiss on his chin. "No, just very, very certain."

Her certainties over the past months were not to be ignored. In the aftermath of that final haunting, Savannah's intuitions had been amazingly accurate.

"I miss them," she confessed, her mind going back to that time when the old house still stood. "I miss Emily and Nathan."

"Is that why you dedicated the book to them?"

"It only seemed fitting."

"I think that wherever they are, they appreciate your gesture."

"I'd like to think so. I do know that wherever they are, they're happy and at peace."

"Are you sure?"

Turning in Jake's arms, she whispered against his lips, "As sure as I am that I love you. As sure as I am that you love me."

"I do love you, babe. I most certainly do love you, now and forever."